THE CELLAR

Natasha Preston

sourcebooks
fire

Published by Sourcebooks Fire, an imprint of Sourcebooks, Inc.
P.O. Box 4410, Naperville, Illinois 60567-4410
(630) 961-3900
Fax: (630) 961-2168
www.sourcebooks.com

Library of Congress Cataloging-in-Publication Data is on file with the publisher.

Printed and bound in the United States of America.
VP 10 9

PRAISE FOR *THE CELLAR*

"[A] ripped-from-the-headlines novel."

—School Library Journal

"Fans of realistic horror like *Living Dead Girl* (2008) may appreciate this."

—Booklist Online

"A well-written, completely absorbing nail-biter of a book...[with] a powerful, suffocating atmosphere of dread and uncertainty."

—Bookish

"Like watching an episode of *Law & Order: SVU*... I honestly, could not tear myself away."

—Chapter by Chapter blog

"A real treat for avid mystery and thriller fans, the story line pulls you inside the world of a madman and the women he preys on... never a dull moment."

—Teen Reads blog

WHAT READERS ARE WHISPERING ABOUT *THE CELLAR*

"The novel is such an eerie concept, and one of the most original plots I've seen! I found myself unable to put it down."

—Kathleen, ★★★★★

"One of the best books I have ever read. It'll be going on my 'favorites' shelf alongside Sarah Dessen's books and *Stolen*. This book grabbed me and didn't let go."

—Breanna, ★ ★ ★ ★ ★

"[An] evocative and poignant book which Preston fills with a mixture of many emotions; you won't know whether to cry or to laugh!"

—Juwairiyah, ★ ★ ★ ★ ★

"This novel kept me guessing until the very end, and I will not hesitate to read some of Preston's other novels."

—Nicole, ★ ★ ★ ★ ★

"This was a book that had me on the edge of my seat. I couldn't put it down; I finished it the day I bought it! Amazing story, with all the right kind of suspense."

—Molly, ★ ★ ★ ★ ★

"Typically I don't bother writing reviews, but it's so fantastic, I just had to give it five stars. It's one of those stories that makes you want to talk about it with all of your friends. Must read for sure!!!!"

—Ellie, ★ ★ ★ ★ ★

For my fiancé, Joseph, whose support is never ending.

1
SUMMER

Saturday, July 24th (Present)

Looking out my bedroom window, I'm faced with yet another dull English summer day. The heavy clouds made it look way too dark for July, but not even that was going to faze me. Tonight I was going to celebrate the end of the school year at a gig by a school band, and I was determined to have some fun.

"Hey, what time are you leaving?" Lewis asked. He let himself into my room—as usual—and sat down on the bed. We'd been together over a year, so we were more than comfortable with each other now. Sometimes I missed the time when Lewis didn't tell me he was getting off the phone because he needed to pee or when he would pick up his dirty underwear *before* I came over. My mum was right: the longer you were with a man, the grosser they became. Still, I wouldn't change him. You're supposed to accept someone you love for who they were, so I accepted his messiness.

I shrugged and studied my reflection in the mirror. My hair was boring, flat, and never looked right. I couldn't even pull off the messy look. No matter how "easy" the steps to the perfect bedhead look were in a magazine, I never could make it work. "In a minute. Do I look okay?"

Apparently the most attractive thing was confidence. But what did you do if you weren't confident? That couldn't be faked without it being obvious. I wasn't model pretty or *Playboy* sexy, and I didn't have bucket loads of confidence. Basically, I was screwed and downright lucky that Lewis was so blind.

He smirked and rolled his eyes—his *here she goes again* look. It used to annoy him at first, but now I think it just amused him. "You know I can see you in the mirror, right?" I said, glaring at his reflection.

"You look beautiful. As always," he replied. "Are you sure you don't want me to drop you off tonight?"

I sighed. *This again.* The club where the gig was being held was barely a two-minute walk from my house. It was a walk that I had done so many times I could make it there blindfolded. "No thanks. I'm fine walking. What time are you leaving?"

He shrugged and pursed his lips. I loved it when he did that. "Whenever your lazy brother's ready. Are you sure? We can give you a lift on the way."

"It's fine, seriously! I'm leaving right now, and if you're waiting for Henry to get ready, you'll be a while."

"You shouldn't walk alone at night, Sum."

I sighed again, deeper, and slammed my brush down on the wooden dresser. "Lewis, I've been walking around on my own for *years*. I used to walk to and from school every day, and I'll do it again next year. These"—I slapped my legs for emphasis—"work perfectly fine."

His eyes trailed down to my legs and lit up. "Hmm, I can see that."

Grinning, I pushed him back on the bed and sat on his lap. "Can you take your overprotective boyfriend hat off and kiss me?" Lewis chuckled, and his blue eyes lit up as his lips met mine.

Even after eighteen months, his kisses still made my heart skip a beat. I started liking him when I was eleven. He would come home with Henry after football practice every week while his mum was at work. I thought it was just a silly crush—like the one I also had on Usher at the time—and didn't think anything of it. But when he still gave me butterflies four years later, I knew it had to be something more.

"You two are disgusting." I jumped back at the sound of my brother's deep, annoying voice.

I rolled my eyes. "Shut up, Henry."

"Shut up, Summer," he shot back.

"It's impossible to believe you're eighteen."

"Shut up, Summer," he repeated.

"Whatever. I'm going," I said and pushed myself off Lewis. I gave him one last kiss and slipped out of the room.

"Idiot," Henry muttered. *Immature idiot*, I thought. We did get along—sometimes—and he was the best big brother I could ask for, but he drove me crazy. I had no doubt we would bicker until we died.

"Summer, are you now leaving?" Mum called from the kitchen. *No, I'm walking out the door for fun!*

"Yeah."

"Sweetheart, be careful," Dad said.

"I will. Bye," I replied quickly and walked out the door before they could stop me. They still treated me like I was in elementary school and couldn't go out alone. Our town was probably—actually definitely—the most boring place on earth; nothing even remotely interesting ever happened.

The most excitement we'd ever had was two years ago when old Mrs. Hellmann—yeah, like the mayonnaise—went missing and was found hours later wondering the sheep field looking for her late husband. The whole town was looking for her. I still remember the buzz of something finally happening.

I started walking along the familiar pavement toward the pathway next to the graveyard. That was the only part of walking alone that I didn't like. Graveyards. They were scary—fact—and especially when you were alone. I subtly glanced around while I walked along the footpath. I felt uneasy, even after passing the graveyard. We had moved to this neighborhood when I was five, and I had always felt safe here. My childhood had been spent playing out in the street with my friends, and as I got older, I hung out at the park or club. I knew this town and the people in it like the back of my hand, but the graveyard *always* creeped me out.

I pulled my jacket tightly around myself and picked up the pace. The club was almost in view, just around the next corner. I glanced over my shoulder again and gasped as a dark figure stepped out from behind a hedge.

"Sorry, dear, did I frighten you?"

I sighed in relief as old Harold Dane came into view. I shook my head. "I'm fine."

He lifted up a heavy-looking black bag and threw it into his garbage can with a deep grunt as if he had been lifting weights. His skinny frame was covered in wrinkled, saggy skin. He looked like he'd snap in half if he bent over. "Are you going to the disco?"

I grinned at choice of word. *Disco*. Ha! That's probably what they called it back when he was a teenager. "Yep. I'm meeting my friends there."

"Well, you have a good night, but watch your drinks. You don't know what the boys today slip in pretty young girls' drinks," he warned, shaking his head as if it were the scandal of the year and every teenage boy was out to date-rape everyone.

Laughing, I raised my hand and waved. "I'll be careful. Night."

"Good night, dear."

The club was visible from Harold's house, and I relaxed as I approached the entrance. My family and Lewis had made me jumpy; it was ridiculous. As I got to the door, my friend Kerri grabbed my arm from beside me, making me jump. She laughed, her eyes alight with humor. *Hilarious*. "Sorry. Have you seen Rachel?"

My heart slowed to its normal pace as my brain processed my friend's face and not the face of the *Scream* dude or Freddy Kruger. "Not seen anyone. Just got here."

"Damn it. She ran off after another argument with the idiot, and her phone's turned off!" Ah, the idiot. Rachel had a very on/off relationship with her boyfriend, Jack. I never understood that—if you pissed each other off 90 percent of the time, then just call it a day. "We should find her."

Why? I had hoped for a fun evening with friends, not chasing after a girl who should have just dumped her loser boyfriend's arse already. Sighing, I resigned myself to the inevitable. "Okay, which direction did she go?"

Kerri gave me a flat look. "If I knew that, Summer…"

Rolling my eyes, I pulled her hand, and we started walking back toward the road. "Fine. I'll go left, you go right." Kerri saluted and marched off to the right. I laughed at her and then went my way. Rachel had better be close.

I walked across the middle of the playing field near the club, heading toward the gate at the back to see if she had taken the shortcut through to her house. The air turned colder, and I rubbed my arms. Kerri said Rachel's phone was off, but I tried calling it anyway and, of course, it went straight to voice mail. If she didn't want to speak to anyone, then why were we trying to find her?

I left an awkward message on her phone—I hated leaving messages—and walked through the gate toward the skate ramp at the back of the park. The clouds shifted, creating a gray swirling effect across the sky. It looked moody, creepy but pretty at the same times. A light, cool breeze whipped across my face, making my light honey-blond hair—according to hairdresser wannabe Rachel—blow in my face and a shudder ripple through my body.

"Lily?" a deep voice called from behind me. I didn't recognize it. I spun around and backed up as a tall, dark-haired man stepped into view. My stomach dropped. Had he been hiding between the trees? What the heck? He was close enough that I could see the satisfied grin on his face and neat hair not affected by the wind. How much hairspray must he have used? If I weren't freaked out, I would have asked what product he used because my hair never played fair. "Lily," he repeated.

"No. Sorry." Gulping, I took another step back and scanned the area in the vain hope that one of my friends would be nearby. "I'm not Lily," I mumbled, straightening my back and looking up at him in an attempt to appear confident. He towered over me, glaring down at me with creepily dark eyes.

He shook his head. "No. You are Lily."

"I'm *Summer*. You have the wrong person." *You utter freak!*

I could hear my pulse crashing in my ears. How stupid to give him my real name. He continued to stare at me, smiling. It made me feel sick. Why did he think I was Lily? I hoped that I just looked like his daughter or something and he wasn't some crazy weirdo.

I took another step back and searched around to find a place that I could escape if needed. The park was big, and I was still near the back, just in front of the trees. There was no way anyone would be able to see me from here. That thought alone made my eyes sting. Why did I come here alone? I wanted to scream at myself for being so stupid.

"You are Lily," he repeated.

Before I could blink, he threw his arms forward and grabbed me. I tried to shout, but he clasped his hand over my mouth, muffling my screams. What the heck was he doing? I thrashed my arms, frantically trying to get out of his grip. *Oh God, he's going to kill me.* Tears poured from my eyes. My heart raced. My fingertips tingled and my stomach knotted with fear. *I'm going to die. He's going to kill me.*

The Lily man pulled me toward him with such force the air left my lungs in a rush as I slammed against him. He spun me around so my back pressed tightly against his chest. And with his hand sealed over my mouth and nose, I struggled to breathe. I couldn't move, and I didn't know if it was because he had such a strong iron grip or if I was too stunned. He had me, and he could do whatever he wanted because I couldn't bloody move a muscle.

He pushed me through the gate at the back of the park and then through the field. I tried again to scream for help, but against his palm, I hardly made a sound. He whispered "Lily" over and over while he dragged me toward a white van. I watched trees pass me by and birds fly over us, landing on branches. Everything carried on as normal. Oh God, I needed to get away now. I dug my feet into the ground and screamed so hard that my throat instantly started to hurt. It was useless, though; no one was around to hear me but the birds.

He tugged his arm back, pressing it into my stomach. I cried out in pain. As soon as he let go to open the van's back door, I screamed for help. "Shut up!" he shouted as he pushed me inside the vehicle. My head smashed into the side of the van while I struggled.

"Please let me go. Please. I'm *not* Lily. Please," I begged and gripped the side of my throbbing head. My whole body shook with fear and I gasped for breath, desperate to get some air into my lungs.

His nostrils flared and his eyes widened. "You're bleeding. Clean it. Now," he growled in a menacing tone that made me tremble. He handed me a tissue and sanitizer. *What?* I was so scared and confused that I could barely move. "Clean it now!" he screamed, making me flinch.

I lifted the tissue to my head and wiped away the blood. My hands shook so much that I almost spilled the sanitizer as I squirted it onto my palm and rubbed it into the cut. The stinging caused me to clench my jaw. I winced at how much it hurt. The man watched me carefully, breathing heavily and appearing repulsed. What the heck was wrong with him?

My vision quickly blurred as fresh tears spilled over and rolled down my cheeks. He grabbed the tissue, careful not to touch the bloody part, threw it into a plastic bag, and shoved it into his pocket. He then cleaned his hands with the sanitizer. I watched in horror. My heart slamming against my chest. Was this really happening?

"Give me your phone, Lily," he said calmly, holding his hand out. I cried harder as I reached into my own pocket, took my phone out, and handed it to him. "Good girl." He slammed the back door shut, immersing me in darkness. No! I screamed and banged against the door. A moment later, I heard the unmistakable roar of the engine and felt a rocking sensation as the van began moving. He was driving. Driving me somewhere. To do what?

"Please help me!" I shouted and repeatedly slammed my fists

down on the back door. It was useless; there was no way the door was going to move, but I had to try. Every time he turned a corner, I fell against the side of the van, but I got up and continued shouting for help and banging on the door. My breathing turned to panting, and I gasped for breath. I didn't feel as if air was getting into my lungs.

He continued driving, and with every passing second, I started to give up hope. I was going to die. The van finally came to a stop and my body froze. *This is it. This is where he kills me.*

After a few painful seconds of waiting and listening to his footsteps crunch on the ground outside, the door flew open and I whimpered. I wanted to say something, but I couldn't find my voice. He smiled and reached in, grabbing my arm before I had chance to jump back. We were in the middle of nowhere. There was a large redbrick house sitting at the end of a stone path; tall bushes and trees surrounded the house. Who could ever find me here? There was nothing around I recognized; it looked the same as every other country lane surrounding my town. I had no idea where he'd brought me.

I tried to resist as he pulled me from the van and pushed me toward the house, but he was too strong. I screamed loudly in one final attempt to get help, and this time he allowed it, which was so much scarier—it meant that he didn't think anyone would be able to hear me.

I repeated over and over in my head *I love you, Lewis* as I prepared to die—and for whatever he had planned for me before that. My heart sunk. What did he plan? He pushed me through the front door and along a long hallway. I tried to take it all in, the color of the walls, where the doors were, in the hope I could escape, but the shock of what was happening stopped anything sticking. From what I could tell the hall was bright, and it was warm, not what I expected at all. My blood turned to ice in my veins, and the pinch in my arms as his fingers dug into my skin stung. I looked down and saw his fingertips sink into my arm, making four craters in my skin.

My body came into sharp, hard contact with a mint-green wall as he shoved me forward. I pressed myself into the corner of the room, shaking violently and praying he would miraculously have a change of heart and let me go. *Just do what he says*, I told myself. If I stayed calm and maybe got talking to him, I could convince him to let me go, or I could somehow escape.

With a small grunt, he pushed a shoulder-height bookcase out of the way, revealing a door handle. He pushed the hidden door open and I gasped as my eyes landed on a wooden staircase inside. My head swam. Down there was where he was going to do whatever he planned on doing to me. I pictured a dirty, dingy room with a wooden operating table, trays of sharp equipment, and a mold-covered sink.

I found my voice and screamed again, this time not stopping when my throat burned. "No, no," I shouted over and over at the top of my lungs. My chest heaved as I gasped for air. *I'm dreaming. I'm dreaming. I'm dreaming. I'm dreaming.*

With his strong grip, he dragged me with ease even though I thrashed around as hard as I could. It was like I weighed nothing to him. I was pushed to the narrow, exposed-brick wall opposite the door. He gripped my arm again, harder, and pushed me halfway down the stairs. I stood still, frozen in shock and not fully registering what was happening.

My eyes widened as I looked around. I was in a large room painted in a surprisingly pretty light blue—too pretty for a crazy man's torture cellar. There was a small kitchen along one end, two brown leather sofas, and a chair in the corner that faced a small television in the middle of the room, and three wooden doors opposite the kitchen. I was almost as shocked by what was actually down here than I was relieved.

It didn't look like a cellar. It was too clean and tidy, everything tucked away neatly. The smell of lemon hit me, making my nose tingle. Four vases sat proudly on the side table behind the dining table and chairs; one held roses, one violets, one poppies. The fourth was empty.

I collapsed on the step, grasping the wall to stop myself from falling down the stairs. The door slammed shut, sending a shiver down my spine. Now I was trapped. I let out a startled cry and jumped into the hard wall as three women stepped into view at the bottom of the stairs. One of them, a pretty brunette who reminded me a little of my mum in her early twenties, smiled warmly but sadly and held her hand out. "Come, Lily."

2
SUMMER

Saturday, July 24 (Present)

She took a few steps up toward me, still holding out her hand as if she honestly expected me to take it. "Come on, Lily, it's okay." I didn't move. I couldn't. She took another step. My heart raced in panic, and I pressed my back farther into the wall, trying to get away from her. What did they want from me?

"I-I'm not Lily. Please tell him, please? I'm not Lily. I need to get out. Please help me," I begged, backing up the rest of the stairs until I came to the door. Turning, I slammed my fists against the metal, ignoring the pain that shot through my wrists.

"Lily, stop! Let me explain," she said and held her hand out again. Couldn't she see I wasn't going to take it? She was fucking delusional if she thought I was going to trust her.

I turned back and gasped at how close to me she was. She held her hands up, surrendering, and took another step. "It's okay. We're not going to hurt you." Tears streamed down my cheeks and I shook my head. "Please, come and sit down, and we'll explain everything." She motioned toward the leather sofa. I looked at it for a minute while I thought through my options—which were seriously limited. I had to know what was happening and who they were, so I raised my shaking hand and placed it in hers.

My body tensed, muscles hurt from trying to control my shaking. Why didn't I just go with Kerri? I should have never walked through the park on my own at night. I should have listened to Lewis when he lectured me on going out alone. I thought he was just being overprotective. He *was* overprotective, but I never thought he had a point. Long Thorpe was a boring town. *Was.*

"Okay, Lily—"

"Stop calling me Lily. My name is Summer," I snapped. I couldn't have cared less who Lily was; I just wanted them to realize it wasn't me and let me go.

"Sweetheart," the girl who had pulled me downstairs said softly, as if she was talking to a child. "You are Lily now. Don't ever let him hear you say you're not."

I gulped. "What's going on? What do you mean? Please just tell him to let me go." I gulped down oxygen as my lungs seemed to shrink. "Why won't you listen to me?"

"I'm sorry, you can't go. None of us can. I've been here the longest—almost three years now. My name is Rose," she said and shrugged. "It used to be Shannen. This is Poppy, was Rebecca, and over there is Violet; she was Jennifer before." What the heck? This was bloody insane. She had been locked up down here for *three years*?

"B-before what?" I croaked.

"Before Clover," she replied.

I shook my head, trying to make sense of what was going on. "Who's Clover? *Him?*" The sick Lily bastard man? "Please just tell me what's going on. What's he going to do to me?"

"We're to call him Clover. You do everything we tell you, and you'll be fine, okay? Never disagree with him and do not tell him your real name. You're Lily now. Summer doesn't exist anymore," she said, smiling apologetically. A strangled sob forced its way out of my mouth, and I fought to keep my diner down. *I can't stay here.* She put her arm on my shoulder and massaged it gently. I wanted to scream and push her off, but I didn't have the energy. "It's going to be okay."

"I-I want to go home. I want Lewis." *I want my nagging parents, annoying brother, and my old, boring life back.*

The other girl, the one she introduced as Poppy, shook her head. "I'm so, so sorry, Lily. You should forget Lewis. Trust me, it's easier that way." Forget him? How could I forget him? Picturing his face was the only thing that was keeping me together. Knowing he was out there and would soon look for me was the only thing stopping me from breaking down.

"We need to escape. Why don't you try escaping?" They all dropped their eyes to the floor at the exact same time, as if they'd practiced it. "What?"

"Some have," Rose whispered.

My blood ran cold. "What does that mean?" I already knew the answer, but I needed her to say it.

"You're the second Lily since I've been here. That's why you need to do what we tell you. Escaping is *not* an option; neither is trying to kill him." She shook her head slightly and stopped talking. I got the impression she wanted to say more, though. Who tried to kill him?

15

They had all given up hope of getting out of here—I could see the defeat in their eyes—but I wasn't going to. I *would* get out and be with my family again. I couldn't think that I would never hear Lewis tell me he loved me again or my brother scream at me to get out of the bathroom.

"Wait, what do you mean I'm the second *Lily*?"

She took my hand and squeezed it gently. "There was another. She was here a month before he found me. One night, she attempted to kill him, but he overpowered her and…" She trailed off, taking a deep breath. "Just don't try anything, okay?"

My heart smashed against my chest painfully. I didn't want to give up hope, but this girl had been here for *three years*.

I gulped and asked the question I was most afraid of. "What does he want from us?"

"I'm not entirely sure, but I think he wants a family. The *perfect* family. He chooses girls that he thinks are perfect, like flowers." I blinked, reeling from her latest bomb. *Flowers?* Was that the reason he renamed everyone after flowers? My mouth hung open. This guy was bloody insane.

She went on, "He likes things that are pure, and he can't stand mess or germs." That's why he was so disgusted when my head was bleeding and why all I could smell down here was the strong, almost eye-watering scent of lemon.

"We have to make sure the house is clean and tidy at all times, and we have to shower twice a day. He comes down to have breakfast with us at eight o'clock sharp, and we need to be showered and have our hair and makeup done, ready for him."

I laughed an entirely humorless laugh, convinced that someone was messing with me. I had to be on a TV reality show or something. "What the fuck is wrong with him?" I shouted, jumping up off the sofa. My legs felt like jelly and Rose easily pulled me back down.

"Don't ever swear in front of him, Lily. Please listen to what I'm telling you," she said. "He brings us fresh flowers when the old ones die…" She stopped, trailing off, and flinched at something—a bad memory? Staring me in the eye, she took a deep breath. "When he falls in love with you, he will want to make love to you."

My heart stopped. I shook my head fiercely as my eyes started stinging. I jumped up again; this time I found the strength from somewhere to rip myself from her quick, tight grip. There was *no way* he was coming anywhere near me. I would rather die. "No! Oh God, I have to get out of here." I turned and sprinted back up the stairs.

"Lily, Lily. Shh, stop it," Rose said frantically and grabbed my arm. She must have been right behind me. "You need to calm down. We don't think he can hear, but we're not positive, so you have to stop."

I heaved and slumped to the floor, sobbing. Rose was half holding me so I didn't hit hard, not that I cared anyway. "I need…I need to go home," I muttered. My body shook with fear. I didn't want him anywhere near me. I had only ever been with Lewis and I wanted to keep it that way. The thought of anyone else touching me made my skin crawl—especially *him* touching me.

"I promise you will be okay, but you need to do what we tell you. We're trying to help you, Lily," Rose said. It took me a few minutes, but I managed to calm myself down a little. Rose was right; I did need to do what she said, just until I could figure out how to get out of here. I had to be calm and think straight, form a plan. There *must* be a way out. Nothing was impossible. I had to play along until I thought of something—it was survival.

I pushed myself up and let her guide me back to the sofa. Rose wiped the tears from my face with a tissue. My eyes fluttered open when she was done, and I saw they were all staring at me, wondering if I was going to freak out again or behave, like them.

"Are you okay, Lily?" the other girl, Violet, asked. It was the first time she had spoken to me, and it was the dumbest question ever. I shook my head. I was definitely not okay. "I'm sorry." She squeezed my hand.

The cellar door swung open, making me jump. My heart rate spiked and my body trembled. He very slowly walked down the stairs, like he was dragging it out for dramatic effect, and stepped under the light. I was able to see him properly for the first time. I gulped as my heart raced a million miles an hour. He had very short brown hair that was immaculately styled; not one single strand of hair was out of place. I was surprised at his strength because although he was tall, he didn't look that muscular. He wore nice jeans and a knitted navy sweater over a white shirt—too preppy and normal for what he was doing to us.

Rose took hold of my other hand and squeezed it. "Hello, Flowers. How is Lily settling in?" he asked, smiling at me warmly, as if he hadn't just kidnapped me. *What the heck is wrong with him?* How could he just pretend like that?

Violet stood up and walked toward him. She narrowed her eyes and shook her head. "This is wrong, Clover, and you know it. You've gone too far this time. She's *so* young. You need to let her go," she said. Her voice was firm, but her trembling hands gave her away. With everything Rose had told me, I was positive they were terrified of him. I respected her so much for speaking up; the other two clearly weren't going to.

The carefree smile dropped from his face, and I stilled. My pulse quickened. His face, now hard and tense, made him look like a completely different person. He looked murderously angry. Reaching out so quickly I almost didn't see it, he grabbed her arm roughly.

Violet winced, her eyes tensed in pain as she looked down at the arm he had in a death grip. "Clover, please don't," she whispered. I didn't want to look at what he was doing or what he was going to do, but my eyes were glued to them, heart pounding, fingertips tingling.

"You selfish bastard," he growled and slapped her across the cheek. Bastard? He said the word, but it was so weird coming out of his mouth; it was as if it was someone else's words. It didn't fit. The slap echoed through the room and Violet hissed through her teeth, gripping the side of her face. But she didn't make a sound. "How dare you speak to me like that after everything I've done for you? We are a *family*. You need to remember that."

My blood ran cold. He wanted me to be a part of his family. He was going to keep me here. I already had a family—parents I'd skipped out on before saying good-bye properly, a brother I'd argued with before leaving.

Violet stood straight and something inside her changed. Her eyes darkened, her nose turned up, and she spat straight into his face. "We're not a family, you *psycho*," she shouted, wrenching her arm from his grip.

The noise that broke through his clenched teeth was animalistic and throaty; no part of it sounded human. I should have ran but fear kept me planted to the floor. Violet fell down, crying in pain from one hard shove. "Get it off me," he bellowed and flailed his arms around frantically. My eyes widened in horror. *It's just a bad, bad dream that you need to wake up from right now*, I told myself. But I didn't wake up.

Poppy jumped up, grabbing the tissues and a bottle of sanitizer from the table beside me. I'd noticed a few other bottles around too—on the bookshelf, kitchen counter, and TV stand. She wiped his face and handed him the sanitizer, and he squirted it on his trembling hand and then rubbed it on his face. Rose and Poppy exchanged a look. I didn't know what it meant, but I knew whatever it was, I wouldn't like it.

He turned to face Violet, and she slowly backed up until she was pressed up against the wall again. I gulped. *What now?* Rose and Poppy moved to either side of me in a protective manner. *Oh God.* I gulped and clenched my trembling hands. *This isn't real.*

Cocking his head to the side, he reached into his pocket and pulled out a knife. I froze. *No!* He was going to kill her. He was going to stab her right in front of us. Why weren't they doing anything? No one was doing anything. Was this what that look was about? Did they know this was going to happen?

"What?" I whispered, trying and failing to look away. Why couldn't you look away from something bad? It's like we're all programed to punish ourselves.

"No, please. Clover, I'm sorry, please don't," she begged, holding her hands out in front of her and crouching slightly in surrender. He shook his head. Deep, heavy breaths burst from his lungs. I could only see the side of his face from where I was standing, but what I saw of it was cold and detached. "You're right. I am so sorry. We are a family. You're my family, and I forgot that for a second. Please forgive what I said. I should have never doubted you." She shook her head. "You've always done what's best for us. If it wasn't for you, we'd all probably be dead now. You saved us. All you do is take care of us, and I treated you badly just then. I'm so very sorry."

He tilted his head and his eyes softened. He stood taller with pride. What just happened? Was that how it worked, stroke his overinflated, screwed-up ego and you had a chance?

I held my breath as time stretched in front of us. The only noise was his and Violet's heavy breathing. Rose and Poppy stood wide-eyed as they waited for his decision. The atmosphere was heavy and tense.

Rose was the first one to relax her shoulders as he lowered the knife in his hand. "I forgive you, Violet," he said and turned to walk away without another word. I watched on, eyes bulging and frozen from the shock and fear. My lips were dry, and my nose stung from the citrus smell of lemon cleaning products.

Rose, Poppy, and Violet silently sat on the sofa and held hands while I stood stock still, like an idiot waiting to wake up.

3
SUMMER

Saturday, 24th July (Present)

"What was that?" I whispered, staring at the closed, heavy cellar door. The thing was thick, like it'd been reinforced or something.

"It was my fault. I shouldn't have questioned him," Violet said from behind me.

I recoiled in horror and turned to look at her. "Your fault? What you said was right. Was he seriously going to *stab* you then?" I wanted at least one of them to say no. Their silence said everything.

"Come and sit, Lily. We'll answer whatever you want to know," Rose said, stroking Violet's shaking hand. I wasn't sure I wanted to know anything.

Gulping my fear down, I sat on the end of the sofa. We just about fit on it all together; he must have bought it especially for four people. I was surprised that it was so comfortable. Everything down here, minus the smell, was comfortable and homey. The soft light-blue of the walls and light wooden surfaces and table made it look inviting. If the cleanly smell weren't so potent, it would be a gorgeous room. It was completely out of place in this psychopath's house.

"What do you want to know?" Rose asked. Her blue eyes were as calming as the color of the walls.

"He was going to stab her, wasn't he?" She nodded once in reply. I took a deep, ragged breath. "Because she tried to stand up for me?" I was aware that I was talking to Rose as if we were alone, but from the second I got down here and she offered me her hand, she'd been the one taking the lead. She was like the big sister.

"That's correct."

I licked my dry lips. "Has he done that before?"

Her eyes darkened, losing that friendliness. "Yes, he has."

"You've seen that?"

"Yes."

"They died," I said just above a whisper.

She nodded, her body tensing. "He's killed, yes."

I looked behind her and saw Violet shrinking into Poppy. He had killed people and no one knew a damn thing. How was that even possible? I shook my head in disbelief. "I don't get it. How does he get away with it?" Surely people would notice someone missing? I'd never seen Rose, Poppy, or Violet on the news or stuck to lampposts.

"The girls he chooses are *usually* living on the streets. If no one notices they're missing, then no one will suspect anything is wrong," Rose said and tucked her dark hair behind her ear. "I ran away from my family when I was eighteen. We had never been close and our relationship was…strained. My father"—her eyes darkened and her posture shrank—"liked to drink and didn't like us." It looked as though sadness and terror suddenly consumed her. "Shortly after my eighteenth birthday, I left home. I just couldn't take it anymore. I'd been living on the streets and in hostels for ten months when Clover found me. I've been here almost three years now." She shrugged like being here was nothing.

I was stunned. How did she do it? I would have gone bloody crazy after three weeks. My chest tightened so much I felt like I was gonna collapse. This wasn't temporary.

"Please don't cry, Lily. It's really not that bad down here," Rose said.

I stared at her, trying to work out if she had actually lost it. She sounded crazy. *Not that bad?* He'd kidnapped us. He was keeping us locked up in his cellar. He would rape us when he "fell in love" with us, and if we dared to fight back, he would kill us. How was that *really not that bad*?

"Please don't look at me like that. I know what you're thinking, but if you do what he says, everything will be fine. He'll treat you well."

She must be crazy. "Apart from raping me, you mean?"

"Don't call it rape in front of him," she warned.

I looked away from her. I couldn't believe what she was saying. How could she think this was okay? It was beyond screwed up, but she was still defending him. She couldn't have always been like that. They must have been a time where she knew it was crazy and hated him as much as I do. How long did it take him to brainwash her?

Poppy, Violet, and Rose stood up at the same time—in perfect synchronization—and walked to the kitchen area. They spoke in hushed voices. I could barely hear their whispers, but from the way that Violet looked over, it was obvious they were talking about me. I didn't even care. I didn't even try listening. They could say whatever they wanted, but I was never going to think it was okay to be down here or that *Clover* wasn't a psychotic arsehole.

Someone would find me soon. I wasn't on the streets like they were. I had a family and friends—people that would know I was missing. Soon enough, the police would be called and they would start searching. Who would be the one to realize first? My parents when I didn't return home? Or Lewis when I didn't answer his calls or reply to his texts? Would he even try to contact me any more tonight? If we were out separately with our friends, we wouldn't usually text each other until we were home, or if we did, it would only be once or twice.

Squeezing my eyes together, I tried to push the image of Lewis's face out of my head. I couldn't even think about my parents. Gulping down the rising lump in my throat, I pressed my fingernails into the palm of my hand. *Don't cry.*

"How long have you been here, Poppy?" I asked.

She half smiled and walked the few steps from the kitchen table back to the sofa. Sitting down beside me, she squeezed my clenched fist. "Just over a year. Mine is a similar story to Rose's. I was living on the streets when he found me, and I was eighteen too." An adult. Was that why Violet got so angry? Not that it mattered how old any of us were. It's not like she could know my age. How young do I look? Did *he* even care?

"Why me then? It doesn't make sense. I'm not an adult like you." If he was even kidnapping adults, maybe it didn't matter as long as he got his *family*. I shook my head, blood boiling in anger. "My family will look for me. They'll find us."

"Maybe," Poppy said and gave me another weak smile. Whatever, she didn't have to believe me. I knew they wouldn't just give up. I was *not* spending years down here like they had.

A creaking at the cellar door made my heart jump into my throat and my stomach turn. He was coming back. I listened hard but couldn't hear anything until the slight squeak of the door handle. Why didn't I hear him outside? The air left my lungs. I felt as if I'd been punched in the stomach. *Soundproof.* We couldn't hear anything out there, and more important to him, no one could hear us in here.

Rose stood and walked to the bottom of the stairs to meet him. How could she stand to be anywhere near him? The sight of his adult-preppy appearance and smug face made me want to throw up.

"I'm ordering pizza for dinner," he announced. "I think we all deserve a treat tonight, and we need to properly welcome Lily to the family." My stomach turned again. *He is actually insane and needs locking up.* He turned to me and smiled. "Lily, we usually get two cheese, a pepperoni, and a barbecue chicken. Is that okay with you? I can order something else if you'd like?"

I stared at him in shock. Was he seriously discussing dinner right after he kidnapped me and pulled a knife on someone else? He was sick, evil, and twisted. I didn't want to talk to him, ever. Poppy nudged me discreetly, prompting me to answer him. Taking a shaky breath, I gave in and replied, "T-that's fine."

He smiled, flashing his too-perfect white teeth. Everything about him looked flawless—his skin, his hair, his perfectly ironed clothes, his damn teeth. The phrase "wolf in sheep's clothing" was made for him. "That's perfect then. I knew you would fit in well. I'll go and order now. It won't be long."

Without another word, he slowly walked back up the stairs.

The cellar door had been unlocked the whole time he was down here.

I watched him close the door and heard him lock it, angry with myself, as I'd missed the chance to escape. "W-what?" I mumbled. My eyes stung where I had been too stunned to blink. This was all a dream. It had to be. Things like this didn't happen to me. They didn't even happen to anyone I knew.

Poppy smiled. "It's going to be okay."

I closed my eyes and took a deep breath. The only way this could ever be okay would be if I got out before he laid a finger on me.

I woke up to someone lightly shaking my arm in an annoying way that I was so used to. I smiled and looked over, expecting Lewis to be grinning back at me. My heart sunk when I saw Rose's long, dark brown hair and blue eyes. Oh God, how could I have fallen asleep?

Gasping in shock and at the realization that all this wasn't just a horrible dream, I shoved myself back against the sofa, away from her.

"I'm sorry I scared you, Lily. Clover's here with the pizza," she whispered. "Come, sit with us." I stopped breathing, my lungs felt like they had an elephant sitting on them. Could I sit with him and eat? Did I even have a choice? Rose put her hand on my shoulder and nudged me forward. "Here, you sit next to Poppy." Did he even dictate where we sat?

I tensed as I sat down at the table. He was opposite me and sat there as if nothing was wrong at all. To him this was normal. He never mentioned kidnapping me. It was like to him, I had always been here. Like we really all were family. He really believed we were a family. How bloody delusional was he?

The table was covered in a bright white cotton tablecloth and a fresh vase of pink lilies. The pizza had been removed from the boxes and piled on two large serving dishes on either side of the flowers that I assumed were all for me and my new name.

"Please, help yourself," he said, gesturing to the food with his hand. *I'd rather die.* He made it sound as if I had a choice, but the steely look in his cold eyes—and the flash of the knife he pulled from his pocket still fresh on my mind—told me I didn't. He wanted us to eat as a family, and I knew what he was capable of if I refused.

I reached out and took the slice that was closest to me, quickly retracting my hand so I was as far away from him as possible. He gave me a warm smile, his eyes glowing now. I dropped my eyes to my plastic plate and nibbled at the edge of the pizza.

While Rose, Violet, and Poppy discussed what we would be cooking for dinner the rest of the week, I forced down a few bites in silence. The food felt alien in my stomach. I didn't mind cheese pizza, but this tasted plastic, and I gagged every time I swallowed the mushed-up food.

Rose held her hand up, gaining my attention even though she wasn't looking at me. "Oh, Clover, before I forget, we're getting low on books again."

He nodded his head once. "I'll get you some more."

"Thank you." She smiled and sipped her water. I wanted to scream at her. How could she not see how messed up this was? She was so at ease with him, her body turned toward him slightly while Poppy and Violet faced straight ahead, and I was just a statue trying not to be noticed.

"Thank you for your company tonight, girls. I'll see you in the morning," he said and rose from his seat. "Have a good evening."

My body felt like it had been outside in the snow all day. I was stiff and slow to move. He leaned over and placed a kiss on Rose's cheek and then Poppy's and Violet's. I started breathing faster, gripped with fear. *Not me. Please not me.* I could hear my pulse smashing in my ears, and bile rose in my throat. He bowed his head toward me and turned and walked away.

I let out a big sigh of relief. I couldn't let him touch me. He stopped on the top of the stairs and unlocked the door. I didn't take my eyes off him as he left the room and locked the door from the other side. I wanted to make sure he really had left.

Rose and Poppy got up and gathered the plates together to

clean up. There was only one of him and four of us. We could overpower him if we worked together. Had they tried that before, or were they always too scared? I wasn't even sure if Rose would want to.

"Come and watch a movie with us," Poppy said. I looked up at her and realized they had cleaned everything away and Rose was now sitting in front of the TV.

I joined them on the sofa and stared at the screen, but I didn't take anything in. Wrapping my arms around my legs, I sunk back into the sofa to try to make myself disappear. Nothing felt real anymore.

Hours must have passed, because Rose switched the TV off and they all stood. "Lily?" Violet said in a soft voice, as if she were talking to a child. "Come on, we need to all get showered and go to bed. I'll show you the bathroom. You can go first." She led me to the bathroom and gave me some pajamas. I didn't even question why I was showering instead of collapsing in bed. Whose pajamas were they anyway?

She left me to it. There was no lock on the door. I wished there was so I could shut myself away from them all. Turning the shower on, I ran my hand under the water until it warmed up. Why was I doing this? *Because he could kill you without question or hesitation.* Stripping out of my clothes, I stepped into the shower and sunk to the floor. I burst into tears, gasping for breath as my cries turned hysterical. I gripped my hair and closed my eyes as my tears mixed with the hot water.

When my tears had dried up and my head felt like it was going to explode, I forced myself to get out of the shower and get dressed. Crying wasn't going to get me anywhere, and I didn't want any more attention than I was already getting. I wrapped the fluffy towel tightly around myself—it smelled fresh, like it was just out of the washer—and opened the bathroom cabinet. I noticed straight away that there were no razors—in their place were two pink boxes of waxing strips. Nothing in the cabinet could cause any damage—to anyone.

Closing the door, I made the mistake of looking at myself in the mirror screwed to the front of the cabinet. My eyes were bloodshot and puffy. I looked like I had been in a scrap with a cage fighter. I spun around, not wanting to see how awful I looked any longer, and pulled on someone else's pajamas.

"Are you ready for bed?" Rose asked as I walked back into the room. I nodded in response and wrapped my arms around myself. "Okay, I'll show you where you'll sleep." She led me into the room beside the bathroom. The walls were painted light pink and the furniture was all white. There were four single beds with pink quilt covers and pillows. On the bedside tables were identical light pink lamps. It all matched too well, like it was decorated for quadruplets. "This one is yours," she said and pointed to the bed against the wall on the left. *Mine.* I had a bed. This was supposed to be home.

I was too exhausted to argue, so I numbly walked over to the bed and climbed under the cover. Closing my eyes, I prayed sleep would come soon and take me away from here, and that when I woke up I would be in my own room.

4
LEWIS

Sunday, 25th July (Present)

Missing. I repeated the word over and over in my head. *Lewis, we need to go now. Summer's missing.* That was what Henry said. His face was pale as he explained that his sister—my girlfriend—hadn't been seen for hours.

It was almost three o'clock in the morning, and we had been driving around and looking by foot for four hours. Summer didn't go missing. The longest she's gone without anyone being able to see or hear her was the ten minutes it took for her to shower. I couldn't think of a single reason why she would take off and not tell anyone.

My brother, Theo, drove slowly through the streets. In any other situation, I would be shouting at him to put his foot down or let me drive. Now I wanted to tell him to go even slower. It was pitch-black out and the dim streetlights barely lit any of the bloody ground below them. We could have missed her a thousand times because we couldn't see properly, but I couldn't go home and do nothing like my parents suggested. Sitting and waiting would drive me mad.

"Lewis, you okay?" Theo asked again. That same stupid question was shot at me about every ten minutes. What did he think? *Of course I'm not fucking okay!*

"No," I mumbled. Where was she? Summer didn't run off; she wasn't the type of person to run from anything. She was strong-willed and stubborn. I couldn't even argue with her properly because she would sit on my bed and tell me to calm down so we could talk and sort it out. She dealt with problems straight on—it was what I both loved and hated about her. Sometimes I just wanted to be pissed off, but she made sure we fixed it.

"We'll find her, bro."

"Yeah." I agreed with him but I wasn't so sure. I hoped we would more than anything, but I had this sick feeling in the pit of my stomach that wouldn't go away. Something definitely wasn't right. "She could be anywhere by now." It had been over seven hours since she was last seen, and since then, absolutely nothing. It was as if she'd just vanished.

"Summer wouldn't run off," Theo said.

My heart dropped to my feet. *I know.* "That's what I'm afraid of. She wouldn't run off…someone must have taken her."

"Don't do that, Lewis. Look, we don't know anything yet." He was right; I didn't know for sure. But I did know Summer. "Do you want to carry on and go into town or turn back and go the other way?"

"Other way." Kerri'd said Summer had turned left at the club. We had checked there before coming this way, but we could have missed something. Double-checking couldn't hurt. Jesus, triple-checking couldn't hurt. I wanted to search every inch of the town ten times so I knew for sure I hadn't missed anything.

The police had people out looking around the area where she

was last seen, but because it hadn't been over twenty-four hours, they were reluctant to put too many officers into it. I had never been so damn angry as I was when I found out they were waiting twenty-four hours when she could be anywhere, going through fuck knows what, before they would take it seriously.

Apparently a bunch of our neighbors had started their own search and were going door to door, hoping that someone had seen something. They knew Summer; they knew she wouldn't run away. Everyone I knew, except Summer's mum, was out looking. Dawn was told to stay home in case Sum turned up or called. I wouldn't want to be in her position.

I pulled my phone out of my pocket and checked it for the millionth time—no missed calls. I sighed and held down number 2—speed-dialing her phone again. It started to ring, like it did before, and I held my breath. *Please answer, baby.* Her voice filled the car, her voice mail told everyone to leave a message and if you were Channing Tatum, yes, she would marry you.

"Babe, please call me back the second you get this. I just need to know you're okay. I'm going crazy here. I love you, Sum." I hung up and clenched the phone in my hand. *This is bad.*

We drove through the night and into the early morning. My eyes stung from being so tired. As soon as the stores opened, Theo bought some food and energy drinks. I hadn't been home since we got that call at the nightclub, so I was still in my jeans and shirt.

"I'll pull over here and we can check the back fields and the park by foot," I told Theo.

He nodded, stuffing the last of his sandwich into his mouth. "You sure you don't want anything to eat?"

I shook my head as I pulled up in the parking lot beside the church. "Not hungry. Let's try the park first." He got out of the car and headed over to the gate. I followed, quickly overtaking him. "Summer," I called out. Of course, she wasn't going to be here. If she were, she would have been found by now. "Come on, Theo," I shouted over my shoulder. He didn't seem to have the urgency I had, but then, he wasn't in love with her.

With every passing minute she was missing, I was even more lost. I felt sick and my heart wouldn't fucking slow down. I had no clue what the hell I was going to do if anything had happened to her. "Lewis," Theo said, "what about down there?"

I looked to where he was pointing. The overgrown footpath that ran beside the park and between acres of farmland and fields. I nodded and headed that way. Worth a shot—anything, anywhere was worth a shot. The park had been searched a lot, but the overgrown path wouldn't have been searched thoroughly enough in the dark. Whatever happened, I wasn't giving up until we had her back.

"Anything?" I asked Dawn as I walked through the door. We had found nothing. No trace at all—all my hope was pinned on her.

She shook her head and whispered, "No." That one little word felt like being stabbed. Her eyes were bloodshot from lack of sleep and crying, and I pictured Summer the same, waiting for us to find her. The remains of Dawn's day-old makeup were smudged under her eyes and down her cheeks. "The police are starting a proper search today, though. They'll find her." She nodded her head as if she were telling herself the same thing, convincing herself.

"Right, I'm going," Summer's dad, Daniel, announced. He stopped as he saw me. "Oh, Lewis. Anything?" I shook my head. It was as if she just vanished. His shoulders were slumped, and from someone who was always strong and positive, it made me fear the worst. "I'll be back later," he said and gave Dawn a brief kiss on the cheek. He looked as exhausted as I felt.

"Are you hungry?" Dawn asked, staring into space. "Your mum's making food. I don't know what."

"Thanks, Dawn," Theo said. "Why don't we go to the kitchen?" He led her through, wrapping his arm around her back to help her like she was a sick old lady.

I didn't want to hang around. I just wanted to find out what the plan was and get back out there. Sitting around eating wasn't going to get Summer back. "Theo, Lewis," my mum gushed, throwing a tea towel down. "Sit, sit."

"Thanks for cooking, Emma," Dawn said. Mum smiled sadly, her eyes showing how scared she was.

"I don't want to sit. I just want to know what I should be doing. Is someone coming to sort a proper search out yet?" I asked. Surely the police had a plan rather than just sending everyone out looking randomly?

"They've already been, sweetheart," Mum replied. "They're

starting with a thorough search of the area they believe Summer was last—"

"How do they know that?"

"Know what?

I sighed in frustration. "Where she last was?"

Mum shrugged. "I'm not sure, a combination of the direction she went in, where a young girl would go, and how long it was before Kerri called her and noticed she wasn't answering to work out how far away she was likely to be. I don't know *exactly*."

"So they're just guessing? They don't even know Summer and they're *guessing* where she was likely to go?"

"Lewis, calm down," Theo ordered.

"No. Fuck this!" They didn't have a clue and now Summer could be anywhere.

I stormed out of the house. I didn't know where I was going, but I had to get out. My girlfriend was missing, and I had no clue where she was or how to find her. And it didn't seem like the police had the slightest clue where to start either.

"Lewis!" Theo shouted. I heard his footsteps getting louder, so I knew he was following me too. "Wait up." He grabbed the top of my arm and swung me around. "You can't just go running off. Look, I'm going to the town hall, that's where the search is based. Come with me and we can ask as many questions as you have before we get back out there."

I sighed and ran my hand over my face. "Theo, what if she's…"
Dead.

"Don't. She's not; she's fine."

"You don't know that!" I exclaimed. My heart was racing. "It's been hours, and no one's heard from her. She never goes off and—"

"Lewis, stop. This isn't helping Summer, is it? She needs you, so quit the bullshit and do something to *help* her."

He was right. I nodded. My eyes stung but I refused to cry. I needed to be strong for her and falling apart now wouldn't get her back. "You're right." I sighed and my heart dropped. "I just can't lose her," I whispered. As cheesy as it sounded, my biggest fear was losing Summer—in *any* way. I loved her.

"Let's go."

Theo smiled and unlocked his car. "Here." He handed me something wrapped up in a paper towel. A bacon bagel. "Eat." I got in the passenger side and forced myself to eat. Every bite made me want to hurl, but Theo was right—Summer needed me—and I had to be strong for her. I was no good if I was a mess.

"She's okay, isn't she?"

Theo nodded. "She'll be fine." She'll *be* fine. He didn't think she was fine now, but she would be when we found her? I should be able to tell where she was. I love her, so shouldn't I just know what was wrong? *Where are you, Sum?*

We pulled into a tight parking space at the hall, the only one left. The place was full. Were all those people here to help?

The main hall was heaving with people. Right at the front was a long table stacked with maps, bottles of water, and high-visibility vests. Where did all that come from? A picture of Summer was pinned to a board beside the table. The world stopped spinning. I took a deep breath and walked toward the police officers.

Above Summer's picture were the words: **MISSING 16-YEAR-OLD SUMMER ROBINSON.**

5
SUMMER

Sunday, July 25th (Present)

I pushed myself up and wiped my tears away with the back of my hand. I wasn't home; I was still in *that* bedroom. Why couldn't I just wake up properly? All I wanted to do was to be at home with the family that drove me crazy most of the time. I wouldn't even complain about Henry running to the bathroom before me or my dad's crappy attempts at giving me a curfew.

"Good morning, Lily," Rose said from the bed opposite mine. Good morning my arse. This was a morning from a nightmare — one that I couldn't wake up from.

I attempted to smile but I was sure my mouth didn't even move. What happened now? What was I supposed to do today? I wanted to say something to Rose, maybe ask her, but I wasn't sure I even wanted to know. I kind of felt like this wasn't happening to me, like I was in a dream or a movie.

Rose smiled in sympathy and opened the single-width wardrobe beside me. "Here, you can borrow some clothes until Clover gets you some new things."

The blood drained from my face. Rose laid a pair of jeans and an oversized lilac sweater on the bed. I shook my head. How could she expect me to wear the clothes of a girl that had been murdered down here—the Lily before me "No," I whispered. "I can't." I wasn't going to walk around in a dead girl's clothes.

"These are all we have."

"You get used to it," Violet said, holding her own similar outfit in her hand. We all color matched. The tops were slightly different but the same color. We were like a lame group of friends at school that thought it was cool to have matching days. I felt like we should start braiding each other's hair and talk about dreamy boys.

"Okay, I'm going to have a shower. Poppy and Violet, can you explain to Lily, please?" Rose said and picked up her clothes and a towel. Explain what? I doubt I wanted to know.

They waited until Rose left and then sat on my bed. "The morning routine," Poppy said, brushing her dark red, almost brown hair. "We need to take a shower and be ready by eight, every morning. That's when Clover comes down for breakfast."

I shook my head in disbelief. "What? We have to dress up for him?" This was too crazy to be real. "The bloody psycho."

Poppy frowned. "It's not dressing up exactly. He likes us to be clean, dressed respectfully, and have our hair and makeup done for when he comes. He likes us to look nice for him *and* for ourselves."

My stomach turned. I didn't want his idea of looking nice. I liked my jeans and T-shirts. I didn't do girly dressing up, especially not for a sick murderer. "I don't want to look nice for him. Bloody hell, can you hear yourself?"

"Honestly, Lily, neither do I. Trust me, though, it's better than the alternative," Violet said.

I gulped and closed my eyes. The answer to my next question was obvious but, like an idiot, I still asked. "What's the alternative?"

"You don't want to know," Violet said and gulped. My heart started to race. Why didn't I want to know?

"I just want to go home." Tears trickled down my cheeks, and I squeezed my eyes closed. "I want to see Lewis and my family."

"Is he your boyfriend?" Poppy asked. I nodded and sniffed, really unattractively. "Do you love him?"

"Yes." I had been in love with him for ages before we got together. He was easygoing and fun to be around. He could also stress over silly little things and was fiercely protective of the people he loved. We had so many arguments about me wandering around alone. If I'd listened to him instead of brushing off his fears and telling him nothing was ever going to happen in *boring old Long Thorpe*, then maybe I'd be at home right now.

She looked down, her red hair falling in her face. "That's nice."

"He'll find me," I stated confidently. Lewis wouldn't just sit back; he would do everything he possibly could to find me. So would my family. My mum was expert in finding things. Nothing could stay hidden from her—unfortunately for Henry and his porn stash.

Violet smiled halfheartedly. "Let's hope so."

Violet wasn't as messed up as Rose; she sounded different, like she wanted to get out. But did that mean she would help me do something to him so we could escape? I wanted to fire questions at her right away, but I knew I had to find out more. I had to be sure she definitely wanted to get out before I said anything.

Poppy sighed, getting back to business. "Anyway, you need to leave your hair natural." Like I could just pop to the shops for some bloody hair dye! "He doesn't like when you mess with it too much, and you should only wear a small amount of makeup— easy on the mascara." I wanted to throw up. I was being told how to dress. I'd never been told that.

Rose came back into the room and immediately fussed around, straightening her bedsheets and plumping the pillows. I watched her running her hands over the quilt, flattening it, and wondered if I would be doing that after three years. *No.* There was no way I would be down here longer than three days. I had people looking for me. This was temporary, and soon enough the police would find us. They would.

Taking a deep breath to clear my thoughts, I went to the bathroom to shower and get ready. There was no point in having a shower before bed and again in the morning, but I wasn't going to argue over that. I let the water spray over my body for a few minutes and then got out.

Standing in front of the steamy mirror I could almost pretend I was at home, getting ready for a date with Lewis or a night out with friends. I brushed mascara over my eyelashes and worried how much I should use. Not too much that I looked like a hooker, but enough so my eyelashes stood out. Would he punish me for wearing too much or too little? Wow, yesterday my biggest worry was which top I should wear to the gig.

I dressed in the clothes Rose gave me and dried my hair. Looking back in the mirror, I barely recognized myself. I looked exhausted and I felt it too. Dark circles under my eyes made me look so much older than sixteen.

Dropping my head, I turned away. Looking at myself was too depressing. I hadn't even been down here one day, and I already felt like a different person—like Lily. Poppy passed me as I walked out of the bathroom. It was her turn to get ready for *him*.

I stopped in the living room area and watched Rose frying bacon and eggs on the stove. She worked so efficiently, humming as she turned the bacon over. The scene reminded me of my mum making a full breakfast on a Sunday morning. My heart squeezed. What would Mum be doing now? Searching for me? Staring at her phone waiting for me to call or waiting by the front door? Not cooking, that was for sure. I wanted to go back home. I'd even let Mum hug me without pulling away and rolling my eyes.

Rose grabbed a plastic spatula and flipped the eggs over. Everything in the kitchen had been chosen carefully. In fact, everything in the whole cellar had been chosen carefully. There was nothing sharp or dangerous. Nothing we could use to escape or hurt him with. The only thing I could think of was poisoning him. There were plenty of cleaning products. But how could you not smell the powerful scent of bleach? And, even if we did poison him, there was no guarantee he would die down here. If he died in the house, we would eventually starve to death. It seemed hopeless without Rose, Violet, and Poppy on my side, but I wasn't going to give up. There was a way—there had to be—and I just had to be patient and play along with this shit until I could figure it out.

I sat down on the sofa and curled up in a little ball. We couldn't be too far away from Long Thorpe; we didn't drive for long. The police would check this place out. That's what they did when someone went missing, right? They did the door-to-door thing, asking residents if they'd seen anything. I'd definitely seen that on the news before.

A door opened, making me jump and my heart race. My shoulders sagged in relief when I realized it was the bathroom door and not the cellar. Poppy briefly smiled at me and went to help dish up breakfast. I wondered if Rose secretly hated it down here and just put on a really good show. Was she so scared of him that she wouldn't be honest in case it got back to him, or did she really think it's all right down here? The last plate was placed on the table and they both smiled. The food smelled good, and I was so hungry, but the thought of eating made my stomach turn.

The creaky sound from the cellar door echoed through the room and I froze. He was coming. I took a deep breath and clenched my shaking hands together. *Keep it together.*

"Good morning, Flowers," he said and smiled warmly as he came down the stairs. He was holding a beautiful bunch of pink lilies, the same as the ones on the kitchen table but bigger, matching the size of Rose's, Violet's, and Poppy's flowers. I sank back into the sofa as he approached me. "For you, Lily," he said, holding the flowers out. My skin crawled like I was being attacked by ants. *Don't talk to me.*

I looked to Rose, pleading with her to help. She nodded toward the flowers once, and I knew I had to accept them. *Just play along, Summer.* I stood up and slowly reached my trembling hand out and took the lilies from him. "Thank you," I said quietly and stepped back, hitting the side of the sofa.

"You don't have to be so shy, Lily. We're a family. Why don't you put those in water now?" He frowned and his eyes darkened. "I don't want them to die." The other girls looked away quickly and sat down. What was that about? They were acting weirder. Did it mean something?

So I wouldn't make him angry, I grabbed the empty vase and filled it with water. It was made from thin plastic but was a very good glass imitation. Unless you held it, you would never tell. I threw them in the vase and placed it between the weltering red poppies, bright violets, and white roses. Why flowers? I wanted to know everything about him so I could use something to get out, but at the same time I wanted to know nothing.

I sat in the seat I was in yesterday—opposite *him*. Every muscle in my body ached where I'd been tensing up. The physical pain was actually welcome; it was almost a distraction from what was happening.

"Let's eat then," Violet said.

The fried food did nothing to settle my stomach. I wanted to puke. I could feel his eyes on me, studying me. Deciding something? If he wanted to keep me or not? I nibbled on a piece of toast, feeling the most self-conscious I ever had. Why wouldn't he look away?

My mind quickly flicked back to Lewis. Concentrating on him took me away for a minute. I wondered what he was doing. Usually he would still be asleep, but I doubt he would be now. My parents always sat around drinking endless cups of coffee on weekend mornings before they did anything. Would they have made a thermos up while they searched for me? I hoped so, because Mum felt awful if she hadn't had her caffeine fix and was super snappy.

"Lily?" someone called, snapping me out of my daydreaming. *He*, Rose, Violet, and Poppy were all staring at me, and now I couldn't read any of their expressions.

"Sorry," I whispered and moved my food around on the plate to look like I was doing something with it. Did they want something, or was it just because I was in my own world? They went back to their food.

"So, Clover, what have you got planned for today?" Rose asked as if this was a normal situation. Like he was going to reply "bit of kidnapping, maybe a murder or two, the usual." How could she even ask him things like that so casually? I wasn't even sure if she was afraid of him anymore.

He smiled at her, almost lovingly. "After I've caught up with a few things for work, I'll be going out." He worked? Well, of course he did; he must have to work to support five people. He didn't seem like a particularly social person, though. Where would he be going out?

"Why don't you tell Lily about your job? She looks a little confused," Rose suggested.

Here goes. Pretend it's not real and he's talking about a film. As much as I wanted to shut off and go back home in my head, I needed every piece of information I could get.

His eyes flicked to me and he smiled. I tried not to turn my nose up in disgust. He looked warm and friendly. It was hard to believe he was the same man who kidnapped me and stabbed a woman to death just yesterday. If I passed him on the street, I wouldn't look at him twice, but I wouldn't be cautious around him either. He just looked so normal.

"I'm an accountant for a law firm in town." I managed to swallow the laughter that threatened to burst out. He worked for a *lawyer*. How ironic. The other side of him––his job––it all seemed so normal. No one would guess that this well-dressed, polite accountant led a secret sadistic second life. He must sit at his desk every day, chat with his coworkers, and do his job, then go home to the women in his cellar.

"You should eat now, Lily. We don't want you getting any slimmer." He stared at me for a second, daring me to disobey him.

Gulping the fear away, I cut off a small piece of egg and popped it in my mouth. I didn't want to make him angry like Violet did, so I forced the food down and prayed I wouldn't be sick. I wanted to lose weight to piss him off, but I wouldn't. The food slid down my throat making me gag. *Chew.*

"Right, Flowers, I need to leave for work. Have a good day and I'll see you for dinner. Roast chicken tonight, Rose."

"Yes, Clover," she said and nodded her head.

He stood up and kissed Poppy, Violet, and Rose on the cheek. *Please not me.* My heart was beating out of my chest. "Good-bye,

Lily." He walked up the stairs, and I breathed a big sigh of relief. What was I going to do when he eventually tried to kiss me like that?

"Come on, Lewis," I muttered. He always made things better, whether it was bringing me my favorite food when I didn't feel well, helping me study for exams I was convinced I would fail, or having a word with Henry if he said something out of line. I knew it was too much to expect him to fix this too, but I couldn't help it.

Poppy arched her eyebrow. "How long have you been together?"

"Just over a year and a half, but I liked him for ages before that."

She smiled, her eyes lit up, and she seemed genuinely interested. I wondered what her story was. "Where did you meet?"

"He's friends with my brother, they met when they joined the same football team. At first he thought I was just Henry's annoying little sister but as we both grew older he started seeing me differently. Thankfully."

"I hope you get back to him," she said sincerely and then walked away. *So do I.*

Sunday, January 4th (2009)

I walked into Henry's room to grab a movie for me, Kerri, and Rachel. He was playing PlayStation with Lewis, as usual. I rolled my eyes. They looked so into it, shooting at something. Zombies? *Bloody losers!*

"Hey, Sum," Lewis said, smiling at me as he looked up. Butterflies flitted around in my stomach. I bit my lip.

Don't say anything stupid. "Hey," I replied, trying to stay casual

when I was happy dancing in my head. I'd liked Lewis for for-
ever, and recently he had been looking at me differently. Well,
he seemed to be anyway. I just hoped it wasn't all in my head—
which I was almost 100 percent sure it was.

His light green eyes sparkled and I melted. They really stood
out against his dark, almost black, hair. He cocked his head to
the side. "What can we do for you?" *You could kiss me.*

"Lewis, you just got us killed," Henry yelled, scowling at
him. You'd think he had *actually* been killed by his over-the-
top reaction.

"Huh?" Lewis looked back to the screen where it said "Game
Over." Oh my God, he just got killed looking at me. Okay,
chill and stop smiling like a creeper. I forced my lips to stay
down as they tried to pull up into the biggest smile. How
could I not smile when this was officially the best day of my
entire life?

"Sorry," Lewis muttered and chucked the controller down on
the bed.

"What do you want, Summer?" Henry snapped, obviously still
angry over his stupid game. *Whatever.*

I walked over to his DVDs and started scanning the titles.
"Need a scary movie," I replied, turning my nose up.

"You don't like scary movies," Lewis said. "You being forced
into it?"

"Yep. Kerri and Rachel want to spend the evening hiding
behind cushions. Idiots." Scary movies were the worst.

Lewis grinned. His perfect white teeth stood out against his natural tan. Why was he so good-looking? It wasn't fair. "Why don't you watch it in here?" he said.

Henry's head snapped up and he frowned. Oh, big bro was not going to like that. "What are you doing?"

I tried to keep the silly grin off my face, but there was no stopping it this time. He wanted us to watch it with him, and I couldn't have been happier.

"This game sucks now anyway," Lewis said and shrugged his shoulders casually. Wait, was he just bored or did he want to spend time with me? Boys say girls were confusing when they're the ones that are total head fucks.

"Fine! I'll go tell them to come in here, and I'm picking the movie," Henry said, sighing in defeat. He walked out of his messy room, muttering something colorful under his breath. Loser.

Lewis patted the bed next to him and smiled. My tummy flipped. Okay, maybe he did want to spend time with me. I walked over slowly and got on the bed, trying not to seem too eager. Kerri and Rachel came bouncing into the room. They seemed happy we were watching in Henry's room. They constantly went on about how Lewis liked me too. I wanted them to be right so badly.

I shuffled over, closer to Lewis so they could all fit on the king-size bed Henry absolutely had to have. We were still crammed together but since I was squished against Lewis's side, I didn't mind at all. In fact I wished my parents weren't such softies and had made Henry get a double instead.

"Oh, come on," I exclaimed. My heart sunk as the title for the movie appeared. *The Texas Chainsaw Massacre*. Much worse than I thought it would be. Now I was going to be all scared and make a complete fool out of myself in front of Lewis. Just great. I didn't even have a pillow to hide behind. I pulled my legs up and rested my head on my knees.

"Er, Sum, he hasn't even pressed play yet," Lewis joked, bumping his shoulder against mine. I elbowed him in the side playfully, making him laugh. Out of the corner of my eye, I saw Kerri raise her eyebrow at me. *Oh crap, if she says anything, I will actually die!*

The film started and that was my cue to hide away and pretend it wasn't happening. Of all the movies my idiot brother could have picked, he chose *this* one. I needed to man up, but every time some crazy jumped out from behind a door I freaked.

About halfway through the movie, I dared to look up. Nothing much was happening but I knew there was still a while to go. Why did people like this kind of thing? They were sick. Something on the screen made a bang and I dropped my head back to my knees. Screw that. I was a baby and completely happy with that title.

I jumped as something brushed the outside of my leg. Lewis's hand? My breath caught in my throat. Okay, that was a better way to make me forget about the movie. I doubt hiding would ever help again after that. I didn't dare look at him, but I sensed his smile.

There was no way I was going to be able to concentrate on the movie now, so I raised my head from my knees. *Just look at him.* Man, I really was a baby. I flicked my eyes up and Lewis looked at me at the same time.

"Okay?" he mouthed, and I nodded. I was more okay with the

back of his index finger drawing circles on my leg. Wow, my skin actually tingled wherever he touched.

"Boo!" Henry shouted at the top of his lungs. My heart leaped out of my chest and I jumped in the air, screaming.

What the heck!

"What's wrong with you?" I yelled. He doubled over with his face planted in the quilt, laughing his arse off. Lewis, Kerri, and Rachel were no better, although I think they jumped too. "Seriously, Henry, I almost had a heart attack."

"Overdramatic wuss," he said, rolling his eyes. I gave him the death glare.

I felt Lewis's body shaking beside me as he laughed. "Damn, that was funny," Lewis said breathlessly, as he continued laughing.

"Yeah, hilarious," I replied sarcastically. My heart was still pumping. My brother sucked. They all did.

Finally the hideous movie finished and Henry went downstairs to get the pizza menu so we could order dinner, since none of us could cook without burning the house down. Thankfully, Mum and Dad left some cash for us. They wouldn't be back from their dinner with Dad's old boring university friend and his equally boring wife until late.

Kerri fake coughed. "I need a drink. Rachel, come help me." Oh. My. God. Can she be any more obvious? I widened my eyes at her and she smiled innocently. *Come on, ground, swallow me up. Please?*

They left and the room fell silent. I literally couldn't think of one thing to say. Everything I thought of sounded lame in my head.

"You're quiet," Lewis said, stating the obvious.

"So are you," I replied.

He chuckled and moved slightly so he was facing me. "Enjoy the movie?"

"Not one little bit."

"Baby."

I rolled my eyes at him and he did that sexy half smile thing. Wow. I heard Henry, Rachel, and Kerri talking at the bottom of the stairs and I wanted to pout that they were coming back so soon. Lewis bit his full lip. "I've wanted to do this for a while."

"Do what?" I asked. He leaned forward and his lips pressed to mine, lingering for only a second. My heart beat so fast I felt like it was going to explode. He pulled back and looked at me. *Oh my God, Lewis just kissed me!* I was in a total daze but he seemed unaffected. He threw one leg over the other and looked up at the door just as they came back.

"What pizza did you order?" Lewis asked. I didn't hear Henry's reply. I couldn't have cared less what pizza he ordered. I bit my lip to try to disguise the huge smile that was making my jaw ache. *I kissed Lewis, I kissed Lewis, I kissed Lewis!* Damn it, why did they have to come back so soon?

6
SUMMER

Sunday, July 25th (Present)

"Let's get this cleaned up," Rose said, clapping her hands together as if it was going to be the most fun in the world. I got up to help, just to have something to do. Rose washed the pans, plastic cutlery, and dishes while I dried them and Poppy put them away. We cleaned and tidied in silence, filling the room with the lemon scent that tingled my nose. I had a million questions I wanted to ask.

Finally, after the whole place was clean, we sat on the sofa. I realized I was acting just like one of them and I burst into tears. I curled up into a ball and sobbed so hard, my lungs started to burn. *This can't be my life.* Never before had I felt so utterly alone.

"Oh, Lily, it's going to be okay," Violet said and rubbed my back.

"N-No. Not okay." I sobbed harder. Tears poured down my face, soaking my knees.

"Shh," Rose cooed. "Take deep breaths and calm down. You're not alone, Lily." *Yes, I am.*

"We're all in this together," Poppy added.

I took a deep breath and tried to stop sobbing. "How can he?" Wiping my tears away, my blurry vision cleared. "He's going out tonight. How can he do all this and still be normal to everyone else?"

Rose sighed. "It's not a pub he's going to, Lily."

"Stop calling me Lily," I snapped.

Rose ignored my outburst as if it never happened. Maybe in Rose's world it didn't. "As far as I'm aware, he doesn't socialize a lot. Most of his time is spent either at work or in here."

"What's he doing tonight then?" I questioned. "And how do you know what he does out there anyway?"

"He is quite an honest person. If you ask him something, he will give you a straight response. Please think about what you ask, though," Rose warned. "Clover doesn't like certain people and what he does occasionally is…" She trailed off, frowning into the distance.

"Is?" I prompted.

"He…disposes of people that do harm."

My mouth fell open. "He *murders* them?" No, he couldn't.

"Yes. That's not quite how he sees it, though. The women, prostitutes, are doing harm. Harm to the innocent families of men that use them."

"Bloody hell, listen to yourself," I whispered, shocked. "You're defending him."

"I'm not defending him."

"Yes you are. You're making it sound like it's okay."

"It's not, and I'm not. I'm just trying to explain how he did, that's all."

"So he spends his evenings out murdering prostitutes?" It couldn't be true. Maybe he only said that to scare them into doing what he said. If prostitutes were being murdered all over the place it would be on the bloody news!

Rose frowned. "You make it sound like he's doing it every night, and that's not true." *How do you know?* Well, it couldn't be true. He couldn't kill on a daily basis and still not have been caught. Surely.

I couldn't believe how calmly *I* was talking about it. Shouldn't I be freaking out and clawing at the door? Should I even worry about how I should or shouldn't think, feel, or act? "How does he get away with it?"

"They're prostitutes, Lily. Most of them have run away from home or have always been alone." But still, for no one to notice. "He thinks they're dirty and represent everything that's wrong with humanity." Rose looked at Poppy and Violet. "We think something happened when he was younger—no one just starts thinking that—but we've never asked." Of course they hadn't. It wasn't worth their life.

"What does he do with them? How many?" I questioned. This was getting crazier by the second. He was like a character from a horror movie.

"I don't know," Violet replied.

"This is crazy. Totally screwed-up crazy. We need to get out of here. We can do it together. I know we can, but we have to work together."

"No, Lily," Rose said sternly, she reminded me of my teachers at school. "We can't. There is no way out, so you need to get this idea out of your head now. You have no real idea of what he's capable of. He has no concept of what is *truly* right and wrong. He can be very…brutal and unforgiving."

A shiver ran through my entire body at her blunt warning. Brutal and unforgiving. I witnessed what he did to Violet, how angry he got and how he threatened her with a knife. How much worse could it get? I didn't want to give up, that wasn't me, but I was terrified.

Rose took a deep breath and stood up. "Now I'm going to clean the bathroom and then we can watch a movie."

Wiping the tears from my eyes, I gulped down the rising sickly feeling in my stomach. "I can't stay here. I need to go home." Why wouldn't they understand that?

Poppy shook her head and squeezed my hand. "I wish you could, Lily. Please don't do anything stupid," she said and got up. Her words whirled around my head. *Please don't do anything stupid.* My mind instantly conjured the image of him holding a knife up to me and it sent a bolt of pure horror right to my bones. I shuddered.

"Which movie?" Rose asked.

Violet shrugged. "Some old romantic chick flick." Was this what would happen every night? I felt a suffocating weight press down on my chest.

Rose put the movie on, and they both sat on the sofa with me. They quickly became absorbed in what was happening on the screen. How could they care about a movie when he was out there preying on some poor girl? I pictured her scared and confused, fighting him for her freedom. Her eyes, completely made up in my imagination, were too wide, popping out of her head in horror. But was he really doing that? For all we knew, he could be going to bingo and just making himself sound scarier to force us to behave and not fight him. My heart clenched. I wanted to know which one was true.

"Can we get normal TV?" I asked, blinking hard to get the girl's eyes out of my mind. Would I be on the news? I must be by now.

Out of the corner of my eye, I saw Poppy shake her head. "No." Of course not. We were literally cut off from absolutely everything and everyone. We completely depended on him. I wished I had never gone out that night. I should have listened to Lewis and my family's worries and let one of them take me. Every time one of them went on about it not being safe to walk alone at night, I would brush it off or tell them to stop being stupid. Looking back, I wanted to punch myself at how cocky I was about it. I felt invincible because I was naïve enough to think bad things only happen to other people.

"We need to start dinner," Rose said and switched the TV off after a while. "Do you want to help, Lily?" *Summer.*

Did I have a choice? "Sure." What else was there to do to pass the time? It was better than sitting down thinking all the time. Although I did like thinking of my family because it took me away from here, I needed to stop sometimes and do something that would distract from how much I missed them. I would give absolutely anything just to talk to them.

"What do you want me to do?" I asked. They had already gotten everything out and were filling two pans with water. They all worked perfectly together. It looked like they were colleagues in a restaurant kitchen.

"Would you peel the carrots and potatoes?" Poppy handed me the peeler, which was plastic apart from the blade in the middle. It didn't look particularly sharp, but it was a possibility. Could it do enough damage, though? Knowing I was probably being watched by one or both of them, I looked away from the peeler and grabbed a potato.

"Do you think we'll ever get out of here?" I asked as I peeled.

Rose sighed and it wasn't in sadness; it was a frustrated sigh. Frustrated with me? "No."

"Do you want to?"

"Violet, can you get me an oven dish, please?" Rose asked, completely ignoring my question.

That's a no then. I felt so sorry for her. He had really screwed with her mind. Rose shoved the chicken in the oven dish and put it in the oven. She was pretending she hadn't heard me, but I knew she would be thinking about it. How could she not? Did she know she was brainwashed?

I'd finished peeling and chopping, so I chucked the potatoes and carrots in the water and turned the electric stovetop on. That was officially the most cooking I'd ever done. Mum would be shocked and proud at the same time; she might even check my forehead to see if I was ill.

The atmosphere had changed; you could cut it with a knife and I knew it was because of my question. They kept their heads down and concentrated on what they were doing. Someone had to say it, though. Rose needed to realize, or re-realize, what he was doing was wrong.

Staring at the water in the pan slowly start to bubble, I shook my head. I had just helped make *him* dinner. I had never even made Lewis dinner before. I smiled at the memory of the one and only time I had offered. He laughed and made a joke about not wanting to be poisoned. I was notoriously bad at cooking.

The time Clover would be back was getting close. I could tell by the way they fussed around, double-checking everything was clean and tidy. My heart beat faster in anticipation. I didn't want him down here, but I almost wanted him to walk through the door so I wouldn't be so on edge waiting for it.

I debated whether I could pretend to be ill, but I didn't want him to check up on me. *Just eat dinner and keep to yourself until he leaves.* This was something I would have to do twice a day on weekdays and three times a day on weekends until I was found.

Finally, *that* sound I had so quickly come to dread echoed through the room—the cellar door unlocking. My hands trembled and my heart leaped into my mouth. Violet gave me a quick smile, telling me it'd be fine. It wouldn't.

"Good evening, Flowers," he said and gave us a charming, *this is all totally normal* smile. That was how he got away with it. He looked so friendly you just instantly trusted him—unless you were down here, of course.

"Good evening," they replied in unison. I busied myself with draining the vegetables while making sure I kept an eye on exactly where he was.

"Is it almost ready?"

"Yes, just serving now," Poppy replied.

I carried two plates over, leaving them to sort out the rest. Rose carried his with a big smile on her face; she probably liked bringing her psycho his dinner.

"Let's eat then," he said cheerfully and tucked into the huge roast dinner.

I forced a bite down, desperate not to draw attention to myself by not eating, but every mouthful made my stomach churn. I kept my eyes on my plate, pretending to eat. All I wanted to do was to fade into the background and not catch his attention. I couldn't relax while he was in the room; my tense body ached.

"How was your day, Clover?" Rose asked.

"Very good so far, thank you. I got a lot done. What about you?"

"Good. We've watched a few great movies." What else are we going to do?

He nodded once. "Well, let me know when you're ready for more."

"We will. Thank you." I wondered if Rose realized she spoke just like him whenever he was down here. They were so formal and polite to each other. It was eerie. "We were wondering if we could have more dress patterns. We'd quite like to make a few summer dresses." My head snapped up immediately. They made clothes? You needed scissors to cut fabric. A plan formed in my head straight away. How poetic would it be if he died the same way as he'd killed—a stab wound?

"Would you teach me?" I piped in.

Clover smiled triumphantly, as if he thought I had finally come around to his sick way of "living." "That's a wonderful idea,

Lily. I'm sure Rose, Violet, and Poppy would love to teach you, wouldn't you, girls?"

"Of course," Rose agreed. My heart leaped with hope. A plan was already forming in my head, almost by itself. I managed to eat a little more food and smile at him almost politely. I could do this. I could play nice, and it was easier now because there was light at the end of the tunnel. We had a way.

Once dinner was over, I expected him to leave, but he took Rose's hand and led her into a room that I hadn't been in before. It looked half under the stairs and couldn't be very big at all. I assumed it was a closet. What was going on? "Where are they going? What's in there?" I asked, looking at the closed door.

Poppy lowered her head and bit her lip. "That's the room where he…" she whispered. Her eyes filled with tears.

"What? Where he does what…" I trailed off, realizing what she was trying to say. My blood froze inside my veins. *The room where he rapes us.* He and Rose were in there now. She went so willingly, no hesitation, no sign of horror in her eyes. "I need to go home," I whispered to myself more than to them.

"You need to stop this, Lily. There is no going home. The sooner you accept that the easier it will be. Trust me. Please?" Poppy said.

All I could hear was the sound of my frantic pulse smashing in my ears. *Shit.* "No." I sat down and tried to absorb everything. Rose was being raped in a room just *feet* from me. But was she? Did she want to now? Surely she couldn't be that brainwashed that she wanted him. I gulped and felt a tear trickle down my cheek.

"Lily?" Poppy put her hand on my shoulder making me jump. "Sorry. Are you okay?" I shook my head and stared ahead at nothing. I felt empty. There would be a time when he would want me to go into that room. Could I survive that? I would rather die than have him near me. If I did die, though, I would never see Lewis or my family again. It was an impossible choice. Either stay alive in the hope of being reunited with my family but be raped, or die never having said good-bye to the people I love but die free of him.

I wasn't sure how long I sat as still as a statue while they were in that room, but it didn't seem that long. The door opened, and I quickly curled myself up in a ball, wiping my tears from my face.

"Good night, Flowers."

"Night, Clover," Poppy and Violet said from beside me. I couldn't talk to him; I couldn't even look at him. *Disgusting, sick bastard!*

Rose sat down and flicked the TV on as if nothing had happened. There were no tears, no acknowledgment of what he just did to her. I didn't dare say anything. Pressing my side into the arm of the sofa, I turned my head so my hair fell in my face, hiding the fresh tears that fell for Rose.

After the movie, it was finally late enough to go to bed. I wanted sleep. I needed the escape. "Lily, do you want to shower first?" Rose asked, and I nodded. Actually, I didn't. I didn't want to shower at all. "Okay."

Without hanging around to talk, I grabbed the pajamas from *my* bed and went in the bathroom. Why was I even doing this?

My second shower of the day lasted longer. I let the hot water cascade over my body and wash away what felt like inches of dried-on dirt. Would I ever feel clean again?

Yawning, I switched the shower off and quickly dried myself. Even though it wasn't really late—only ten at night—I was exhausted. My mind had been working overtime and desperately needed a break. It was strange to think I was looking forward to sleeping here. I would actually like to sleep the entire time I would be down here.

As I walked between the bathroom and bedroom, I glanced back at the stairs leading to the door. How the hell am I ever going to get out of here? I didn't believe it was impossible, like they did, but I knew it wasn't something I could just do impulsively. I had to play it safe because if anything went wrong, he would kill me without thinking twice.

I got into bed and pulled the quilt over my head so I was completely hidden. The bedroom would look quite pretty if it wasn't in the middle of hell. Closing my eyes, I stupidly tried to contact Lewis. I prayed that by some odd miracle he would hear me. But of course, he wouldn't be able to. *Please come*, I begged Lewis in my head and started crying silently.

A loud bang followed by a high-pitched scream woke me up. The color drained from my face and my heart skipped a beat. What was that? I threw the cover off myself and sprinted to the door. I slammed into Poppy, who grabbed my arm and shoved me farther back into the room.

"What's that?" I hissed.

"Just stay in here. He'll want to see someone," Poppy said and followed Rose and Violet out, closing the door behind them. I was alone. The soft light from the lamp didn't do much to lighten the room. I wanted to turn them all on to make it as bright as possible, but I was too scared to move.

"No, no, no," a new voice I didn't recognize screamed, and a haze of fear engulfed me. Who was that?

"Shut up," Clover bellowed. His voice ripped through the room with such force my heart leaped into my throat. I'd seen him shout before, but this was different; this sounded violent and angry.

What was he doing, and who was he shouting at? Everything went silent. I turned my head, angling my ear toward the door, wanting to hear more but not daring to move. My heart pounded in my chest. Was she going to stay down here too? Was she trying to fight back?

I licked my dry lips as I waited for something to happen. I couldn't hear Poppy, Violet, or Rose talking, so I didn't know what they were doing. A very small part of me wanted to be out there, so I would know what was going on.

A sudden crash caused me to jump and I scrambled back on my bed, pulling the cover up and pressing my face into the pillow. I felt like I did when I was home alone and heard a noise, only now the noise wasn't in my head.

"Shut up," Clover shouted again. His voice exploded, and he sounded so mad I pictured him with wide eyes and a red, rage-filled face.

The freshly washed bedcovers smelled of lavender—just like my gran's. I pictured myself as a little child, lying in the middle of the king-size bed, puffy, feather-filled quilt up to my chin, breathing in the comforting smell as I fell asleep to her reading me a bedtime story. In my head I could pretend, but another piercing, guttural scream reminded me where I was.

He wasn't hurting her; he couldn't, not with Rose, Violet, and Poppy in the same room witnessing it. She had to be struggling to escape. He wanted her to stay down here and she was resisting. It would all be okay once he left and she was alone with us down here.

The annoying, nagging voice in the back of my mind was telling me if he wanted her to stay down here, he'd have a bed for her too. Everything was in fours. There was no place for her. But maybe he was going to make a place.

Like a few seconds ago, everything went quiet again. I couldn't stand it. I hated not knowing what was going on, what he was doing, and, more important, where he was. I didn't want him to come in here and see me.

Just leave her here and go. He left me as soon as he'd thrown me down the stairs and told Rose to explain what was going on. Why wasn't he going? I lay perfectly still as I waited to hear something. My breathing was ragged and heavy, and I fought to control it so I wouldn't miss any noise from outside.

I pressed my face into the pillow harder as the tension was threatening to consume me. My heart raced painfully fast and my hands started to shake.

A dull thud that sounded exactly like the time Henry leaned back too far on his chair and fell over. We all rushed upstairs thinking he'd fainted or something. Was that what I'd heard? A person falling? I gulped, whimpering as my mind tried to force me to see the things I didn't want to see. Everyone was fine. Something was dropped. In a minute, I would hear the cellar door open and close and then the girls would come back in the room with whoever else was out there.

My chest rose and fell heavily with every deep breath I took. Just as I'd thought, the cellar door opened and closed, squeaking slightly. Soon they would be back. Someone was going to have to share with the new girl because there wasn't a bed for her yet.

The bedroom door opened, and I leaped up, spinning around and pressing my back into the headboard. Violet, it was just Violet. She smiled, but it didn't reach her eyes. "You okay?" she asked.

"No. You?"

She gulped and her eyes left me. Where were Rose, Poppy, and the new girl? "Lily, you're not like Rose and Poppy. They've given up and you haven't. *I* haven't."

I frowned. Where was this going and what was happening out there? I heard taps running and cupboards being opened. "What?" I asked, only half paying attention as I tried to figure out what was going on in the main room.

"I can't do this anymore," she said and climbed into her bed, turning away from me and pulling the cover over her head.

I wanted to ask her what she meant and see if she was okay, but I heard something slosh around in water and something else being sprayed vigorously. Seconds later an overpowering scent of that lemon cleaner hit me, tickling my nose and making my eyes water.

"Violet, what're they doing?" I whispered, wide-eyed, clutching the quilt. She didn't answer; instead, she pulled the cover up higher and I saw her body curl up beneath the quilt. I took a deep breath and looked at the door. *What are they doing?*

7
SUMMER

Wednesday, July 28th (Present)

Four days. I had been down here for four days and every single one of them had been the same. In the mornings we would shower and make breakfast. The days were spent cleaning, watching movies, and reading. I'd heard nothing more of the dressmaking and I didn't want to bring it up in case one of them became suspicious. The weekdays were best—and best was a stretch, nothing down here was good—because we only saw him twice a day.

On Sundays he would take Rose into that room, Tuesdays it was Poppy, and apparently Wednesday—today—was Violet. I knew the time would come when I would have a day, and I still wasn't sure if I should do something to get myself killed first. Was it already set? They probably knew which day was *Lily's* but I didn't want to know. I didn't want to know any of it. Perhaps I could switch off enough to survive until I was found? I couldn't believe that was something I now had to worry about.

So far he hadn't expressed any interest in me other than a few polite, friendly exchanges. I hoped with every single part of my being that it would stay like that.

Poppy said he didn't like things being "messy." He liked even numbers, things that lined up. No one had mentioned what happened four days ago. I didn't dare bring it up. All I knew was that there were still only four of us.

Yesterday Violet mentioned wanting to get out. She came into the bedroom while I was getting ready for bed, and while Rose and Poppy were doing a final wipe down of the counters—that were already sparkling clean—and said she couldn't do it anymore. The same words she said to me the night *something* happened. This time when I asked her what she meant, though, she told me she "needs" to get out. Needs, not wants.

I've been trying to speak with her alone since, but it's hard with Rose and Poppy always hanging around. Violet whispered that we could speak when they were doing lunch today as we passed each other outside the bathroom this morning.

I sat on the sofa, watching Rose and Poppy pull out pans and ingredients from the fridge as they planned to make something for lunch. Violet was in the bedroom, and I wasn't sure if I was supposed to go in to her or if she was going to come and get me. Which would look less suspicious?

My heart raced in anticipation. I wanted to hear what she was going to say; I hoped she'd have a good plan, but I was also scared that we'd be overheard and that would ruin everything. We literally had one chance at this; if he knew what we were doing, he'd make it impossible for us to try again. We couldn't risk him upping the security any more; I still had one last hope of him leaving the door unlocked by mistake.

Rose and Poppy moved around the kitchen, sprinkling cheese

on slices of bread and heating a pan on the stove. We were having grilled cheese sandwiches? The bedroom door opened and Violet stuck her head out. "Can someone help with my hair, please?" she asked, pulling at the long black strands.

That was my cue. I stood. "I will," I said, giving Rose and Poppy a quick, innocent smile, willing them to believe I was just trying to fit in and be helpful.

Neither of them said a word, they went back to cooking. My body relaxed; they weren't suspicious. I closed the door behind me as I walked into the bedroom and leaned against it. Violet pulled her hair into a neat ponytail.

"Tonight," she said. "We're getting out tonight."

My eyes widened in shock. I knew she wanted to escape, but I thought it'd be a well-planned-out escape attempt, not a "let's just run for it." "What? Tonight?"

She gulped, her eyes glazed over. "I can't do it anymore, Lily," she whispered, repeating the words she'd said to me a few times before. Her voice cracked with a dark, painful emotion that sent chills down my spine. "I can't shut it off like they can," she said, nodding her head toward Poppy and Rose in the kitchen next door. "They're stronger than me; they've done this for longer. Poppy keeps telling me I'll get through it and learn to live down here but it'll never be living. 'Be Violet' is what she says; everything that happens, happens to Violet and not Jennifer. I *can't* do it, though I can't switch me off. Tonight, I *have* to leave." Was that why they kept telling me to accept I was Lily? Were they training me to let go of Summer so I could survive what was coming? I bet that was why they never called each other by their real names. "Tonight," she said.

Tonight before he raped her again. "How many times has he taken you in that room?"

Her eyes flicked to the floor and she blinked rapidly. When she'd composed herself, she looked up. "Three. I won't let there be a fourth."

"How long have you been here?" She was the only one that I hadn't spoken to about her life outside here, but she never volunteered any information.

"A little over six months." So I had about six months. "I met him outside Top Shop. Apparently he'd met a couple others there too, so Rose said. It's a homeless favorite spot because of the shelter."

I played with my fingers, biting my lip. She was opening up, finally. "How did he...get you here?" I asked, hoping she wouldn't close up.

"He offered to buy me a coffee from a late-night café in the city. We never reached the café." Shit, not only did he kidnap people, but also he pretended to help them to get them down here. He just grabbed me.

"I'm sorry."

"I used to think living on the streets, scared, cold, and alone was the worst thing in the world." She laughed humorlessly. "How wrong was I?" I wanted to ask how she ended up on the streets, but her eyes filled with tears and she clenched her fists; she looked like she was going to crumble.

"How do you want to escape?"

Her posture changed instantly; she stood taller, businesslike. "We need the key. He keeps it in his left pocket; I've watched him put it in there a few times while he's walked down the stairs. I'm going to smash him over the head with a vase," she said, laughing wickedly at something I didn't understand. Either that or she was starting to lose it. "I have these in case things go wrong." She pulled out a pair of scissors from her pocket. They were much smaller than I'd imagined; the blade was only as long as my thumb. Too small to cut material but he probably didn't want to give us anything too big and sharp, and we didn't have anything else.

"Okay," I whispered. It all felt very wrong, Violet was leading with emotion, but I hadn't been raped, so I wasn't going to judge or try to stop her.

"You move by the bottom of the stairs when he's in the room. I'll hit him, hard, and grab the key. The second he falls you run as fast as you can to the top of the stairs. I will be right behind you. This has to work. I can't go through it anymore, and I don't want you to either." She shook her head. "It's only supposed to be lost *women* down here, not children." I frowned. I didn't think of myself as a child, but clearly she did. She said it as if he was breaking another law as well as kidnap, rape, and whatever it's called for locking someone up in your cellar. I was the age that made me a child in the eyes of the law, but over the age that would make him sign a register. Age didn't matter to me down here; it was all wrong.

I took a deep breath. "All right, I'll run for the door."

She smiled so briefly I almost missed it. "Good girl. We're all set then." *Are we?* I didn't feel all set. I had a horrible feeling in the pit of my stomach. It was the thing my dad told me to listen to when making a decision. It's what made me go back and change a question on my test and not fail it. There was more at stake than passing a class here.

"Let's get back out there. They'll be finished soon and wonder what's taking us so long." She left the room and I wanted to pull her back. Surely we should go through it more than that? Shouldn't we discuss what could go wrong and what we could do about it? We needed to think through more scenarios, like Rose and Poppy trying to stop us.

Violet left the door open and I watched her walk confidently over to the kitchen and cut the sandwiches that Rose put on the chopping board from the pan. She was doing a better job of pretending than she thought.

I felt sick as I watched him walk down the stairs. If Violet was right, the key would be in his left pocket right now. The means to my escape was feet away from me, but it was in the pocket of a psycho. Violet's eyes flicked to me, and she gave me a quick nod. She hadn't given me much to do—she was hitting him over the head and grabbing the key; all I had to do was, the second he fell down, run to the top of the stairs.

There should've been more for me to do, but she knew him better. I used to think I would be able to protect myself, but I was naïve, so I was taking my lead from her and doing whatever she said. The butterflies in my stomach felt like bats. I was terrified that something would go wrong and we'd never get the chance to get the key again.

He stepped beside the table, the end farthest away from the stairs, greeting us and smiling like this was all normal. I had no problem moving away from him. He made me feel sick and I wanted to be as far away from him as I could possibly get.

Violet stood against the counter, her hand very close to the handle of a frying pan. My heart leaped. *Please let this work.* I wanted to go home so badly that I ignored everything telling me this was too risky.

Clover faced Rose. "How was your day?" he asked.

I stopped listening to their conversation when Violet's hand circled the handle. *Come on.* I knew I was supposed to run when she hit him, but he was standing between her and the stairs. What if he managed to grab her as she tried to get past him? I had to stay to help her too. I could kick him if he tried to get up. I wasn't strong, but I would give it a go. She was risking everything to help me; I wanted to help her if I needed to as well.

Before anyone had time to blink, and more important, before Rose and Poppy had time to register what was happening, Violet struck him over the back of the head with the pan and he launched forward.

No one made a noise. I expected Rose and Poppy to scream— they weren't expecting it—but they didn't. Clover stumbled a grand total of two steps, and by the time he'd corrected his balance, Violet was beside him as she made a run for the stairs.

He snatched her arm in his iron grip. She screamed.

8

SUMMER

Violet's eyes widened in horror as she realized he hadn't gone down like she'd planned. *This is why we should have discussed different scenarios,* I screamed at her in my head. Now we were never getting near that key and he would make doubly sure the door was locked at all times.

I pressed my side into the banister and dug my nails into the wood. What were we going to do now? Breathing suddenly became too hard, and I felt like I was drowning. Tears sprung to my eyes as I realized I wasn't going home.

"Clover, I'm sorry. I don't know—"

"Shut up," he growled. Spit flew from his mouth. He managed to keep his posture calm and controlled, relaxed even, when he sounded so murderously angry. What was he going to do now? The image of the knife he kept in his pocket flashed through my mind. He wouldn't really use it, though, would he? It was just to scare us into behaving.

Out of his pocket came that same knife, the blade shining proudly under the light directly above. I gulped and I wanted to close my eyes through his threat and until he left but I couldn't not watch. My back hurt where the edge of the banister dug in as I tried to get farther back.

Violet raised her trembling hands and shook her head. "Please don't. I'm sorry."

"I've already given you a second chance, which isn't something I offer lightly. There are no third chances, Violet." He spoke so calmly it sent a chill down my spine. Without another word from either of them, he took a step forward. There was no hesitation when he shoved the knife into her stomach.

My legs gave way, and I collapsed to the floor, gripping the wooden banister as if it was my lifeline. I tried to scream, but when I opened my mouth, nothing came out. Tears streamed down my face and I blinked hard to clear my vision. *It's a dream, it's a dream*, I repeated over and over in my head. *Wake up. Wake up!*

Violet gasped hard, desperate for breath, and slumped to the floor, limp and lifeless. She was dead. I had never seen a dead body before, only fake ones on TV. I stared at her, dazed. She was *dead*. It was over quicker than it would've been if we were in a movie.

His head snapped around and he faced Rose and Poppy. "Clean this up. Now." Turning back, he bounded up the stairs and out the door, locking it behind him.

Poppy pulled me up, dragging my stunned body to the sofa, where she then pushed me down. "Shh, stay here." There was no danger of me going anywhere. I literally couldn't move, not an inch. It was as if my body had seized up.

I looked on in shock, breathing heavily, wide-eyed as Rose and Poppy gathered a bucket, mop, and what looked like another bucket full of cleaning supplies. "Oh God, she's really dead," Poppy whispered, almost in disbelief.

Rose squeezed her shoulder and brushed her fingers over Violet's face, closing her eyes. "Get the body bag, Poppy." My eyes bulged and my throat dried. "Get the body bag, Poppy" were five words that instantly burned themselves into my memory. They had done this before.

A small pool of blood had started to form beneath her body. I couldn't take my eyes off the bright red liquid. Rose took Violet's hand and kissed it. "Good-bye, sweetheart," she whispered. I gagged, slapping my hand over my mouth as I ran to the bathroom.

Rose and Poppy were struggling to pick up Violet when I came back in the room; there was no way I was going to offer to help them put someone in a body bag. They carefully laid her down and pulled the sides of the bag up. Even though they struggled to move her, they never asked for my help. They either didn't want to make me so soon or they just knew it wasn't happening.

I stared as they moved in tune, working around each other perfectly, as if they'd done it a million times before. How many times had they cleaned up after his murders? A shiver ripped through my body, turning my blood cold. Would I have to see something like that again?

My eyes fixed on the small sliver of Violet I could still see. She looked peaceful, as if she were sleeping. Of course, I knew she wasn't. Rose zipped the bag up, and I sagged in relief, mentally thanking her for creating the plastic shield between Violet's face and my eyes. But I knew I'd never forget it. My head pounded and heart raced as I struggled with what I'd just witnessed.

"Good-bye," Poppy whispered and placed her hand over where Violet's heart was.

I watched in horror as they stood up and collected a bucket, filling it with water. They were going to mop up the blood and then it would be like it never happened.

The water in the bucket quickly turned pink as it mixed with the blood; it looked like one of my mum's cocktails, and I tried to pretend that's exactly what it was. My stomach turned when Poppy lifted the mop to rinse it, a string of blood stretched between the floor and the sponge pad and dripped back to the floor.

The horribly strong metallic smell bulldozed its way through the eye-watering lemon scent and I gagged. As quickly as the blood had poured onto the floor, it was gone. They were fast but thorough—not one spot was left unclean. *How many times?*

If it weren't for Violet lying in a bag in the corner of the room, you would never know someone had just been murdered here. That was the scariest, most horrific thing I had ever witnessed, and they just cleaned it all up as if they were mopping muddy footprints. Their brief moment of sadness seemed long gone.

"He'll be back to get the body after he's had a shower," Poppy said, sighing and looking at Violet. *The body.* She wasn't even a person to them anymore. Was that why they get through it and how they're able to be so calm now? See a body, not a person. I tried. I pictured Violet—*the body*—with no face and no name. I took everything away from her until she was just a lump of meat. But I still wanted to collapse and scream until I lost my voice.

I sat back down and gripped my hands to try to stop them from shaking. "How many people has he…you know?" I whispered. *Murdered.* Poppy looked away and I gritted my teeth. Violet wasn't the first; he'd done it before. That was what I'd heard the other night. I whimpered, curling into a ball on the sofa.

Rose lowered her head and replied, "Eight since I've been here, including Violet."

9
CLOVER

Saturday, March 25th (2005)

Loneliness was like a terminal disease. With every passing day you faded just that little bit more. I had felt as if I were dying for the past four years and I'd had enough. Combing my hair one last time, I slid my wallet in my back pocket and picked up my keys. The girls' room was finished and had been for three days now. There was just one thing missing before I would be ready for them—their clothes.

On the way to the department store, I stopped off at my local florist to buy a bunch of yellow tulips for my mother. They were her favorite. I never liked them, but I appreciated their natural beauty and purity.

"Good morning, Colin," Mrs. Koop said and smiled from behind the fresh-flower-filled counter.

I returned her smile and inhaled the fresh aroma of a mixture of flowers. "Good morning."

"Would you like your usual?"

I nodded once. "Please."

"Coming right up, dear." She turned her back and gathered a handful of bright tulips, tying them with yellow ribbon. "How are you doing?"

"I'm fine, thank you. And yourself?"

"Oh, same old, same old," she replied and gave me her motherly smile. "That'll be ten pounds, please." I handed over cash. "Thank you. Have a lovely day."

"And you, Mrs. Koop."

I drove to the graveyard, smiling to myself. The sun was shining and it was a beautiful day for early March. It wouldn't be too much longer and I would be alive again. I wouldn't drown in the silence and emptiness of my home anymore.

For a minute I sat in the parking lot and stroked the tulip's delicate, silky petals. No man had tampered with them or damaged them. They were pure and innocent—something that wasn't often found in this world of greed, disgrace, and self-gratification. The wrong people were protected while the innocent were left to be picked at like a lion's prey. I wanted to stop that. I wanted *my* family to be protected from the outside evil. *I will stop that. I will protect them.* I knew how and I was willing to do it. It seemed as if I were the only one out there willing to do what it took.

Getting out of the car, I walked along the familiar path. Mother's grave was at the end of the graveyard in the right-hand corner. There was a space beside her reserved for me, so that we could be together again in the end. I placed a patchwork blanket down and knelt on it. Gazing at the perfectly soft petals, I smiled, appreciating the purity of nature's most beautiful creation.

Turning my attention to my mother's grave, I placed the flowers over her heart. "I miss you," I said aloud. "I hope you don't feel that me getting the family I have always wanted will affect what

I feel for you in any way." I kept my focus on the flowers. "I love you very much and I always will. Nothing will stop me visiting you or putting you first. I won't ever forget what you taught me, and I promise you I will continue striving for what you wanted for this world. I won't let them win, Mother. I promise you that."

The sound of a young girl's laughter caught my attention. She walked beside her parents and what must have been a brother. Her long blond hair hung down her back like a light golden waterfall. *She* was the reason I would never give up the fight. Innocent little girls like her that in a few years would be tainted beyond repair.

"No, Mum," she shouted, "I don't like Backstreet Boys anymore; they suck."

I smiled at the innocent, fickle comment. She could only be about ten or eleven, not long until she discovered boys and would have to contend with other girls fighting for the attention of the one she liked.

Her mum laughed. "Sweetheart, yesterday you bought their poster."

"Well, that was yesterday." Her parents shook their heads, both smiling with pride and amusement. The boy hung back a step as if embarrassed to be with them. He held his cellphone out in front of him and mindlessly tapped away at it.

As quickly as they appeared, they were gone, out the other side of the fence. That was all I wanted—except I wouldn't sit back and allow my family to be corrupted, unlike that girl's parents. Soon enough, their beautiful little girl would become just another one of *them*.

I stood up and gathered the blanket, now eager to get to the city and shop for the girls' clothes. I felt a pang of guilt for leaving my mother to shop for other women, but I needed this. I couldn't go on alone anymore. "Good-bye, Mother. I'll visit again soon." As I walked back to my car, I looked around for that family again, but they had disappeared. My heart ached for that poor, young, golden girl.

I had been shopping with Mother many times, but this was very different, exciting. This was *my* choice and no one else's. I could dress them how I wanted—respectfully, modestly, but also modern. I walked into the department store and was hit by the feminine scent of female perfumes in an array or brightly colored bottles.

As I followed the sign to women's clothing, I wondered what the girls would smell like. Would they always have their own scent, or would it merge into one the longer they were all together? Would we eventually have the same smell? Would mine change to accommodate theirs into the mix, or would they change to accommodate me? I almost couldn't walk in a straight line I was so excited and anxious. I wanted it all now.

A group of teenage girls squealing over a picture of a male model drew my attention. There were three of them, all wearing revealing and tasteless clothing. How on earth could their mothers allow them to leave their houses looking like that? The loudest one had a dark orange/brown tan and heavy makeup. Society had gone downhill if women thought it appropriate to act and dress like disgusting little whores. My eye twitched.

Swallowing my hate, I turned and walked away. I stopped in women's clothing and began looking for the perfect outfits. "Can I help you?" the shop assistant asked. She wore a distastefully short skirt and low-cut shirt. No wonder the younger generation of women dressed like little whores if they see career women dressed that way too.

I smiled. "Yes, please. I'm looking for matching skirt and cardigan sets."

"Oh, okay. Well, we have this one here," she said, unable to hide her surprise, and gestured with her hand at a floral set beside me.

"Perhaps something a little more modern. It's for my...fiancée." Taking a deep breath, I closed my eyes for a second to enjoy how that sounded. *Fiancée.* Could I have that? A normal fiancée? No, probably not. No one but Mother would understand what I was trying to do, not straight away, but I wanted a family to share my life with.

"Of course, here are the more fashionable two-pieces." I followed her to the next rail. Now these were perfect. Soft pinks, greens, and blues would make them look respectable but be in keeping with their age.

"I'll have four of each of those three."

"Four of each?"

"Yes, please."

She frowned and flicked through the rail. "What size?"

"A ten, please." Ten was a healthy size, not like the six young girls aspire to these days.

"Are these all, sir?" she asked, holding the clothes in her arms.

I nodded. "That's all. Thank you." Their underwear had been ordered via the Internet. I didn't have any business looking through that in a shop. I paid for the clothes with cash. "Thank you for your help."

"No problem. I hope your fiancée likes them."

"I'm sure she will." Grabbing the stuffed bags, I left the shop.

I went straight home, eager to hang them and view the finished product. Moving the waist-high bookcase out of the way, I unlocked the door to the girls' home. Their place was beautiful, and although it wasn't huge, it had everything they could ever want or need. It was big enough for them to live comfortably, and the separate bedroom made it more bungalow-like. I was proud of what I had created—all for them.

Walking into their bedroom, I hung one set of each color in the four wardrobes and smiled. I had made sure I spent more time in their room, getting it perfect for them. I was doing the right thing. Would Mother think so too? Would she want me to be with anyone else? I shook my head. I had come too far to turn back. I needed this. I was owed this.

The bedcovers matched and the beds lined up, two against both walls facing each other. Between the beds were two bedside tables and two single-width wardrobes on each side. Each girl had her own space. Just a year ago, this was an old cellar, housing boxes of junk and old furniture. Now it was a beautiful home for four beautiful, pure women.

Climbing back up the stairs, I closed and locked the door and pushed the bookcase back across. The door was hidden, matching the wallpaper; you would never know it was there, and the placement of the bookcase meant the door handle was out of view.

Taking a deep breath, I tried to calm my nerves. Not long until I could pick up Violet now. Turning around, I saw something that made my heart sink. The ornate crystal vase now held a bunch of dead tulips. My breathing became heavy and sharp, and the tips of my fingers tingled. Dead, they're *dead*. The only truly pure thing in this world and they died.

A fog of red smoke engulfed me and I was lost.

10

SUMMER

Thursday, July 29th (Present)

"Poppy, what's this?" he spat. His nostrils flared and a vein on the side of his neck poked out. I jumped at his random outburst. *What's what?* I looked around. Nothing was out of place. Nothing was ever out of place. Looking back at him for a clue, I saw him staring at the dead poppies, breathing heavily.

"I'm sorry, Clover. I couldn't help it," she whispered. Couldn't help what? What the hell was going on? He looked at her with an icy glare that made my heart freeze. Was he going to kill her?

"I-I'm sorry, Clover. They just died." The fear in her voice terrified me. The flowers died. Of course they bloody did; they were in a vase underground. I couldn't believe what was happening. It was too stupid.

He slowly walked over to Poppy, watching her like a predator. "*You* didn't look after them," he growled. *Look after flowers.* Was he actually insane?

Poppy flinched and shook her head. "I-I did but they. Um, they—"

"Don't mumble," he shouted, making us all jump. "You let them die."

"No, I didn't. I swear. I didn't. I'm so sorry, Clover," she whispered, pleading with wide eyes for him to understand. He stepped forward, backing her against the wall. What the hell was he doing?

Rose wrapped her arm around me and held me tight. "It's going to be okay," she mumbled under her breath. Was it? Would he kill her for the dead *flowers*? How could he assume they wouldn't die anyway? I cowered into Rose's side.

Poppy held both hands up. "Clover, I promise I took care of them; they just died."

His nostrils flared again. He raised his hand and slapped her across the face sharply. Poppy whimpered and clutched her cheek. I couldn't believe what I was seeing. How could he get angry over *that*? It didn't make any sense.

He grabbed the flowers out of the vase and threw them to the floor. I jumped deeper into Rose's side and buried my head in her shoulder, peering at the scene out of the corner of my eye. What was he doing? Just as I thought he was about to do something to Poppy, he spun around on his heel and ran from the room. It was only when the cellar door slammed shut that I pulled back from Rose.

"It's okay, Poppy," Rose soothed, holding her hand out and stroking her arm to comfort her.

Poppy nodded and took a deep breath. "I'm okay. Lily, you're shaking. It's all right now, I promise. I'm fine." *I'm not.* "Come and sit," she said, exchanging a glance with Rose. They were about to explain what the hell that was.

I sat on the sofa and hugged my legs to my chest. "Why did he do that?"

"He doesn't like when they die," Poppy whispered.

I almost laughed. He had no problem murdering women, but he didn't like flowers dying. "He doesn't like when flowers die," I repeated, testing the words. Seriously, how fucked up?

Poppy sighed. "I don't know why exactly, but he says flowers are pure and beautiful. Nature is beautiful and clean. I think that's why he's doing all this." She waved her hand around, gesturing to the prison we were trapped in. "This is his idea of a perfect, pure family."

"Locking four girls and four bunches of flowers in a cellar?"

Poppy half smiled. "I'm not saying it makes sense. Not to us anyway, and it's just my theory."

"I think it's an accurate theory," Rose said.

I shook my head. "What's wrong with him?"

Rose scratched the top of her head. "I don't know, Lily."

"Summer," I snapped. Rose flinched, and I instantly felt guilty. It wasn't her fault. "Sorry, I just don't like being called that."

"You are Lily now. I'm sorry. I'm only trying to help you. If you keep holding on to who you used to be, you'll go crazy. Accept this life. It'll be a lot easier once you do." Rose got up and walked into the bedroom. I dropped my head to the floor. I would never accept this life, not ever.

As soon as Rose took her clothes into the bathroom to shower, I sprinted for my bed. I didn't want to talk to her again tonight. Poppy followed me and sat on the end of *my* bed. "Lily, you need to shower first."

I got in bed and pulled the cover over myself. "How the hell will he ever know? Screw the shower. It's ridiculous." I didn't want a bloody shower. I wanted to go home. At the very least I wanted them to be normal and make it a little more bearable down here. Violet was murdered, right in front of me, and neither of them had mentioned it beyond the little "It'll be okay" remark they'd said right after they cleaned up her blood.

They either didn't care or they really had managed to shut everything out. I couldn't do that. Every time I closed my eyes I saw her lifeless body on the floor. I could still hear her scream as he stabbed her. She tried to get us out because not only could she not do it anymore, but also she was concerned for me. She didn't want me to go through what he had already done to her three times.

I felt sick with guilt. I should have been stronger and told her we would shut ourselves out and be Violet and Lily together until we were found, then maybe she would still be here. I missed her much more than I should miss a virtual stranger, but I felt like I'd known her ages. She let me in and told me things about her that she clearly didn't speak about; she tried to help me escape. I felt so alone without her.

Friday July 30th (Present)

I woke up in complete darkness. The quilt covered most of my head, making me uncomfortably hot. I threw the cover off and sighed. Last night I dreamed of Lewis. He was here too, only we weren't trapped, and I wasn't scared of him. Lewis and I were lying on that sofa watching movies. He was playing with my hair, the way he had done a million times before. *Clover* wasn't here, but Rose and Poppy were. I wanted it to mean that Lewis would find us. I wished it were a sign that we were going to be okay.

I forced myself to get out of bed, and seeing the small, obsessively clean, matching room made me realize how far away from home I was. My room was messy, really messy to a point that when I tidied, I didn't know where anything was anymore. Taking a deep breath, I tried to stop myself crying. I was tired of crying and feeling exhausted. It wasn't getting me anywhere. I needed to focus and stay strong if I had any chance of getting out of here. I had to play family.

The bedroom door flew open and Poppy walked in. "Oh good, you're up. You need to—"

"Shower and get ready," I said, finishing her sentence. "Yeah, I know." Poppy gave me a quick, fake smile and walked out of the room, probably to clean for the millionth time this morning. I wondered what he would do if he came back and the whole place was a mess, if we smeared food on the walls and emptied the trash on the floor. Violet should have been in the room too, running around getting the final things ready for breakfast. Rose and Poppy didn't even seem to notice; they picked up the slack as if Violet—Jennifer—had never even been here.

I emerged from the bathroom exactly how I was instructed to

look and dress, and sat down on the sofa. How had they not gone insane by now? Years of doing this every single day and they were still sane. I couldn't imagine what I'd be like if I was still stuck in three years' time.

"Want me to do anything?" I offered.

Rose turned and smiled warmly, seeing me for the first time. "No, thank you. We're all done. Why don't you have a seat? He'll be down soon." She said everything in such a matter-of-fact way. *Open your eyes, Rose.*

I sat down and played with my fingers—waiting. The seconds ticked by on the clock, and I tensed. He was coming soon, but I didn't know how soon. That noise I feared so much rang through my ears, and the cellar door was unlocked and pushed open. Now. I held my breath and my heart hammered in my chest.

"Good morning, Flowers," he said and walked down the stairs.

"Good morning," Rose and Poppy replied. They said it so in tune, as if it was their line in a play. That was how I was going to look at it. I was a part in a play. It was all make-believe and I just had to go along with it until we were found.

He stopped at the bottom of the stairs and looked at me. "Good morning, Lily." His voice was firmer—challenging me. He wanted me to say it. His face reddened as he waited.

I stood up. My hands started to shake. "Good morning," I replied quietly and forced myself to look into his cold, muddy brown eyes. He smiled triumphantly and ran his eyes over my body. I squirmed under his gaze. My skin crawled at the way he looked at me. I didn't dare look away; I didn't want to give him the satisfaction of making me uncomfortable. If that was even what he was trying to do. Would he even care how I felt? No way. He couldn't.

"You are a very beautiful young woman, Lily." My stomach turned. I clenched my fists, digging my nails into the palms of my hands. In the eyes of the law, I was still a child. I felt dirty and violated as he raked his eyes down my body. "Let's eat then," he said. "This smells wonderful, girls."

I let out a sigh of relief that his attention had been turned to something else and sat down. The food did smell good, but I couldn't stomach anything. He placed something at the end of the table. A newspaper. My heart leaped. Would I be in it? The urge to grab it and see was overwhelming, but I was too afraid.

We ate mostly in silence, answering the odd question. The newspaper was taunting me. I wanted to reach for it and see what was going on outside this prison.

"Well, that was lovely. Thank you. I'll see you tonight for dinner." He left without giving Rose or Poppy a kiss. I was glad for them, even though they didn't seem bothered either way.

It wasn't until he had locked the door that I reached for the paper. I flicked it over and gasped. On the front page was a recent close-up picture of me. It was taken just a few weeks ago at my aunt's birthday dinner. Lewis was also in the picture, but he had been mostly cut out so the focus was on me. I wished they had left him in so I could see his face. All I had was a small part of the side of his head, not even enough to see his eye. I could see his styled black hair, though.

I stroked the picture where he should have been and closed my eyes. Tears streamed down my face, making a soft thud as they landed on the paper. As hard as it was to see that picture, to read about myself, at least it meant people were looking for me. People were searching, and it was only a matter of time before they found me. But how much time could I cope with?

"Is that Lewis with you?" Poppy asked, peering over my shoulder. I nodded, not trusting myself to speak without breaking. She put her hand on my shoulder and gave it a little squeeze. "I'm sorry, Lily." *Summer.* "We'll watch some movies tonight. Okay?" *Right, for a change!* The way she said it was as if that was a treat rather than the only thing we had to do.

"Sure," I replied.

Poppy smiled. "Clover's bringing popcorn for a movie night tonight." Bringing. He was staying down here too? My heart sunk. I nodded and went to get a book from the large bookshelf so I had something to do and so I could fall into another world and leave this one for a while.

I started reading *The Time Traveler's Wife* to pass the time as quickly as possible. Every second down here seemed to drag on for hours and hours. As I flicked over another page, I wondered: how many books would I finish before I got out of here? Tens? Hundreds? Thousands?

"Lily, we need to start dinner," Rose said, placing her hand on the top of the book to get my attention. I looked up, stunned. I had been reading all day. Smiling to myself, I vowed to read my time away every day until I was found.

"Okay," I replied, placed a bookmark in the book, and put it back on the shelf. If I had been at home I would have slung it on my bed, but he was weird about cleanliness and tidiness, so I was too scared to be messy.

When dinner was in the oven, we cleaned up and made sure everything was perfect. Rose and Poppy were so obsessed with things being perfect it scared me. "I'm just going to brush my hair," I told them and walked away. I wanted to be in another room when he came down. The anticipation was too much; my heart felt like it was going to explode as I waited for him to come down.

I sat on the bed and took deep, calming breaths. Just play along. That was all I had to do. *All.* As if that wasn't already too much. A murmur of voices filtered through to the bedroom, and I knew he was out there. Pushing the fear deep down inside me, I pulled the door open and forced myself to try to smile.

"Ah, Lily, so nice of you to join us," he said and smiled. "Come and sit. Dinner's almost ready, right, Rose?"

"Two minutes, Clover. I'm just serving now," she replied.

Ignoring him as best I could without making it obvious, I helped Rose and Poppy serve dinner. When I sat down, he stared at me. I sank down in the seat and pushed my food around the plate. I felt uncomfortable. Everyone had finished eating before I had even had half, but I couldn't force anything else down.

"Are you not hungry, Lily?" Poppy asked.

"Not really. I'm a little tired actually." I wasn't tired, not physically anyway. I wanted to be anywhere but in his company. Whenever I looked at him, I saw him stabbing Jennifer.

"Let's watch the movie now, and we can all relax," Rose said as she quickly tidied up. If there were a world record for cleaning, Rose would easily hold it. Was that what three years here did to you?

Poppy poured the popcorn into a large plastic bowl and we all crammed on the sofa. It was large enough to fit four people, but because I wanted to be as far away from him as possible, I pressed my side into Poppy's. He was sitting in between me and Rose—still too close to me. I held myself in such an awkward position my muscles started to ache.

I had watched *The Notebook* with Lewis. He complained through the whole thing. If there weren't any cars, fights, or nudity, he really wasn't that interested. I'd do anything to be back with him and listen to him whining about how boring it was.

Clover threw his arm over the back of the sofa and I cringed. My heart was racing and I couldn't concentrate on the film anymore. About halfway through the film, his fingers brushed my hair so lightly I barely felt it. I seized up. *No!* Gulping, I looked down at my lap and closed my eyes, pretending I was anywhere but here. I tried to control my breathing—in for three seconds and out for three seconds—anything to take my mind off what was happening and calm my racing heart.

He stroked my hair until the film finished, and then he got up, said good night, and left. I rushed to the bedroom and dove under the cover. My skin felt like a million bugs were running all over it. I curled up and burst into tears, sobbing into the pillow and soaking it within seconds.

11

LEWIS

Saturday, July 31st (Present)

It had been seven days since Summer went missing, and I had barely slept at all. I took as little rest as I could survive on and spent the rest of the time searching. I looked awful and could see the worry on my family's faces. Finding her seemed hopeless, but I wouldn't ever stop. Although the search area had widened, there was still no trace.

Summer's face was all over the local and national news every day, and people from all over had turned up to help look for her. I'd heard that the first few days were vital to find evidence of what had happened. I didn't know what it meant for our chances that it had been a week. If there was something somewhere, fingerprints or DNA, then would it have washed away in the wind and rain? How long could it hang around? I desperately wanted to know, but I was too terrified to ask.

Someone must know something or have seen something. It was impossible to just vanish. Although we knew Summer must've been taken, there were no suspects, no real ones anyway. Time wasters had phoned in many times with their theories and suspicions, but none of them had led to anything.

I arrived back at Summer's house, where I was meeting up with her family and mine for a quick, early dinner, and then I was going back out. Two days ago, I gave in and agreed to stop and go back to Summer's house to eat, rather than grabbing something on the run. I felt guilty every time I stopped. What if I missed something because I turned back?

"Lewis," Mum said, giving me a hug as I walked through the door. I hated being around them all. Not because I didn't love them but because they seemed to cope better. They slept and ate, and I could barely breathe. "Honey, you need to sleep more." She frowned, looking over the dark circles under my eyes. I looked like shit, but who wouldn't in my situation?

Ignoring her comment, I walked into the kitchen, where Dawn was keeping herself busy. She grated cheese, stopping every few seconds to stir beans on the stove. She hadn't stopped doing something for the last few days—keeping herself busy to stop herself from going crazy waiting. The house phone was beside her wherever she went; if she moved an inch, it went with her. "Lewis, have a seat. It's almost ready," she said, glancing at me for a second before returning to her stirring.

My dad sat at the table looking over a map with Daniel and Henry. Daniel looked up and half smiled. "We're just going over the areas that aren't in the official search." That was something that bothered me. Although the search had widened, what if it wasn't wide enough? What if Summer was just a mile out of that area—or even a few feet? That was why we had widened our search. The area closest to us was more than being covered with the official search, which now included the wide forest area. The reason you searched a forest was if you were looking for a body.

I sat down and tried not to think about the possibility of Summer being dead. She couldn't be dead. I couldn't picture her cold and pale. I couldn't even force myself to believe her being dead was a possibility. Until I knew otherwise, she was alive and well.

"Apparently this part of town is where runaways go," Dad said, pointing to the town that was about twenty minutes away.

"Summer didn't run away," I said, frowning at his suggestion.

"I know that, Lewis, but that doesn't mean we shouldn't check it out. It may be that someone there has seen her with someone." The person that took her. "Okay, let's go then."

"Ah, ah! Not until you've eaten. I'm serious, Lewis," Mum said. Her eyes were wide, stern. I felt like a kid being told off for swapping the sugar for salt.

I inhaled my food, barely tasting a thing, and within minutes I'd finished. It wasn't until I had eaten that I realized how hungry I had been. "Okay, now?" I said, pushing my empty plate away. "Let's go."

Dad, Daniel, and Henry stood up. "Lewis, you pick up Theo from home and then go to the east side of town; the three of us will start west, and we'll meet in the middle. Stick to the back areas first. If there's something to be found, it's most likely going to be there," Dad said. He was good at things like this, organizing people. I don't think he knew what he was doing more than any of us, but he could think calmly and logically while I just wanted to run around and search every little corner of the world. Daniel and Henry had also been calm, unlike Dawn. I think they were trying to stay strong and refused to believe we wouldn't find her alive.

"Theo's ready?" I asked. There was no way I was waiting around for him.

Dad nodded. "Ready and waiting, so let's get a move on."

I pulled up outside my house and honked the horn, tapping the steering wheel impatiently. *Come on, Theo.* The front door opened and my brother walked out. I put the car in first, ready to go as soon as he got in.

"So we're going into town?" Theo asked. I pulled away as soon as he shut the door.

"Yeah."

He nodded and looked out of the window. Unless we were talking about finding Summer, we barely spoke at all. We used to talk about most stuff. Theo was only a year older, so we were close, but not right now. Everything we used to talk about and care about was nothing now; none of it mattered anymore.

"What's the plan?"

"We search east to west and meet Dad, Daniel, and Henry somewhere in the middle."

"You have pictures of her?"

Only about a thousand on my phone. "Yeah." I had a copy of the same one the press released. It was a close-up of Summer.

Her golden-blond hair framed her beautiful face. She had these deep emerald-green eyes that always smiled. I loved waking up to those eyes, right before I snuck out of her room.

"Lewis…"

"What?"

"How are you doing? Really doing?"

Terrible. Not knowing where she was or how she was torture. All I wanted was for her to be safe. Sighing, I replied, "Fine." Theo frowned and turned back, looking out of the window. "What do you want me to say, Theo?"

"The truth."

"The truth! The truth is I feel like I'm fucking dying. There, is that what you want to hear?"

"Yes," Theo replied. "We'll find her."

I drove through town and thought about Theo's words, *We'll find her*. I had no doubt that we would find her, but when? Anyone could have her and I didn't even want to imagine what she was going through. I gripped the steering wheel, my knuckles turning white. What if someone was hurting her?

"Park in there," Theo said and pointed to a run-down multistory parking garage. Colorful graffiti covered almost every inch of the dull concrete structure. My car probably wouldn't be here when we returned. A couple weeks ago, I would have never parked my car in a place like that. Now I couldn't have cared less if it exploded.

I parked in the space closest to the exit, and we walked into town, taking back streets. "I don't really know where to start."

Theo scratched the top of his head. "Me neither. Maybe behind the main street?" We walked between two shops and along an endless street. A couple of teens sat on the doorstep of a piercing shop, giggling to themselves. High, no doubt.

"Excuse me," I snapped, having no patience to wait for them to come down from whatever was hilarious. "Have you seen this girl? Her name's Summer Robinson. She's sixteen."

The girl squinted her bloodshot eyes as she looked at the picture while the boy seemed to take great pleasure in looking Summer over. I clenched my jaw and forced myself to stay calm and not punch his fucking face in. The straggly girl shook her head and gave me a lopsided grin. "*Nopes*, sorry, dude." *Nopes?* She sounded like a thirteen-year-old trying to invent new in words at school.

"Never seen her, but I wish I had," the guy slurred. I hoped Summer wasn't around here with low-life scum like him.

"Thanks," Theo mumbled and pushed me past them.

I had a horrible feeling that we were just wasting time here. Even if someone had seen her, would they say? This seemed like a place where everyone respected everyone else's wish to disappear. It wasn't Summer's wish to disappear. She didn't want to go.

Theo and I walked around for an hour and a half, asking anyone we stumbled upon to look at the picture. Of course, no one had seen a thing, or so they told us. "I don't know what to do now." I admitted. I should have known.

"We keep looking. That's all we can do."

"Okay, let's meet up with the others and try somewhere else."

I missed her so much it physically hurt, like I was being punched in the gut over and over. All I could do was look, and that hurt even more. I had promised her I would never let anyone hurt her, and I failed her.

Sunday, August 1st (Present)

I woke to the bright sun glaring down on my face. Looking across at Summer's alarm clock, I gasped and bolted upright. Shit, I overslept! It was almost ten. I threw the cover off and jumped out of bed. Fuck, how could I sleep in so long when Summer was missing? Chucking yesterday's clothes on, I ran downstairs. Why didn't anyone wake me?

"Lewis, come sit down for breakfast," Mum called as I sprinted past the kitchen to grab my backpack. Today I was concentrating my search in the smaller forest near the park.

"No time," I replied.

"Lewis! Come and get something now," she snapped.

I sighed and darted into the kitchen. "Just throw something together for me then!"

Dawn sat at the kitchen table staring blankly into a full cup of coffee. The phone sat next to the mug. It hadn't been more than a few inches away from her since Summer went missing.

Mum handed me a plastic shopping bag full of food. "Thanks," I mumbled and sprinted out of the house. I had food in the backpack, but I wasn't planning on eating anything in there. It was full of Summer's favorites—sports drinks, malt balls, gummy bears, a Cadbury's Fruit and Nut bar, and gingerbread men.

111

I stepped outside and was taken aback at the amount of people outside the house. News reporters lined the waist-high brick wall around the house. "Lewis, Lewis," the crowd shouted all at once. Flashing lights exploded from their cameras.

Ignoring the questions fired at me, I hopped in my car. Just as I turned the key in the ignition, the passenger door opened. "I'm coming with you," Henry said and buckled his seat belt. I nodded and sped off, telling myself, *Today I* will *find her*—but I said that every day.

12
CLOVER

Friday, March 11th (2005)

I parked the van in the darkest corner in the abandoned parking lot and walked toward the department store. I had never felt so alive before. Very soon she was going to be mine and I couldn't wait to take care of her. *My* perfect Violet.

It was warm out for March, but even so, the street was deserted. For the past two nights she had been huddled in the doorway of a dated shoe shop. I walked along the alleyway between the corner store and bank. As I had hoped, Violet was sitting against the door of Bentley's Shoes.

"Hello," I said, smiling at the most beautiful creature I had ever seen. I would never admit it aloud, but she eclipsed my mother with her looks. She was pure and innocent, and I was drawn to her immediately.

She gasped and looked up, startled. "Um, hello." Her eyes were pools of light blue tropical ocean, and I knew her wispy dark brown hair could be tamed into a sleek, presentable style. "Can I help you?"

"I would like to take you for a coffee." I smiled.

Her mouth dropped open. "Why?" She frowned, her eyes darkened. "I'm not like that, you know?"

I held my hands up. "No, no, that's not what I meant, and I'm glad to hear you're that type of…person. I would just like to buy you a hot drink and perhaps something to eat. There's a twenty-four-hour café just down the street."

"I don't get it. What do you want from me?"

"Nothing." It's *you* that *I* want to help. "Please, just let me buy you a late dinner?"

"Just dinner?"

I nodded, smiling. "Of course."

She hesitated and then rose to her feet slowly. "Okay."

My heart leaped. "Wonderful. Let's go."

"I'm Catherine."

Catherine didn't suit her at all. She was Violet. "Colin," I replied and offered her my hand. "Are you hungry, Catherine?"

"Yes," she replied, smiling and dropping her eyes to the ground.

"Well, the café isn't far." She walked beside me, leaving a gap approximately a foot from me. I didn't like it. "How long have you been living out here, Catherine?"

"Um, a year almost."

"That long?" How on earth could her so-called family allow her to sleep on the dirty, dangerous streets for even one night? "A beautiful young woman like yourself shouldn't be sleeping in the cold. You should be looked after. Cherished."

Violet blushed, hiding her face behind her hair. Her shyness was endearing. It wasn't something I was used to. Mother was a very strong and forceful person. The other women that I had encountered sold themselves on a daily basis. Violet was the first sweet and innocent woman I had met.

"Where is the café?" she asked.

"Not far. You've never been?"

She shook her head. "No, I stick to the other side of town, where there's more people."

"This side isn't bad, Catherine, just a little neglected. The café is decent."

She looked back over her shoulder and bit her lip. Was she considering running back? The streets were deserted, with the exception of a few homeless people littered in shop doorways.

"How far?" she asked again and glanced back behind her. My van was in sight, just a few feet away. We were almost there. "I think I should go back."

We were by the back door. I reached into my pocket and unlocked the van. Violet gasped as the door clicked unlocked and the sidelights flashed. "What…?" She shook her head and her eyes widened.

"It's okay, Violet. I'm going to take care of you."

"Violet? What? I'm not…" She took a step back, glancing over her shoulder, looking where to run. I sighed. She didn't understand what I was trying to do, what I was trying to save her from—yet. Her body trembled and she flopped to the ground. I did a double take. She'd fainted. Quickly opening the back door, I picked her up and laid her inside.

I carried her slender frame and placed her down on the sofa.

She had woken up as I carried her down the stairs and had been crying ever since. She looked around, eyeing the room in shock. Even though she was crying, shaking, and had makeup running down her face, she was still a very beautiful woman. "Violet?"

"N-Not Vi-Violet. I'm not," she said, stuttering and gasping for breath.

"Please stop crying, Violet," I said. "Calm down. Everything is going to be all right."

She took a few deep breaths, concentrating hard as she tried to relax. Her occasional sobs pierced through me like a knife. Strong women didn't cry. Mother had never cried. "What do you want from me?" she whispered.

"A family."

Her eyes widened in horror. "I'm not having your baby!"

"A baby? I never said I want that." *Did* I want a child? No. Certainly not now and not with someone I barely knew. "Violet, I don't want a child. A family isn't defined by offspring. I want the five of us to be a family. I will take care of you all, and in return you will take care of me." That was how a family functioned.

"What? Five? What five?"

"That'll come later. Please make yourself at home here. I built this for you, for all of you. Violet, don't be afraid of me. I want to help you, to care for you."

"Why do you keep calling me that?"

I frowned. "Your name?"

"Yes."

"Well, because it's your name," I replied and smiled. "Now,

I'll come down for breakfast at eight in the morning and again for dinner at six thirty in the evening. I'm afraid my work will keep me away in the week, so it will only be the weekends where we will eat lunch together." Violet stared at me with a blank expression, her mouth hanging open in the most unladylike way. "Please do not look at me like that."

Her mouth snapped shut. "Why are you doing this?"

Sighing, I stood up. Which part had I not been clear on? "I've explained that. I would like a family and I would like to save my family from…" I stopped, searching for the appropriate word to make her understand. "Corruption, pain, humiliation."

"Oh," she replied, taking me by surprise. Was she understanding now? "I don't feel those things. I just want to go."

"Violet, if there's one thing I do not like, it is people being ungrateful." Her mouth dropped open again, and she raised her eyebrows. This girl had a face of a million expressions.

"Now please, allow me to explain how things are to be done." Her eyes widened and she nodded numbly. "Good. I will take care of you. I'll take care of everything. In return, I expect you to keep your home clean and tidy at all times. I cannot abide dirt and mess; it's *disgusting*." Her eyes widened to the point where they began to water. "You're to shower twice a day—germs spread fast." I raised my eyebrows.

"Yes, okay," she whispered.

"I will provide you with everything you need—food, toiletries, entertainment. We're a family, Violet, and soon you won't be alone here."

She gasped quietly. "I won't?"

"No, you won't. I know this is a lot to take in. It's very new and very exciting. We will both need an adjustment period, so for a few days, just get used to your surroundings. On Monday, we'll test-drive our routine. Okay?"

I could tell she had a million other questions but now was not the time. "I'll let you get some rest and settle in. Oh, would you like the tour or can you show yourself around?"

"I can show myself," she whispered, sitting rigid on the sofa.

"Very good." There was just the living area in the main part of their home, with a bedroom, bathroom, and our room to the side of the living room area. It was quaint, perfect for my four flowers.

Saturday, March 12th (2005)

"Good morning, Violet," I said, as I walked down the stairs. Nerves bubbled in my stomach. I wanted her to be okay and for everything to be all right. I had explained everything to her yesterday, but I wasn't sure if she fully understood. She sat on the sofa huddled into a ball. Seeing her like that reminded me of how she used to sit on the street. "Are you all right?"

She looked up at me, gaping as if I had grown a second head. "I'm fine," she finally replied. I smiled wide, my heart soaring. *She is mine.*

13

SUMMER

Saturday, July 31st (Present)

I woke up and my head felt fuzzy, like I'd been wasted the night before. My throat was sore from crying so much. I could still feel his hands on my hair—it made my skin crawl. I didn't want him to touch me ever again.

"Lily, are you okay?" Rose asked and sat down on the bed.

Summer. "Fine," I lied.

She nodded and broke into a warm smile. "You need to have a shower. Clover will be down for breakfast in half an hour." I should just let him kill me.

Sighing in defeat, I got up. I didn't want to give up. I was stronger than that. The image of a huge reunion with Lewis and my family made me hold on to hope that I'd get out. Whatever was going to happen down here, I could go along with it because I would eventually get out and go home. *Think of this as if it's happening to someone else. It's happening to Lily, and I'm not Lily.*

I grabbed the clothes that were hanging on the front of *my* wardrobe and went to the bathroom. Black boot-cut trousers and a light blue shirt with matching cardigan. Even though the clothes looked fairly modern, they still made me look older—in my twenties. They were a size too big too, but that was good;

it meant my figure wasn't shown off. I didn't want him looking at me.

After taking a quick shower, I dressed and tried to mentally prepare myself to put on the act again. I used to spend ages in the shower, but now they barely lasted beyond five minutes. The natural-looking makeup was my next step. What I really wanted to do was plaster a ton of it on my face just because he didn't want me to. How could he think he got a say in how I looked? I didn't even let Lewis determine how I wore my hair or makeup.

"Lily," Rose called through the door at the same time I heard the creaking of the cellar door opening. "Come on."

Panic gripped me. I swung the door open and stepped into the main room. I didn't want him to come look for me if I wasn't there when he entered. He walked down the stairs with confidence. It threw me every day how normal he looked. Weren't people like him supposed to look like monsters? There should have been something physical that gave him away—but he looked normal.

"Good morning, Flowers," he said cheerfully. I replied, saying good morning instantly. I did it at the same time as Rose and Poppy, so he wouldn't single me out again. He sat down in his usual seat and waved his hand, gesturing for me to sit opposite him. I held my breath and sat down.

Did anyone suspect there was anything odd about him? Someone must have. As far as I knew, he lived alone. Did anyone find that weird? A fairly antisocial thirtysomething living alone? I prayed that someone would see through his perfect-gentleman act long enough to raise the police's suspicions.

"This looks incredible," he said and smiled at Rose. It was fucking scrambled eggs on toast! "So, I'm going shopping to get some new clothes for all of you." Someone must find *that* strange, a grown man shopping for a load of women's clothing alone. Although they would probably just think he was a cross-dresser. After all, that was easier to assume than what was really going on.

"That sounds nice, thank you," Poppy responded. He looked over to me so I smiled, praying it looked like a smile and not a grimace.

"I hope you'll like what I buy."

Rose grinned. "I'm sure we all will." *Unlikely.*

"Good. The clothes you have on at the minute are all fine for now, but if you would bag everything else up, I'll take it when I return tonight. Please make dinner for eight o'clock tonight."

We fell into a silence that they all seemed comfortable with. I forced a few bites of egg down and nibbled on a slice of toast. He looked at Rose differently than Poppy; there was more there. If he wasn't so cold and dead inside, I would almost think he genuinely loved her. Why her? "Do you think you would be able to get us a new mascara too, please?" Rose asked.

I nearly laughed even though there was nothing funny about this situation.

When their plates were empty and I sat back, he stood up. "I'll bring you a paper again today," he said. Another paper. *Please let Lewis be in it.* Or anyone. I just wanted to see someone I love.

After kissing Rose and Poppy on the cheek, he took a step closer to me. My heart stopped and my breath caught in my throat. What's he doing? He stopped right in front of me. I bit down on my tongue. He leaned down and pressed his lips to my cheek. I tensed every muscle in my body and fought against the growing urge to be sick. I wanted to scream. He pulled away after a second and walked away.

As soon as I was out of his sight, I sprinted to the bathroom. My skin was crawling, and I felt sick and dirty. Lifting the toilet seat, I threw up. My skin felt dirty, like I'd rubbed mud and crap on my cheek.

"Lily," Poppy said and knelt beside me. "Everything's going to be fine. Come on, calm down, you need to be strong."

I slumped back against the wall and burst into tears. I just wanted to go home. "I-I don't want him to touch me," I said, stuttering my words. I had to get him off me.

"Shh," she soothed and handed me tissue to wipe my eyes. "I don't either. You just have to do what you have to do." That was it? *Just do what you have to do*? Let *him* do whatever he wanted. "This is, hopefully, only temporary, until we're found. Just hang in there, please." "Hopefully" wasn't good enough, but it wasn't like we had anything but hope.

I nodded and pushed myself up. *Pull yourself together.* "Okay." Poppy smiled and nodded her head toward the door, gesturing for me to follow her. Taking a deep breath and giving myself an internal pep talk, I stepped out of the bathroom. "Are we watching a movie?"

"Rose and I plan on reading, but you can watch a movie if you like."

I shook my head. "I'll read too." Getting lost in another world sounded good—whether that was on the TV or in a book. I chose the thickest book on the bookshelf and sat down. When I was only a few chapters in, Rose put her book down and got up. She walked to the kitchen area and slipped on her rubber gloves.

I stopped reading to watch her. The place was clean—it actually made operating rooms look like landfills. Poppy didn't clean as much as Rose did, and it didn't seem like Rose was doing it just so Clover wouldn't flip out either. Rose was as obsessed as him. She sprayed surface cleaner on the counter and worked the cloth in circular motions. The room quickly filled with a stronger scent of lemons. *It's not even dirty!*

Glancing around the room, I saw that excessive cleaning wasn't his only thing. The bookshelf between the bedroom and bathroom door stored books in alphabetical order by title. It was the same with the DVDs. Everything sitting on the shelves under the stairs looked the same distance apart. Did he go as far as measuring how far apart they needed to be? Surely no one was that OCD.

Turning my head, I looked back toward the kitchen and saw everything there was lined up and matched too. *Freak!* The three vases of flowers held almost-dead roses and poppies. *My* flowers were the only ones still standing tall. What was the point of keeping flowers when down here they would just die so quickly? What a waste of money.

Lewis used to bring me sunflowers—because they reminded him of me, apparently—though that was usually only when he was in trouble. I would have given anything to be home staring at Lewis's flowers instead of in this prison looking at lilies.

"Right," Rose said as she put the rubber gloves back in the cupboard. "We need to sort through our clothes now. Clover wants them all bagged up by the time he gets back." New clothes from him. *Well, at least they won't be hand-me-downs from someone he's murdered.* She smiled and held up two black bags, as if this was something fun she had been looking forward to doing. "Come on then."

I reluctantly followed them into the bedroom and opened *my* wardrobe. Rose shook the bags and laid them out in the middle of the room. There wasn't much space at all; the walkway between the ends of the beds was only wide enough to fit one person through at a time.

"Everything?" I asked.

"Everything," Rose confirmed. "I'll do Violet's as well as mine."

We bagged the outfits in silence. Rose and Poppy exchanged a few knowing glances that I didn't get. I frowned and asked, "Why is he doing this?"

"I don't know, Lily," Rose replied.

"Summer!" I exclaimed.

Rose sighed and shook her head. Maybe all this was easier for her to accept because she had cut ties with her family years ago, but I hadn't. I loved my family, as much as they drove me crazy. I couldn't imagine not seeing them again.

"Lily is your name now," she said, her eyes hard and stern. I glared at her. *Maybe you gave in to that sick freak but I won't!* We stared at each other, neither of us backing down. Poppy kept her head down and busied herself sorting the clothes. She wasn't as messed up as Rose. I bet if she had the opportunity to get out, she would take it.

Rose finally sighed. "Let's just get this done. I'll take this bag out." She took the tied bag from Poppy and walked out of the room. *Whatever.*

"What's wrong with her?"

Poppy half shrugged. "Three years is a long time to be down here." Three minutes was a long time to be down here. "We need to stick together." That wasn't the first time Poppy had said that, and I started to wonder if she said it so much to try and convince herself. We stuck together and what would happen? We would magically appear back home? Realization slammed me in the chest. No. She wasn't talking about escaping—she was talking about surviving. My heart dropped. I thought we were on the same page.

I stuffed the last of the clothes from my wardrobe in the bag roughly. This was stupid; there were *three* of us and *one* of him. We could smash him over the head with something—a chair, the TV, anything—but I couldn't do it alone.

Lifting the heavy black bag, I carried it into the main room and dropped it next to the other one. Two black bags held all the clothes we had, and they were just hand-me-downs from the previous dead girls. I froze. Where were my clothes? I hadn't even thought of where they were. Did he take them? Did it even matter?

"Good work, girls," Rose said. "I'm going to start some knitting. Want to join in?" Poppy nodded. "Lily?"

"I don't know how to knit." *I'm sixteen, not sixty!*

"That's not a problem. We can teach you. Poppy, grab Lily a new set of needles and we'll get started."

I closed my eyes and took a deep breath. Don't cry. "What's the point of knitting?" There wasn't anything knitted in the cellar, so what did they do with what they made?

"We don't knit for ourselves; we knit for others."

"What?" I replied.

"Clover donates the garments to charities." *Or so he tells you.* He could be burning them for all they knew.

"Wouldn't it look weird, a grown man with knitting stuff?"

Rose frowned. "I don't think so, and I believe he donates through charity bags." Ah, so no one sees him; the bag is picked up from outside his house. Smart sicko.

Rose's knitting lesson lasted an hour and was very in-depth. It was boring, but I sucked at it, so at least my mind was distracted for a while. That was probably why they did it too—anything to stop your mind wandering to what was actually happening. Survival.

We had just finished making dinner when the cellar door unlocked. The blood drained from my face and I felt dizzy. He was coming. Did he have another newspaper? Please say the press used a picture of me with someone else. I didn't care who; I just needed to see someone I loved.

He strolled down the stairs, looking around at the three of us.

"Good evening, Flowers," he said. Gulping, I took a step back. My heart raced. "Here are your new clothes." He placed at least a dozen bags down beside the black bags and smiled. "All packed up, I see. Very good."

Rose and Poppy walked toward the bags, grinning with excitement. *Act like them.* I took a small step closer, making sure I could see where he was and pretended to look in the bags too. The room was too small to be as far enough away from him as I wanted. Wherever I was, he was too close. "Now, I want you all to change into the clothes in this bag and hand me the ones you have on now."

Now? I didn't want to look in the bag and see what he wanted us to wear. At least it wouldn't be anything revealing or degrading—not degrading in the sexual sense anyway. Anything we had to wear to suit him was degrading.

Rose nodded. She was so obedient, although I'd seen what he did if you weren't. "Okay," she said and took the bag from his hand. "Come on, girls." I walked into the bedroom in shock. Were we really doing this? Rose tipped the bag upside down and four outfits fell out. They were all exactly the same. Smart gray trousers, a dusty pink high-neckline camisole, and matching pink cardigan. It looked like something you would wear to work.

"All the same," Poppy said, stating the bloody obvious. Was that what he wanted now, us to match too?

"Let's just change quickly," Rose replied. "They're all the same size, just grab one."

I picked one set up and checked the label—size ten. Why didn't he just get the size we wore? Oh God, were we all supposed to be this size?

"You look beautiful, girls," he said, smiling at us as we walked back into the main room. *Psycho, psycho, psycho!*

Rose beamed. "Thank you, Clover, and thank you for the clothes." I wanted to grab her and shake her. She either needed some serious medical help or an Oscar.

Clover stepped forward, took Rose's hand, and kissed her knuckles. "You're very welcome." My stomach turned for her, but she didn't flinch.

"Lily," he said, turning to me. "Don't worry. We'll soon have your weight to where it should be."

To where it should be. I clenched my jaw and forced a smile. There was no way I wanted to put *on* weight, especially not for him. If he wanted me bigger, I wanted to be smaller.

"And, Poppy, you look incredible too."

She bowed her head. "Thank you."

He clapped his hands together, looking incredibly pleased with himself. "Well, shall we eat?"

I shoved the stupid needle through the stupid hole, or whatever the hell Rose called it, and the whole thing came undone—again! I wanted a distraction, not something that was going to make me want to hang myself. "I'm done with this," I growled and threw it to the floor.

"Lily, you'll get there," Rose said and laughed.

"I don't want to get there. I. Want. To. Go. Home!"

Rose looked at Poppy. "I think we should give it to her."

"Give me what?" I snapped.

"Clover bought a paper. It was in one of the bags. We didn't want to give it to you yet because you were so upset earlier, and we didn't want to make it worse," Poppy explained.

I sat forward, my eyes widening. "Where is it?"

"I'll get it." Poppy walked into the bedroom and came back with a national newspaper. "Here."

I grabbed it from her and turned it over to the front page. My heart stopped. Lewis. It was a picture of us both, taken in the spring when we went to Alton Towers theme park. The headline and article faded into nothing and all that I could see was his face. He looked so happy with a big smile that lit up his eyes. His arm was around me and his head tilted toward mine. Suddenly wearing clothes for a psychopath didn't bother me as much. I could do that if it meant I had a chance of seeing Lewis again.

I was so absorbed in the paper that I didn't notice he had come back until I heard a deafening scream. I jumped in shock and looked up to see him shove a girl down the stairs. She fell halfway down and landed in a heap at the bottom. I clutched the newspaper to my chest.

He stood above her, hovering over her skinny frame. "Filth," he spat. "Filthy whore!" Like when he said *bastard*, *whore* didn't sound like his word; it was like when you hear a ten-year-old call someone hot. Grabbing the girl's hair, he yanked her up. She screamed in protest, gripping her long dark hair.

"Let me go. Please, let me go," she begged and sobbed violently.

"Shut up," he screamed and slammed her back against the wall. "Filthy whore," he repeated.

My heart beat so loud I could barely hear what he was saying. "Poppy," I whimpered, pressing my body into hers. I almost felt safe; it reminded me of when I was little and I hid against my mum's body at the firework display.

"Shh," she whispered.

He pinned her against the wall and she cried out in pain. "No, please."

"Shut up, just shut up." She cried and turned her head to the side as Clover leaned in and spoke. "People like you make me sick."

"Please let me go. I won't say anything." Tears streamed down her face, making her makeup run.

"You're disgusting. You're all disgusting."

"I-I'm sorry. Please, let me go." He shook his head and pulled a knife out of his pocket. I gasped.

I watched the scene in horror, unable to look away. She sobbed loudly, desperately, and shook violently. "Please, no, please."

We should do something. I went to step forward, but Poppy pushed me back. "No," she hissed.

He pulled her hair again, making her scream and thrash around as she tried getting out of his grip. Like with Violet and without hesitation, he plunged the knife into her stomach. I gagged at the same time she screamed a deep, feral scream. Closing my eyes, I shrank back behind Poppy.

Suddenly all of the sounds were amplified—his deep, ragged

breaths and her spluttering and gagging. Within seconds, her noise stopped, and after a thud to the floor, his noise was the only thing left.

He killed her.

I didn't dare open my eyes. I was too scared of what I would see. "Clean this now." His loud, angered voice cut through me, making me tremble. He ordered us around as if we'd done it.

Poppy leaped forward, causing me to stumble and my eyes to fly open. He ran up the stairs and slammed the cellar door. Very slowly, I looked down and almost threw up. My body shook in fear. Rose and Poppy gathered the cleaning things and got to work. I would have loved to be inside their heads when they were cleaning up a murder. They didn't give much away on the outside. Was it easier for them because they didn't know her?

They were a whirlwind: Rose mopped up with purpose, her lips pursed as she worked with ruthless efficiency, dodging me. Poppy was more reserved; she still looked like she was only cleaning up dirty footprints but she had slightly more emotion. She at least looked a bit sad. We didn't even know the poor girl's name. Did she have a family? Children? She was a person and she had a life. He just took it as if it were nothing.

I turned around slowly and walked back into the bedroom, closing the door behind me. I didn't want to see him come back for her body or watch Rose and Poppy act as if nothing was wrong. I climbed into bed and cried into the pillow.

14
CLOVER

Friday, July 15th (2005)

"Good morning, Violet. I have some news," I said as I walked downstairs. It was very exciting news. I didn't like there only being two of us. The table was unbalanced. Three seats were empty.

She looked up from the worktop where she was whisking eggs. "News, Clover?"

"Yes, another surprise. You'll find out later, perhaps in a day or so." Violet was a bright young woman. After I brought Poppy back two days ago, although I'd not seen her since, she would know my surprise was another family member. Poppy just needed a little readjustment time; Violet was helping her settle in, and I was sure she would be right as rain soon enough. As desperately as I wanted her out here with us now, I could give her a few days. I'd waited so long for this, I could give Poppy time. "What's for breakfast? Scrambled eggs on toast?"

"Oh, okay. Yes, scrambled eggs."

I smiled. "One of my favorites."

"Can you cook?"

"I can. Mother taught me." My eyes widened and I mentally chastised myself for giving away too much. I didn't ever want to speak of Mother in front of my new family. I wanted that part of my life separate. "How long will it be?"

"Five minutes. We're running low on food."

"I have the delivery coming tonight. I'll bring it down later."

"Thank you."

I sat down at the table, looking at the empty seats. My fingers tapped away on the wooden surface as if they had a life of their own. I was anxious and restless. It wasn't supposed to take so long; we should have a full family by now. As fond as I was of Violet, I couldn't bear it to just be the two of us for much longer.

She sat down, placing our food before us. "Thank you, Violet. Can I ask you a question?"

"Yes," she replied.

"Are you lonely?" Her eyes dropped to the table, telling me that she was. "Violet, answer me please," I prompted. "I don't like when you hold something back."

"Yes. I am. I'm sorry."

"I thought so, and please don't apologize." I could barely contain my excitement of bringing Rose and Lily back. Four beautiful, pure flowers. "Is Poppy not good company?"

Violet's eyes widened, alarmed. "She is. It's just taking a little time to settle in. I promise she'll be fine, though."

"Oh, I know she will. It's natural to feel apprehensive when this is so new to her. Is she healing?"

"Yes. Her head is still sore so I let her sleep in."

"I thought you had." I sipped my orange juice. "What are your plans for today? I haven't forgotten those extra books. I'll make sure the bookshelf is full soon enough."

"Thank you. I was planning on reading." She poked around at her eggs. "Clover?"

"Yes?"

She bit on her lip nervously. "I used to knit, and I was wondering if you would consider getting me some needles and wool?"

"You can knit?" I was told that my grandmother was a skilled knitter, but Mother never took it up—not that I could remember, anyway.

"Yes. My gran taught me from a young age. I used to make cardigans, scarfs, gloves, socks, anything really. It's calming, relaxing, and I like that I can make something unique. There aren't enough handmade things around anymore. Everything's mass production now."

I smiled. "You're right, there's not. I don't know what I'm getting, though. Perhaps you could write a list for me?"

Her eyes lit up, causing my heart to skip a beat. "Of course. Thank you. I'll knit you a winter hat."

"That would be lovely, Violet, thank you. Anyway, I need to leave for work. What is for dinner tonight?"

"Lasagna and salad. Does that sound okay?"

"That sounds perfect." I walked around the table and kissed her cheek. "Thank you for breakfast, and have a good day reading."

"You're welcome, and have a good day at work," she replied, beaming at me. I nodded my head and left the room.

Saturday, July 16th (2005)

Parking in the small lot behind the self-storage place, I scanned the street opposite. *Where are they?* I frowned. Had I missed my chance? I hoped not. I hoped I hadn't missed Rose and Lily simply because I hadn't acted fast enough, but it wasn't time before.

"Come on," I whispered. My heart was heavy. The thought of them alone somewhere out there was awful, especially when I had a safe home and a family waiting for them. Someone stepped in front of my view and tapped on the window.

I jumped back in surprise and wound the window down. A young woman wearing very little leaned down. "Can I help you?" I asked. My voice was tighter than I intended, but I knew what she was.

She smiled and tilted her head to the side. "Do you wanna go somewhere?"

I felt sick to my stomach that she assumed I wanted anything to do with her—or any of them. Images of that woman and my father flashed through my mind. *Dirty whore.* "I have a wife," I said, testing her morals.

She shrugged. "And?"

And? My lip curled and every nerve ending burst into angry flames. "Get in," I said. There was no hesitation from her, even after my less than warm response. She strolled around the front of my car and got into the passenger side. Her cheap perfume turned my stomach.

"The forest isn't far if you take a left at the crossroads," she said.

I tightened my grip on the steering wheel. "I know a place," I replied.

As I drove home, I thought about Mother. Would she feel proud that I hadn't given up? Since her death I hadn't been as dedicated to her cause as I should have been. I didn't particularly want to be; this was my time to have a family and a fresh start. It was selfish of me. I was desperately unhappy being alone and wanted a family more than anything, but I couldn't help the reaction women like her gave me. I couldn't help the uncontrollable urge to fix it.

I pulled into my driveway ten minutes later and turned off the engine. My heart fluttered and stomach turned. I didn't think I would be back here so soon. This wasn't supposed to be my life now. I wasn't so naïve that I thought that I could turn my back on everything Mother and I had built, but I wanted something that was just for me too.

"We're at your place?"

"Yes," I replied. "I have a room."

She giggled. "Sounds kinky. That's extra, you know?"

I ignored her and got out. Where was her self-respect? She had lost it along the way. I wondered at what age she turned into a whore. More and more teenage girls were making little tarts out of themselves. It was hardly surprising why some lose their morals; it seemed to disappear with their innocence.

Leading her into the house, I pulled back the bookcase and opened the door. "Wow, you got a sex room down there? BDSM?" Ignoring her again, I gestured with my head for her to go down first, and she walked ahead without hesitation.

At the bottom of the stairs, she turned fully and saw the girls. "What the…?"

"Stand against the wall," I ordered.

She jumped back and pressed herself into the concrete wall. "What are you going to do?" she asked. "And who are they? I don't do that sort of thing."

"You do not ask the questions. Close your eyes. Now."

"No. Look, I just want to go, okay? I won't mention whatever you've got going on here; it's none of my business."

"Close. Your. Eyes." To my surprise, she did. "Good-bye," I whispered and pulled the penknife out of my pocket. Her eyes flew open, and I leaped forward, plunging the knife into her gut.

An ear-piercing scream echoed through the room as one of the girls cried out. I kept my eyes on the whore, watching her slump to the floor. Letting out a sigh of relief, I turned around. "It's done. It's over." My blood was singing in my veins and my body relaxed.

Violet stared at me in horror. "What did you do?"

"What I had to. Don't worry, Violet, it's over now. She's won't be able to hurt anyone ever again. I took care of it. I will always take care of it." I couldn't help it.

"B-but what? Clover, it's…wrong," Violet whispered. Her eyes were wide, scared, and her hands trembled with shock. *Wrong*, I repeated in my head. No, what the whore did was wrong. I'd prevented her from hurting anyone else. No child would lose their family because of her now.

My heart raced at a hundred miles an hour. How could she accuse *me* of being in the wrong? My hands clenched into fists of their own accord. I took a deep breath to clear my anger. *She doesn't understand what I'm doing, that's all.* "Violet, you don't understand."

"No," she replied, shaking her head slowly. "No, I really don't."

"I have done nothing wrong. You know what she is, don't you?" Violet nodded her head, showing me she understood the whore was a prostitute. "Good. Do you think they should be allowed to rip families apart? To dress like a tart and give herself to anyone that has the money. Is that right, Violet?"

"No," she replied, a tear trickled down her cheek. Finally, she was starting to get it.

"That's right, it's not. Poppy?" I looked over to where Poppy was sitting frozen on the sofa, shaking. "Do you think they should get away with it? After all, the police do nothing to prevent it." Poppy shook her head stiffly. Her eyes were as wide as her mouth was hung open. I smiled. "You see. What I'm doing is…righting a wrong." I scratched my head. "Now, we need to clean this up."

"Clean it up?" Violet squeaked.

"Yes. Fill a bucket with hot, soapy water, get bleach and garbage bags." Violet and Poppy stayed still. "Now," I snapped. I knew there were still body bags in the cupboard under the stairs. I'd bought no more since Mother died, but I knew now I would have to.

I returned to Violet with the body bag. She and Poppy had already made a start. I pressed my fist to my mouth and dropped the body bag beside them. "Put it in that," I murmured against my fist. Blood seeped from the wound in her gut, making my stomach turn. My breathing became shallow and my skin crawled. I felt dirty, as if the whore's germs were crawling over my body.

Fleeing from the room and locking the door, I sprinted to the shower and got in with my clothes still on. Peeling my soaking clothes from my body, I grabbed the sponge and scrubbed until I my skin was red and raw.

Sunday, July 17th (2005)

I parked the car in the same spot as yesterday and got out. They were here tonight, huddled together on a bench. Closing my eyes, I sighed in deep happiness. Both of them were beautiful. Lily had long light blond hair, a golden veil, and Rose was the exact opposite with shoulder length jet-black hair. Neither was more attractive than the other, though; they were perfect.

I got out, barely able to hide my joy. "Hello, ladies," I said. They both jumped, startled. "Sorry, I didn't mean to frighten you."

"It's okay. We didn't see you coming, that's all," Rose said.

"Where are you headed?"

"Um." Lily hesitated. "We're trying to make our way to London." London? They were miles and miles away from the capital. "It's taken us almost a week to get this far and we've only come fifty miles. We're trying to earn money where we can, but it's hard."

"Well, I don't know if this would help, but I live about forty miles out of London. I'd be prepared to take you that far if you like?"

Rose's eyes lit up. "Really? That would be great."

"Of course. I would quite enjoy the company on the long drive anyway. I've just stopped to get a drink and sandwich. Would you like one too?"

"Yes, please," Lily replied, grinning wide. "I'm Bree, and this is Sadie."

I smiled tightly. "Bree, Sadie, shall we head off?" They nodded in unison, as if they had practiced, and walked with me to my car. I drove home and felt light, complete. Four flowers. Four perfect, innocent, beautiful women. My family was complete.

15
SUMMER

Tuesday, December 14th (Present)

Rose was cleaning the bathroom so I took the opportunity to speak to Poppy in private. It had been nearly five months since I was kidnapped and thrown down here, and I hadn't given up hope—even after turning seventeen yesterday. No one knew and he didn't mention a thing, although he would definitely have found out. I didn't want to celebrate anyway.

"Poppy," I hissed under my breath when she didn't look up from her book as I hovered over her. "When did you give up hope of getting out?" It was something I had wanted to ask thousands of times but didn't dare. She was my only hope of doing something to escape, and I wasn't ready to hear it if she didn't want to. Five months was long enough. Five months was too close to the average of six to eight months it took for him to "fall in love" with his "flowers" and rape them. I couldn't beg her to help me escape too soon—before I was sure I could trust her and knew she wanted to get out—but I was dangerously close to going into *that* room.

She shifted on the sofa uncomfortably, as if I'd asked her something really personal. *It's a damn simple question and the answer is never.* "It's not about giving up, Lily; it's about surviving," she replied. "I don't know if we'll ever get out of here—alive—but going along with all this is the only chance we have." There had to be another way.

"Do you think your family is looking for you?"

She shook her head and dropped her eyes to the floor. I knew she didn't have a great relationship with them, but surely no one would give up on their child, especially if that child was missing. "I know they're not. We had a huge falling-out, and my parents said if I left I should never come back. I used to think my brother would look for me. He probably did for a while, but I doubt he would still be looking."

"I'm sure they didn't mean what they said. People say lots of things when they're angry." I'd said some horrible things to my parents, especially in my early teens. I would give anything to take them all back now.

"Maybe." She half smiled and looked so sad it made my eyes fill with tears. I couldn't imagine what it was like to think your family didn't care. "Your family will be, though. You never know, maybe they'll find us all."

I nodded. "Yeah, they'll be looking. I know Lewis won't give up until he finds me." He was definitely too stubborn to. Henry and Theo used to argue over which one of us was more stubborn and take bets on who would back down first in different situations. I used to win, but I still think Lewis is more stubborn. "We will get out of here," I said to myself as much as her.

She squeezed my hand. "We will." *When?* I had to get out before he touched me.

"Why did you leave home?" Poppy swallowed hard, it was

obviously still hard for her to think about. "Sorry, you don't have to talk about it."

"No, it's okay. It's just that I haven't ever spoken about the details before; everyone else down here seems to respect each other's privacy," she teased and winked. I smiled apologetically.

"When I hit my teenage years, I started going out a lot and got in with the wrong crowd. They took me to raves and shared their alcohol. I thought I was so cool at the time, and I loved how confident it made me." She smiled and shook her head at the memory. I could relate to that—minus the bad crowd thing. I wasn't confident and was always more outgoing when I'd had a drink, although I only drank a little bit, until I got that warm, tipsy feeling.

"Of course my parents didn't like it. They tried grounding me, taking things away, getting other family members involved, but I wouldn't listen to anyone. My new friends understood me, or so I thought. Every time I stumbled in drunk after midnight, my family became even more frustrated. I guess in the end, they'd had enough. We had a big argument and they were telling me I needed to get help and stop going out. I packed a bag and left. I can still remember my mum's words, 'You need help, Becca, so if you leave this house now, don't even think about coming back.' Those words still haunt me now. I should have stayed. I wish I could turn back the clock and storm up to my bedroom that night rather than out of the front door." She sighed. "Now I'm here."

I didn't want to admit it, but Poppy suited her better than

Becca. Maybe that was just because I had only ever called her Poppy, though. Her family must be going through hell, especially after ending things like that. We had to get out; Poppy and her family deserved a second chance too.

"Right," Rose said as she closed the bathroom door behind her. "All done. Shall we watch a movie?"

What else was there to do? We had already watched every film we had twice. He buys and sells DVDs online once a month. We had about forty movies, but with little else to do, we quickly went through them. I was starting to hate my favorite movies.

"Yeah, whatever," I replied and flopped back into the sofa, preparing myself for yet another night in front of the TV.

Wednesday, December 15th (Present)

I toweled myself dry as quickly as I could and pulled on the size-too-big clothes. I wondered if he would ever give in and buy clothes that actually fit me or if he was too determined that I should be a size ten. Not that it really mattered.

As soon as I was ready I grabbed the door handle and ripped it open. We were running late and Rose still had to get ready. She darted in as soon as I was out. Her eyes were wide and face pale. *Shit, what would he do if we weren't ready?* I didn't know that—I'd never asked—and I didn't ever want to find out.

Poppy was frantically whisking eggs in a bowl. I was thankful that the psycho loved scrambled eggs on toast so much—it was quick and easy. I opened the loaf of bread and pulled out eight slices to toast.

"You okay, Poppy?"

She nodded her head; her hair flew about when she was trying too hard to convince us both that she was fine. "Pop the toast under the grill now, please."

I did what she told me to do. My heart was working overtime. I didn't like how nervous they were. They were usually so at ease with him. How could Rose be okay with things down here when she was clearly still scared?

The cellar door unlocked at the same time Rose came out of the bathroom and we finished dishing up breakfast. I grabbed two places when I felt something lightly touch my back. From the faint smell of his woody aftershave, I knew it was him.

"Breakfast smells incredible," he said. I tensed and smiled over my shoulder, trying to pretend his touch didn't make me feel ill. I turned and he stepped back, allowing me to move away and put the plates on the table.

My heart rate slowed down as soon as I was away from him. How much longer could I manage to keep away from the psycho? He sat down, followed by Rose and Poppy, and we started eating in silence. He chewed slowly, distracted.

Finally he looked up and asked, "How was your evening last night?"

Depressing and boring—the same as every other night. "Good. We watched a few feel-good movies," Rose replied. "How was yours?" Feel-good movies down here were *Saw* and *The Texas Chainsaw Massacre*. Nothing could be worse than being locked up by the Clover freak.

He half smiled, eyes darkened, and his eyebrow twitched. It was a sinister look that made my blood run cold. What had he done? Had he killed someone? Did he enjoy doing it, or did he just feel he *had* to? I didn't think I would ever be able to understand his reasons, even if he explained them to me until the end of time. He was so intelligent, though. If Poppy and Rose were right and he wanted to change the world for the good, he could have done it the right way. Everything about the façade made you trust him. He looked normal, kind, trustworthy, and dependable. I didn't understand why he was so fucked up.

I shook my head. Why was I even trying to understand the creep? Shrinks would have a field day with him.

"What happened?" he snapped. I jumped at his sudden outburst and looked over my shoulder to where he was looking. Oh no. The poppies were a dark, dull red and draped lifelessly over the vase. My heart started pounding. Neither the lilies or roses looked particularly good either; they had browned at the edges and started to droop. They were all dying—of course!

He pushed his chair out roughly; it scraped along the tile, making me cringe, and slammed down on the floor. Rose and Poppy stood quickly but I was frozen, completely terrified of what I knew he was about to do. "What. Happened?" His eyes were wild and looked almost glazed over. He was like Dr. Jekyll and Mr. Hyde; his moods could flip in an instant. It was times like this I wondered how much control he had over the flower thing. After all this time he must know what was going to happen. Why did he continue to do it?

"We're very sorry, Clover. They died," Rose said. Her voice was soft and soothing, begging him to understand something that she shouldn't have to explain about and apologize for.

"Died," he repeated slowly. His breathing switched and became deep and ragged, as if he was fighting for control—making me question if he could help it all over again. "Yes, they died. They died because you can't take care of them properly." He slammed his fists down on the table so hard that the glasses of orange juice fell over, spilling down the table and onto the floor. *Of course, they fucking died. They're flowers!* They were in a cellar with no natural light. How could someone so intelligent not grasp that? Or did he fully understand but couldn't accept it? Nothing about him was simple or straightforward. I used to think I was quite good at reading people, but he was something else.

I backed up as he took a step toward my side of the table. *Don't come over here.* Rose and Poppy closed in and the three of us stood together. If the three of us worked together, we could get out. In the state he was in, though, I wouldn't risk trying anything.

"Do you have anything to say?" he asked. He spoke calmly and his voice was smooth like silk. But that was scarier than if he was shouting. He was too calm and controlled, but I knew any second he would let go and flip out. He was like a dog playing with a balloon; you knew it would pop but not exactly when.

None of us said a word. It would probably just make him angrier anyway. He walked around the table in the opposite direction. Rose and Poppy were between him and me. Raising his hand, he slapped Rose across her cheek. She gasped and stumbled to the side. Poppy steadied her and we all took a step back. I could hear my rapid breathing and tried to calm it down. What the hell is his deal?

He shoved Rose out of the way and grabbed Poppy's hand, pulling her closer. *No!* A sharp slap to her cheek sent her flying into the table. She cried out and held her stomach where it had hit the wood.

"You. Will. All. Learn," he growled and leaped forward, pinning me to the wall.

My breath caught in my throat and I flinched, closing my eyes as I preparing to be hit. *Lewis, Lewis, Lewis,* I screamed in my head, needing to mentally go somewhere else. His fist connected with my jaw and I fell down. Pain exploded in the side of my face. Pressing my hand over my mouth, I took a few deep breaths through my nose. Don't scream and give him the satisfaction. My jaw throbbed and tears welled in my eyes, but I refused to cry. I wouldn't let him know he'd hurt me.

My mouth filled with the metallic taste of blood and a stinging sensation pulsed from the inside of my cheek. I must have cut it against my teeth. I swallowed, knowing him seeing blood would make him worse. Slumping to the floor, I closed my eyes. *I can't do this for much longer.*

"Clean up. Now," he ordered. I flicked my eyes open just in time to see him disappear up the stairs. Jumping to my feet, I ran to the bathroom and rinsed my mouth out. Knowing he was gone, I allowed myself to spill the tears that pooled in my eyes. I sank to the floor, feeling so scared and alone it made my heart ache.

Thursday, December 16th (Present)

I sat on the sofa with Rose and Poppy. We had the TV on but none of us were watching. We anxiously waited for him to come back. He hadn't come down for breakfast today. The thought of him coming was scary, but the thought of him never coming back was worse. If he left us, we would starve to death down here.

My jaw was bruised and swollen, and inside, my mouth was so tender I could only eat soft foods. The purple dusting across my face was a constant reminder of how messed up he was and how much danger I was in. Every time he hurt me or someone else, I seriously doubted any plan of escape. I realized that was why Poppy didn't want to do anything; she didn't think for one second we could make it.

"What are we going to do?" Poppy asked. "He's getting worse, Rose, and you know it."

There was something completely terrifying about them when they were worried. They had seen so much and were used to how it was, but now they were scared. I wondered if it was because of me. He chose someone who had a family. Was the outside world closing in on him? They were both distracted; when they watched the TV, their eyes were blank—thinking, worrying.

Rose shook her head. "I don't know, but I'm sure everything's going to be fine. We stick together as usual."

I was seriously sick of them saying everything was going to be fine. Why did they even say it? They had clearly accepted this was their life, and it was not fine. Something inside me erupted and I jumped up. My blood boiled.

"Rose, take a fucking look around, will you? We're locked up in some psycho's cellar. How the hell is this fine?" I shouted. "Will you wake the hell up?!"

"Shh, Lily. You don't know where he is," she said in a hushed shout.

I took a deep breath and ignored her calling me Lily. Lily was someone in his sick fantasy and I was not her. "Oh my God. Think about it, Rose. We can't hear crap until the door opens. You really think he can hear us? Instead of playing I-wanna-be-Mrs.-Crazy, can you please just act like a normal person? We. Were. Kidnapped."

"I am very aware of the situation, Lily, but what do you want me to do?" *Was* she aware of the situation?

I clenched my fists. What the hell was wrong with her? "I want you to get your head out of his arse and think of something we can do to escape. I want you to stop acting like this is normal. Why don't you want to get out? If we all work together, we could overpower him."

"That has been tried before," Poppy said, cutting into the argument.

"I know. You've both said it has, but not by all three, or four, at the same time. Sure, one he can take on one no problem, but how is he going to stop all three of us? Just think about it: we can attack him and escape. This can work." What was I saying? Two minutes ago this was impossible and now I was rallying the damn troops.

The cellar door creaking open made me jump. My heart leaped

152

and stomach sank. "This can work if we do it together," I whispered, begging them with wide eyes.

"No, Lily," Rose replied. I turned away before I screamed at her again.

He was carrying three bunches of flowers and mumbling to himself. I couldn't work out exactly what he was saying but I caught what I thought a few words were. *Bodies* and *camel* but it couldn't have been that. Well, not the second one anyway.

Rose took a deep breath and smiled warmly. She looked confident and relaxed but her hands tapped against the side of her thighs and she held herself stiffly. "Good afternoon, Clover."

He jumped, startled, as if he wasn't expecting us to be here. "G-good afternoon," he said, stuttering as if he was surprised we were right there. He never stuttered. He was so confident and smooth, unless he was freaking out about flowers. How could he have been surprised to see us? What did he think, that we had popped out to the corner store?

"Have you come for lunch?" Poppy asked, her eyes flicking to the clock. It was only twelve, so he should have been at work.

The way he was acting was so erratic—talking to himself and being completely unaware of everyone around him. His eyes darted around the room, taking everything in. I gulped and noticed Poppy took half a step back. "Flowers," he said and held them out.

"They're beautiful, Clover, thank you." Rose stepped forward and took all three bunches out of his hand. *So, we're just pretending this is normal? No questions?*

I followed Rose and Poppy to the kitchen area and filled the vases with water. Out of the corner of my eye, I watched him. He eyes darted around the room, every few seconds flicking back to the door. Who was he expecting? The police? He was acting weirder than before. It was unlike him and I had no idea how to act. Was it best to ignore him completely?

"So, Clover, would you like some lunch?" Rose asked.

"No, thank you," he replied quickly and smiled.

Without another word, he kissed Rose and Poppy on the cheek and looked at me. I held my breath as he closed the short distance and kissed my cheek. The palms of my hands stung, and I only realized once he moved away that I had been digging my nails into them.

"Good night, Flowers," he said from the stairs and continued mumbling to himself. *Phone* and *bodies*.

"Good night?" Poppy repeated to Rose. Did that mean he wasn't coming down here anymore today or did he just have no idea of the time?

Rose shrugged and took one last glance at him before he was gone through the door. "I'll make us all a nice hot chocolate." *Oh, that'll fix everything, Rose!*

I drank my hot chocolate quickly, burning my tongue and barely tasting it. I tried to focus on something other than his lips on my skin, but I could still feel the light pressure on my cheek. I felt dirty. "I'm taking a shower." I needed to feel clean again, if that were possible now.

Turning the shower on first so it would heat up, I stripped off my clothes. The temperature was too hot, but I forced myself to get in. No matter how hard I scrubbed my body, I still felt disgusting. It was as if he had been etched into my skin. I idly wondered how long ago Rose stopped scrubbing her body, if she ever did. She seemed to like it down here. I would never get to that point. Ever.

16
CLOVER

Wednesday, May 9th (2007)

I sat at the unbalanced table with Violet, Poppy, and Lily. There should be four flowers sitting with me. I couldn't help my eyes flicking to the empty seat. My Rose was missing. It felt wrong and I couldn't relax.

"Is everything okay, Clover?" Lily asked. Love and concern shone in her eyes; it made me feel a hundred feet tall. Lily was beautiful. She had been part of the family for two years now and was someone to look up to for the other girls. Poppy and Violet looked up to her.

"Everything's fine," I replied, smiling through my unease. I ate silently, listening to their conversations, only joining in when necessary. My foot tapped on the floor rhythmically. *This is wrong.* I needed to see Shannen, and I needed to find Rose.

When everyone had finished their meal, I excused myself and made my way to my room to get changed for the night. I needed to see my Shannen. That girl seemed to occupy my every thought—she never left my mind. She was the one I thought of when I fell asleep by myself every night. I wanted nothing more than to look after her—but I wanted her in the house with me. I had only known her for three weeks, but she already meant so much more. Shannen was my one and only chance at a traditional relationship.

I dressed in smart black trousers, a gray sweater, and slipped on my long, black coat. Everything had to be perfect. I combed my hair, spraying hairspray on thick, so not one strand would be out of place. My appearance had never been so important as it was tonight. I wanted to be the best I could be for her. I wanted to give her the world, to share my world with her.

The drive to the supermarket next to her hostel was short. I wanted it to be longer so I had a few more minutes to calm my nerves. It wasn't something I was used to, nerves around women. I half liked it. Parking the car, I spotted her immediately as she walked out of the hostel and toward the field behind it.

My heart rate spiked. She was very beautiful even though she wasn't looking after herself as well as she should. I would help her with that. We would look after each other. I walked behind, watching her long brunette hair blow softly in the warm, early May breeze. She turned suddenly, no doubt finally hearing my footsteps crunching over the stones.

"Hello again, Shannen," I said.

Her cheeks flushed light pink and she smiled. "Hello, Colin. I'm going to sit by the trees. Would you like to join me?"

"That would be lovely."

We walked in silence across the grass field to the trees at the back. I sat down beside her, ignoring the uneasy feeling in my stomach caused from sitting on the dirty ground. "How has your day been?"

"The same," she replied, shrugging her shoulders and looking at the floor. "I'm glad you're here, though." She blushed through her admission, and I knew then we were perfect for each other and this would work.

I took her hand and squeezed. She shouldn't feel shy with me; I wanted her to be confident and relaxed. "Me too. I missed you today."

Everything was different with Shannen. She was the one. I knew that; she just made me feel…happy. A part of me felt guilty for feeling more for her than the other girls, but I couldn't help it. Shannen was perfect, everything a woman should be. I wanted her to live with me, to be my wife—my everything. She reminded me a lot of my mother, so I knew she would understand about the girls.

"How was work?" she asked. Her question was genuine—she really wanted to know. That was what I loved the most about her. She cared so much about people even though others have treated her badly. Her family had turned their backs on her, but she was still kind and caring.

"It was good, thank you, although a very long day." She nodded, playing with a blade of grass. I closed my eyes and took a calming breath; she had no idea how dirty that was. Anything could be on that grass. "What have you been doing today?"

"I read a little and then came out here."

"And how was everyone else in the hostel?" I frowned as I thought about the incident she described two nights ago. Some vile whore had hit her while trying to steal what little money she had left, leaving behind a faint red handprint on her left cheek.

She shrugged, looking down at the floor. "They were fine."

"Don't lie to me," I snapped, instantly regretting it as she flinched.

She stood, ripping her hand from mine. "I should go now," she whispered, wrapping her arms around herself.

I rose to my feet quickly, panicking that she was going to walk off and leave me. "No, Shannen. I'm sorry. I shouldn't have snapped like that. I just hate the idea of anyone treating you badly." I took her hand and squeezed it, being careful not to hurt her tiny frame. "Forgive me, Shannen, please?"

She smiled and nodded. "Yeah, I forgive you. It's okay. Want to go for a walk?"

"Absolutely."

We walked along the footpath. Every time I came to see her, we would meet in the field and then go for a walk. I led her around the lake—our usual route—and slipped my hand into hers.

"It's beautiful tonight."

"Yes, it is," I agreed.

"My dad used to take me outside in the evenings and we'd watch the stars appear in the sky," she said and looked down at the ground. Her voice was filled with sadness and regret. She had never mentioned anything about her family, other than that they fought and she left.

"What happened, Shannen? How did you end up here?"

"Please don't," she whispered. "I don't want to talk about it." I nodded, pushing away my anger at her not answering my questions. My girls answered my questions, always.

"Look, why don't you stay with me for a while? At least until you get yourself sorted out."

"I appreciate that, Colin, but I can't."

I sighed in frustration. Why couldn't she just do what I wanted? I wasn't used to it and I didn't like it. "Would you like to get a late dinner somewhere?" I asked, frowning at her tiny, fragile wrist. She bit her lip as she considered my offer. "Please? It'll be my treat. I'd like to."

A wide smile stretched across her beautiful face, one that made me stop breathing. "Okay. That would be nice, thank you."

We arrived at my favorite Indian restaurant that my parents used to go to when I was little. My father loved his curry and often took us—that was before he slept with that whore and ripped our family apart. "A table for two, please," I said to the waiter.

We were seated in the corner of the restaurant and handed menus. "Thank you." I turned to Shannen once the server had disappeared, giving us time to browse the menu. "Order whatever you like." She smiled and scanned the menu. "I think I'm going to have a tikka masala. Have you chosen?"

"The same, please," she replied.

I closed my eyes. *You are made for me, Shannen.*

"So, how long have you been working in accounting?"

"Oh," I replied, pleasantly surprised at being asked a personal question. "About five years now, I suppose. What did you do prior to the incident with your family?"

"I was working in the diner my mum works at. My father lost his job and we needed money, so I quit college to work." She frowned. "He always needed more money." What did that mean? Her father didn't sound particularly decent. A man takes care of his family, not the other way around. I wanted to pry further, but I didn't want her to close up again. It would take time, and we had plenty of time.

Our conversation was easy and with little gaps of silence between, I knew I had made the right decision—Shannen was not going back to that hostel. I'd lost count of the number of times she'd made me smile and laugh—I hadn't laughed in years. Shannen was my future, my one chance. I had the drive back to convince her that I was the best person to take care of her. We could make this work; I would make her as happy as she made me. I vowed to.

Holding the restaurant door open, I let her leave first. Her arm brushed against mine and I gasped at the electricity. We had a connection, a real connection. "Thank you for dinner, Colin," she murmured, a light blush warmed her perfect, defined cheeks.

"You're welcome. It was my pleasure." Yes, it certainly was my pleasure. I never knew how incredible I would feel at something so normal as taking the girl I was fond of to dinner. How many dates had I missed out on over the years? It wasn't a feeling I'd ever had before, but I was desperate to keep it—desperate for Shannen to give us a chance.

We got back in my car and words failed me. My heart beat wildly and I felt sick with nerves. How was she going to react to me taking her home? To get to the hostel, you had to drive past my road, so I knew I could get her almost home before she started questioning me.

"You're cold," I said and switched the warm air on.

She rubbed her hands together. "Thank you. For everything."

"You're welcome. I had a lovely time."

A small, shy smile pulled at her lips. "So did I."

I drove slower than usual, delving into a conversation about what Shannen studied at college to calm my nerves. My house was close; I could see my red tile rooftop over the hill. *This is it. Now or never.* Slowing down a little too sharply, I pulled into my driveway and turned off the ignition.

"What are we doing here?" she asked, biting her lip and looking at my home out the window.

I turned to face her and smiled. "This is my house, Shannen. I just need to use the bathroom before I take you back. Come in for a minute." I watched as her eyes darted to my front door, hesitating. "I won't be long." After a second, she made up her mind and nodded, opening the door. She trusted me—I had won her trust.

"It's a lovely house," she said as I let us both in.

"Thank you." I was glad she liked it. I wanted her to like it and feel at home. I'd let her redecorate if there was anything she didn't like. Perhaps we could do that together—redecorate and turn the house into *our* home rather than just mine. "I'll show you to the living room where you can sit for a minute."

She sat down on the green sofa and I couldn't help sitting beside her. I liked it, the both of us sitting in our living room. "Don't you need the bathroom?" she asked and smiled.

"Shannen, I must confess…I don't really need to use the bathroom. I'm sorry I lied, but I just needed to get you in here so we can talk. I've brought you home." Her eyes widened in horror, and she stood up, gasping. I leaped to my feet and grabbed her arm before she had the chance to run. "Let me explain. Please."

"No, get off," she shouted, frantically trying to pull her hand out of my grip. Her hair flicked in all directions, hitting me in the face as she tried to get away. "Please, let go."

"Calm down," I ordered.

"Let me go." She thrashed her body again and pounded her free fist against my chest. The thuds of her punches didn't hurt—she didn't have much strength—but it angered me. I was trying to help—how dare she? I clenched my jaw, grabbed her other hand, and slammed her against the wall. All I could hear was my pulse pounding in my ears. I didn't want to hurt her, but she left me no choice. Shannen's piercing screams seemed like background music. Her blatant disrespect drove me insane. I knew what Mother would do, and I could almost hear her barking the order, *Kill her.*

"Please, please no." I didn't like begging. Mother didn't like begging. It was for the weak.

Kill her. Do it now.

Shannen's eyes bulged as I held both of her hands in one of mine and pinned my other hand over her mouth. I was fighting myself for control. I wanted to kill her—the knife was in my pocket—but I wanted her too. I wanted her and Mother wanted me to kill her.

She whimpered against my palm. I closed my eyes and concentrated on steadying my heavy, ragged breaths. *She'll be everything I want once she understands. She's not bad. She doesn't mean it.*

Slowly, I cracked my eyes open. It wasn't until I saw her terrified expression and her tear-stained face that I realized how vulnerable she was. Shannen was scared and didn't know what I was offering or how I felt. My heart swelled.

"Everything's going to be okay," I whispered. "I need you to trust me. All I want is to look after you. You're home now, sweet Shannen." I lowered my hand and stroked the side of her face, looking into her eyes. *Please believe me.*

She gulped. "I believe you'll look after me, Colin, but I can't stay here with you." My face fell. Did she not hear what I told her? She was home. This was where she belonged. "Sorry, I can't do this. I have to go now." She took one step away from me, and I felt complete panic. I couldn't let her walk away from me.

She had barely made two steps when I grabbed her from behind and clamped my hand over her mouth. Her muffled cries tore me apart and I realized this couldn't work out how I wanted it to—not yet at least. I shoved her into to the drawing room and into the corner.

"Don't try anything," I snapped and pushed the bookcase out of the way. She stood still, frozen, as I unlocked the door to the girls' room. Grabbing her arm, I pulled her with me, dragging her down the stairs.

"No," she yelled once she realized what was happening. I didn't want this to happen either; my heart was heavy and my eyes stung with the loss of the life I so desperately wanted with her. But I had no other choice. I couldn't lose her and this was the only way.

Poppy, Violet, and Lily rose from the sofa and the movement startled Shannen. She screamed, her legs gave way, and she slumped to the ground. "Explain everything to her, Lily," I ordered and walked back up the stairs. *No! No, no, no.* I closed the door and locked it before sliding down the wall. Gripping my hair in my hands roughly, I cried in agony. I wanted her to be with me, but now she was Rose.

17
CLOVER

Monday, January 17th (Present)

I watched the clock on my desk and the second it ticked over to five, I shut my computer down and grabbed hold of my briefcase. I needed to leave immediately. My girls wouldn't have dinner ready for another two hours, as per my request, so I had time.

I drove the thirty minutes to the city with my heart in my mouth, tapping my fingers against the steering wheel. It was already dark, but the hostel was just outside the city. This shouldn't take long anyway.

It had been too long since we had been a complete family— almost six months now. It's the longest we'd been incomplete. I felt anxious. I drove in the traffic, turning off before it got too bad in the city center. The winding road led to a small train station the hostel was nearby. I parked between the hostel and a block of derelict flats.

Come on, Violet.

She had to come along soon. I had waited so long for her. Lying back against the seat, I glanced out of all the widows and checked the mirrors. The orange glow of the dashboard lit up the clock—thirteen minutes past six. I could only stay another five or ten minutes. My heart raced with anticipation. I wanted her to appear. I needed her.

At 6:22, just as I was about to give up for the evening, I finally spotted her. Her hair was as dark as night and draped all the way down to middle of her back. *Violet.* She took my breath away. This *was* her. She started walking in my direction with her backpack hanging from her shoulders.

I opened the door and she sprung to life, jumping back in surprise.

"I'm sorry. I didn't mean to frighten you," I said, raising my hands to show her I didn't mean her any harm.

She shook her head. "No, that's okay. I wasn't really paying attention." Smiling briefly, she shrugged her bag back on her shoulder. "My fault."

"Do you need a lift somewhere?"

"Um." She hesitated. "I think I'll be okay but thanks."

I pursed my lips. *I'm trying to save you.* "You'd be doing me a favor. I've just got off the train and can't remember my way into the city in the dark."

"You're not from around here?"

I shook my head. "No. I had a meeting and decided to park here and take the train the rest of the journey. I have yet to find my way around the city. Where are you headed?"

"I'm not sure. City probably."

"Do you know it well?"

She nodded. "Yes."

"Well, would you like a lift? You can direct me to wherever you want to go and point me in the right direction once you get out."

"Okay then," she replied and smiled. "Thanks."

I got back in the car and she got in the passenger side. I drove off as soon as she was inside. "So where do you live?" she asked.

"Not far, we'll be home soon." I locked the door. "Violet." She laughed and shook her head. She was laughing at me? Did she find this funny? I frowned. What did she think? I'd had it with the soft approach. Their reactions were all the same at first, so it didn't matter how I saved them—direct and to the point gave me less of a headache.

"You need to turn left at the lights, that'll take you on the ring road around the city."

"Violet, we're going home."

Out of the corner of my eye, I saw her face slowly fall. "What?"

"Please don't worry. I'll take care of you."

"Are you being serious right now?"

"Of course." Her eyes widened in horror as she registered what was happening wasn't my idea of a joke. "I told you not to worry, Violet."

She shook her head. "What the fuck? I'm not Violet. You've got the wrong person." I sighed, gritting my teeth through her choice of colorful words. Her face cracked as my words properly sunk in and a steady flow of tears streaked her face. "Please let me go. I'm not who you think I am. I'm not this Violet, I swear. My name is Layal."

"I know who you are," I replied.

"No, you don't. Let me go. Now!" she snapped, pulling at the door handle in vain.

"Don't you *dare* be so disrespectful. I'm saving you." She flinched. "Just be quiet and everything will be fine. Just be quiet." She shrank back against the passenger side door and her knuckles turned white, still gripping the handle. My own hands tightened around the steering wheel. Her deep, unattractively loud sobs came frequently, and I ground my teeth together, trying to ignore her pathetic cries.

"W-Why are you doing this?" she muttered, stuttering over her words.

"Violet, I'm saving you," I repeated. *Why can't you see that? Look at what your life is.*

For the rest of the journey she was silent. Her cries died down to the occasional hiccup, and she stared emotionlessly out of the windshield. Finally, she understood what I was doing. I smiled; the stress and anxiety oozed from my body.

"Not long now," I said as we turned down the road leading to my house. "The girls will be happy you're home."

She pressed her hands to her mouth, muffling a cry. "Who?"

I smiled. "The girls. You're going to love them. Here we are," I said, pulling into my drive. "Are you ready to meet them?"

"No. Look, just let me go now and *I promise* I won't say anything. I won't go to the police, I swear to you. Please. Please just let me go."

"Violet, please just trust me and trust what I'm trying to do. The girls will be able to explain everything." I switched off the engine and unbuckled my seat belt. "Right, let's get inside."

I unlocked the car and shoved my door open. Violet jumped out and sprinted around the car, toward the road. "Help," she screamed. "Help me!" I lunged forward and grabbed a fistful of her coat. "No. Get off. Let go, you freak!" Her voice was loud and high-pitched. It rang through my ears.

I pulled her against my chest and clamped my hand over her mouth. "Be quiet, Violet," I growled in her ear. I felt stressed, like a volcano ready to erupt. She was pushing me to the limit. I dragged her to the house and unlocked the door. "Enough now," I whispered. She whimpered beneath me. "Almost there." I pushed her through the house. "I'm going to move the bookcase. Are you going to stand there nicely, or do I need to restrain you?"

She gulped and her eyes widened. "I'll stand here," she whispered hoarsely.

I smiled. "Good." Releasing my grip, I watched her move one step away from me and stop. I pulled the bookcase out of the way and unlocked the girls' door. "Come," I said, pushing the door open. She was frozen on the spot, staring at the open door. "Violet, *come*."

"But…" she whispered. Sighing in frustration, I grabbed her wrist. Why couldn't she just do as she was told? "No!" She gasped and thrust her body around, trying to get out of my grip. "No. Please don't."

I held both of her arms tight and pushed her down the stairs with me. For someone so slim she was strong. Rose, Poppy, and Lily all stood, waiting. "Good evening, Flowers," I said. Violet's body stiffened and she planted her feet into the floor. "Please make Violet welcome and help her settle in. I'll be back for dinner very soon." I let go of her and walked back up the stairs. I needed to get clean.

I returned to the girls' room after showering and picking out the wool Rose requested. The room was filled with the warming smell of a fresh shepherd's pie. It took me back to my childhood, before I was six, when Mother would make incredible home-cooked meals. That all changed the second we caught Dad with that whore, of course. Sitting down as a family and having Mother dish up large helpings of hearty food was one of the things I missed the most.

"Good evening, Flowers," I said, stopping at the bottom of the stairs.

"Good evening," they replied in unison. Violet sat on the sofa staring at the floor, a statue.

I frowned. "Is Violet okay?" I asked Rose. She was supposed to help her settle in.

Rose nodded. "She'll be fine. She's just getting used to something new."

I smiled. Of course. The adjustment period. "Dinner then?"

"It's ready," she replied and smiled. "Violet, come sit at the table. Dinner's ready." Lily helped her up and led her to her seat. My heart swelled. Lily was perfect—she was now everything I wanted her to be. Somewhere between my worry of finding Violet and the countrywide search for *Summer*, I'd forgotten to pay attention to her flourishing. I'd missed that and I was overcome with guilt.

"Eat, Violet," I said. Everyone was almost finished, but she had barely touched any of hers.

Lily looked up. "I don't think she's that hungry. We can save hers for later." Violet couldn't have eaten for a while, and she was thin. Her clothes would probably hang off her frame the way Lily's still did. "It's only her first night, after all," Lily added.

"You'll make sure she has something later?"

"Yes."

I nodded and turned my attention back to my own dinner. "Oh, your yarn is on the bottom step."

Rose smiled. "Thank you. I'll put that away when we're done."

I finished and waited for the girls. *Everything is going to be fine. I am in control.* Rose and Poppy got up to clear the table and I stopped Lily from helping. "Come, Lily." I walked ahead. She had shown me that she was the thoughtful, caring person I wanted, and now it was my turn to show her how much she meant to me.

She appeared at the door. Her posture was stiff, as if she wasn't breathing, and her eyes were wide. "It's okay, don't be nervous." I closed the door behind us. "Please relax. I'm not going to hurt you. Everything's going to be perfect now, can't you see that?" I led her to the bed, and she sat rigid on the edge. "Did you shower this morning?" She nodded and I smiled, stroking her long blond hair behind her ear. "That's my girl."

She blinked rapidly and a few tears fell from her eyes. "Shh," I whispered and unbuttoned my shirt. "Don't be afraid. I love you, Lily."

18
SUMMER

Tuesday, January 18 (Present)
I couldn't move. My body shook to the point where it ached and felt numb. Nothing felt real anymore. I didn't want anything to be real anymore. The bedsheet was wrapped tightly around me and I clung to it as if it were my lifeline. It smelled of him. *I smelled of him.* I desperately wanted to get that smell off, but my damned, traitorous body wouldn't move.

A distant voice drifted through the room, and I raised my head. "Lily. Lily, shh, it's okay," Poppy said softly. "It's going to be okay." I opened my mouth to speak but nothing came out, just a low creak in the back of my throat. "Don't worry, it'll be all right." *It won't bloody be all right!* "You want me to help you to the bathroom?" In my zombie state, I nodded and Poppy helped me up.

Somehow, we made it to the bathroom, but I don't remember getting here. I felt like I was underwater, the floor felt uneven, and everything was swimming. I couldn't believe that had just happened to me. I knew it had, but it didn't feel real.

Standing on the bathroom floor still in my socks, I gripped the sheet tighter around myself and stared at the floor. *Why can't I feel anything?* I couldn't even cry. I should be crying. Poppy turned the shower on and placed a fresh towel on the side of the sink.

"Call if you need me, okay?" she said and walked out, closing the door behind her.

Letting go of a sheet shouldn't be hard but I couldn't do it. As the only thing that was covering me—protecting me—I couldn't let the damn thing go. Taking a deep breath I gave myself a little pep talk, *You can do it. Just drop the sheet and get the smell of him off you.* Taking a deep breath, I let go and it dropped to the floor.

I stepped in the shower, eager to be free of his aftershave. The hot water ran over my whole body, washing him away with it. Why didn't I fight him? I didn't want it, but I didn't do anything to even attempt to stop it. Would it have been worth my life? Yes. Knowing I had done nothing made me feel sick, dirty, and worthless. If I'd have fought, at least I would have died knowing I didn't ultimately allow it to happen. But it was too late now. I couldn't turn back the clock and change anything. It was now something I would have to live with. I sobbed.

Too scared to do anything about it, I'd let him. My legs turned to jelly. I slumped to the floor and started crying. Grabbing the sponge, I frantically scrubbed my skin until it turned bright red. I felt dirty, and no amount of scrubbing was going to change that.

When my skin was too sore and I winced with every touch, I dropped the sponge, stood up, and turned the shower off. I cried as I wrapped the towel around me and the cotton rubbed against my sore, broken skin. My body shook from the shock, and although I'd had a hot shower, I felt cold—freezing cold.

Every time I closed my eyes, I saw his face looming over me. The way he looked at me—*lovingly*—make me sick. I gagged, slapping my hand over my mouth. Running to the toilet, I made it just in time to lean over it and empty the contents of my stomach.

"Lily," Poppy called through the door. She spoke so softly, like I was a newborn baby. I gripped the towel and pulled it around me tighter. My heart raced in my chest. I didn't want anyone to see me. "Can I come in?" Nothing came out when I tried to talk, just a quiet squeak. I sat down on the toilet seat and gripped the towel.

Poppy pushed the door open and peered around the side. I turned away, not wanting to see the pity in her eyes. She knelt down in front of me, and I tensed. "This is going to be a stupid question, but are you okay?" she asked. I shook my head, wrapping my arms around myself. She was right, that was a stupid question.

"I'm sorry. I know this isn't much, but it never lasts very long, I promise." It wasn't much at all. The length of time didn't matter; I didn't want him anywhere near me for *one* second.

"Shh, I know. You don't need to say anything." Poppy wiped the tears from my face. I didn't even have the energy to push her away. "Come on. I'll take you back to the bedroom. You need some sleep."

I stood beside my bed and let Poppy dress me in some pajamas. It was as if I had forgotten how to do everything. She guided me down on the bed and tucked me in. I felt like her daughter. Violet was already asleep, and I wished I was too.

I wished I could speak to Lewis, even for just a second, just to hear his voice. Pressing my face into the pillow, I cried silently. The bed shook where my body heaved from my sobbing. I could still feel him on me. As ill as I felt, I couldn't even get up and be sick. My legs were too heavy, and I just wanted to curl up and sleep.

Closing my eyes, I pictured Lewis's face, his smile, his laugh, and the way he said my name. I could still hear it perfectly in my head. *Sum.* He was too lazy to say my whole name most of the time, but it still gave me butterflies every time he said it. And the way his eyes lit up when he said it, like he was so happy just to say my name.

When I was with Lewis, it was special. He made me feel special, like the only girl in the whole world. He was soft and gentle. With him it meant everything. I was safe and loved. I cried harder, remembering how amazing it felt with him. I would never have that again. Now it was messed up and dirty. *I* was messed up and dirty, and Lewis would never look at me in the same way again. How could he?

I buried my head in the soaking wet pillow and squeezed my eyes closed again. All I wanted was to fall asleep and forget everything. Now I had nothing left for him to take from me, though. Did it really matter what he did to me now? I curled up tighter, making myself as small as I could, and hugged my legs. I cried until I'd run out of tears and my throat burned. Eventually, I was so exhausted that I fell asleep. The only thing that kept me from falling apart was knowing *that* wasn't my first time—that he hadn't stolen that from me too.

Saturday, May 2nd (2009)

Lewis looked nervous. He kept biting the inside of his cheek. *Why is he nervous?* My heart was beating a million miles an hour, and I felt like I was going to faint. He straightened up on my bed and tightened his arm around me. We had the house to ourselves as my parents were away for their anniversary and Henry had a date with a weird girl who laughed at all his sucky jokes.

Tonight Lewis and I were going to have sex for the first time. It was also my first time ever, and I was almost sick with nerves. What if I did something wrong? I was totally in the deep end here, and he just kept saying everything was fine. Apparently I couldn't mess it up. I didn't want to prove him wrong.

"You okay?" I asked. I still didn't know why he was scared—he'd done it before!

"Yeah." He nodded and wiped his hand on his jeans. "You?"

"I'm fine," I whispered. I was ready and had been for a little while now, but everyone said it hurts the first time so I was scared. Hurt how much?

We spoke a few times about when, and I didn't want it to be quickly before my parents got home from work or in the back of a car, so we planned on tonight. Shouldn't he make the first move? I looked up at him through my eyelashes. What if he had changed his mind? I mentally laughed at myself. What seventeen-year-old guy changed his mind about sex?

"You're nervous," I said, blushing.

He nodded. "A bit."

"Why?" He shrugged, giving nothing away. "Lewis?"

"I dunno, it's just different this time. And you're a virgin." *Oh, sorry!* I frowned, and he laughed. "That's not a bad thing, Sum."

"I know," I replied, narrowing my eyes.

"Would you rather wait?"

"No," I whispered. "Would you?" He smirked, his eyes dancing with amusement. "I'll take that as a no," I muttered sarcastically. He bent his head and kissed me. My tummy flipped over and over again. His lips pressed against mine forcefully but somehow gently at the same time. It was dizzying. "I'm ready now," I muttered against his lips.

He groaned and tangled his fingers in my hair. "Wait, should I have roses scattered on the bed or something cheesy like that?"

"Yeah, because every girl wants a thorn sticking in her butt on her first time. It'll be special. I don't need all the cheesiness." His lips covered mine suddenly. After a second, I kissed him back and we fell onto the mattress. My clothes just seemed to disappear. He was good at this. I felt stupid, not really knowing what to do.

Lewis was gentle as he pushed inside me, *really* gentle, but it still bloody hurt. Closing my eyes, I gripped hold of his back. I loved how he made me feel, that we were like one person right now, but I couldn't ignore the pain. I bit down on my lip and he stilled. "Do you want to stop?"

"No!" I blushed at how desperate I sounded, but it was true—I really didn't want to stop. I wanted to get past the hurting part. "I like being this close to you and, anyway, I'll be okay after a few minutes." *I hope. Kerri better be right!* He kissed me again, and I was too lost, too wrapped up in him to think about the pain that was very slowly subsiding. It was perfect, even without the candles and roses.

I cuddled into his side with my head on his chest. "You okay? Does it still hurt? You're not still in pain, are you? I can get you something," he rambled, drawing random shapes on my back with his fingers.

"Lewis, chill, I'm fine."

"You said it hurt."

"It did, but I think I'll survive." I rolled my eyes.

"So you're in pain, but you won't take anything for it because it's not a pain that will kill you?" He shook his head and looked at me in amusement. "I think your stubbornness has reached a new level."

"Or," I said, "I'm just not a big baby. Besides it's a nice pain, and it doesn't really hurt that much now."

"You're such a weirdo," he teased and kissed my forehead.

I laughed. "Yeah, love you too."

19
SUMMER

Thursday, January 20th (Present)

Poppy woke me up in the morning by stroking my hair and whispering, "Lily." *Summer, Summer, Summer, Summer, Summer!* I squeezed my eyes closed and a tear escaped, dripping onto the pillow. Wrapping the cover around me tightly, I pressed my face into the pillow. *Leave me alone.* "Hey, it's okay. Don't cry. He's already gone," Poppy said. I heard her put something down on the bedside table. I raised my head and saw a hot mug of tea and a plate of toast. I could eat here? And he was gone?

"What?" I asked, blinking rapidly to clear the tears in my eyes. We never ate in the bedroom.

"He's already been down for breakfast. We told him you're not feeling well so you were sleeping in. Try and eat something, okay?" I nodded my head. I felt sick but my stomach groaned, begging for food. "I'll leave you to it. Call me if you need anything." She walked out of the room and closed the door. I gulped down the panic at her leaving me. I wanted to be alone, but I didn't feel safe. None of us were safe down here, but we were safer together. He couldn't just magic his way in here—appear in front of me—but it still scared me. He had so much control over us.

I sat against the wall and pulled the cover over me for protection.

The steaming mug of tea looked so inviting; I picked it up and took a sip. After a few mouthfuls, I felt a little more human. My gran was wrong, though: a cup of tea couldn't fix everything. It was just a normal thing to do and normal didn't happen down here much.

Yesterday felt like it was a bad dream. Did it really happen? Sometimes I thought about something so much that it didn't seem real anymore. Or something was so shocking that it couldn't seem real. I knew I should keep myself busy to take my mind off it, but I was too drained. I felt like I had nothing left inside me. Summer was slipping away, and I clutched at that carefree, stubborn teenager with my fingertips. I wouldn't let her go. I couldn't be Lily.

My skin crawled and a shudder of disgust rippled through my body. I jumped out of bed and grabbed clothes and a towel. "I'm showering," I muttered on my way through to the bathroom.

"Okay," Rose replied, looking up from her book the sofa.

I turned the shower on as hot as it would go and sat on the floor and waited for the steam to tell me it was hot enough. Would I ever feel clean again? *Don't think about it...Summer.* Stripping out of my clothes, I stepped into the shower. The water burned as it hit my skin, and I gasped in shock. I clenched my teeth together and held on to the wall, digging my short nails into it. The water was unbearably hot; it felt like being stung all over by bees, but I wouldn't move.

When I was red and sore, I got out and loosely wrapped a towel around my aching body. The soft material rubbed against my delicate skin. It stung so much it brought a tear to my eye. The mirror on the wall next to the shower had steamed up and, thankfully, I couldn't see myself in it. I used to think they were crazy to happily shower twice a day, but maybe they just didn't feel clean down here.

The only tight fitting clothes I had were a pair of white cotton trousers and a thin, light green long-sleeved top. I brushed my hair, dragging it from the roots to the tips, counting to one hundred. My mum used to tell me to brush it one hundred strokes when I was little. I treated it as a game—shouting the numbers out until I reached one hundred. This time I did the same and counted in my head. I wanted to go back there, to when I was a little kid sitting on my daddy's lap combing my damp hair.

"Lily, are you okay?" Rose asked, the second I walked out of the bathroom. I nodded in reply, even though what I felt was the furthest thing from okay.

Poppy sat on the sofa as Rose got up, and I followed her. I had a feeling she didn't say certain things in front of Rose, and I wasn't sure if that was because she didn't trust her or she didn't want to upset her. "It will get better, I promise. You won't always feel like this."

"Won't I?" I replied.

"You won't. It gets...bearable. I hate it too, Lily. You just need to find something to focus on while it's happening." I tried. "I think about what I want my life to be and for those few minutes, I'm in a different world," she said, smiling fondly at whatever that image was.

"What do you want your life to be?"

"Happy," she replied simply. "I imagine living in a beautiful little cottage with ivy growing up the walls and around the windows. The garden is equally as beautiful, with colorful flowers and a vegetable patch. My husband's a great man who works hard to support his family and I stay at home with our children. I imagine what my pregnancies would be like and how my children would look, our family holidays and playing in the garden. We're happy, you know, really happy."

I managed to smile a little. "That sounds nice." I wanted a life in London with a huge flat overlooking the Thames, a good salary, and lots of cocktail bars. Now I'd settle for anything—a cardboard box—if it were outside this fucking cellar.

"It's silly, I know, but a family and nice little house is all I've ever wanted."

I shook my head. "It's not silly. You can still have that." We just needed to get out of here. Would her fantasy of her perfect life be enough to make her help me? With her help, we could do something to him. I had no doubt Violet would be in.

She sighed and shook her head. "I can't, Lily. It's just a dream. Do you want another cup of tea?" Before I had time to answer, she walked over to the kettle. Boiling water. We could do a lot of damage with boiling water. "Lily, do you want an extra sugar?"

Why would I want an extra sugar? I frowned. "No, thank you."

Poppy smiled and went back to making tea. She should be making tea for her husband and juice for her children. She deserved that life. I sat back and for the first time I *really* realized that it wasn't just me that was losing out. Rose and Poppy may not have had a family when they were taken, but that didn't mean they didn't dream of having one. They could have one now if they weren't down here.

Tea and toast was placed in front of me. I wasn't sure if it was fresh toast or the old one from our room—it didn't matter, though. "Thank you." I nibbled at the toast but my stomach turned. I felt too disgusting to keep anything down.

The new Violet opened the bedroom door and tentatively stepped out. Her eyes darted around the room. "It's okay," I whispered. Wow, I was just like Rose and Poppy, giving false hope to the new girl. She stepped into the room and perched on the arm of the sofa.

Poppy whispered in my ear, "She's not said a word, and she won't talk to us or even listen to us." *Probably because she doesn't want to hear what you have to say.* Violet was still in shock; her wide eyes scanned the room. My chest tightened as I remembered that feeling of being completely lost, confused, and terrified. Violet needed someone that understood her, not someone that would tell her to stay strong and endure it from day one.

"What's your name?" I asked her.

Her head snapped to mine so quickly I jumped in surprise. "Layal," she replied in a voice barely above a whisper.

"Layal's unusual."

"I'm from France originally, moved here with my mum to live with my grandparents when I was two."

I was getting somewhere. At least she had spoken to me. "Why did you move?"

She shook her head, frowning at a bad memory. "My dad was abusive, apparently. I don't remember him at all."

"I'm sorry," Rose said, and Layal shrugged. *Violet,* I reminded myself. I couldn't get caught up in calling her by her name. If I slipped up in front of him, then who knows what kind of screwed-up reaction he would have.

Violet looked up, directly at me, as if she didn't want to acknowledge Rose and Poppy. "What does he want?"

"We think the perfect family, or something like that. I don't understand it. I don't want to understand that psycho." I ignored Rose's deep frown. *Brainwashed.*

Violet look on, turning her nose up in disgust. "He's so fucked up." I nodded in agreement. *You have no idea.* "What did he do to you last night?" I dropped my eyes to the floor and tensed. "He raped you, didn't he?" she whispered. *No! No, no, no, no, no!* I tried to ignore the lump in my throat and picked a spot on the floor and stared. *I will not cry.* "He won't do that to me." I curled up, hugging my legs to my chest. I remembered saying a similar thing.

Rose tucked her hair behind her ears. "Would you like something to eat, Violet?"

"Layal," she corrected. "And no, thanks. Why are we all still here when there's four of us and only one of him?" Good question. Fear. That was all that stopped me and Poppy from trying to escape. For Rose, though, it was something else.

Violet clearly wanted to get out, so maybe it could work. We still both desperately wanted to escape. Poppy would take a lot of convincing, but I think we could win her around. Rose was a lost cause. Whatever we did, we had to make sure it was well thought out and that Rose didn't know a thing.

"We could poison him," Violet suggested.

I shook my head. "Too much could go wrong. We'd have to do it gradually, so he wouldn't taste or smell it, but then there would be no guarantee he'd die down here. I don't want to starve to death." Stabbing him with something, though there wasn't anything particularly sharp down here. Hitting him over the head with something hard, but then the only thing hard enough was the frying pan, TV, or a chair, and who wouldn't see that coming?

"Anyway, how did he find you?" I asked, needing to change the subject because Rose was still around, and I didn't want her to know how much I'd been thinking about escaping.

"I'll make some soup for lunch," Rose announced and abruptly walked away. I watched her go and hoped that when we got out she would be okay. Her family had to come forward and take care of her after everything she's been through.

As soon as she was busy pulling pans out of the cupboard, I turned to Violet and whispered, "We'll talk when we're alone." She looked up at Rose and her eyes widened a fraction as she understood why. I was determined to get out now more than ever.

When Rose called us for lunch, I made myself sit at the table like normal. Even though I felt the furthest thing from normal. My chest was aching. I wanted to curl up in the corner and lie there until we were found.

"Smells good," Poppy complimented.

I looked down at the steam rising off the plate, dancing around and making swirling patterns in the air. I watched it rise until it disappeared, wishing I could float off and disappear too.

"Lily, are you not hungry?" Rose asked.

I had only eaten a few mouthfuls and not even touched the bread roll. "No." Of course I wasn't hungry. Since I had been down here, I had lost my appetite, and after last night, I felt too sick and disgusted to eat anything more than a few nibbles of toast.

She took my plate. "Well I'll pop it in a Tupperware and we can keep it in the fridge for later."

"I won't want it later," I replied.

She smiled. "Just in case."

Rose and Poppy started another one of the daily bathroom cleans. I knew I should help by doing the kitchen or something, but I had no energy or motivation. I wanted to live to get out and see my family again, but with every passing day I cared a little less if I died.

Violet turned to me. "They said he comes down for dinner, right?" I nodded. "We'll do it then. We'll both grab something and hit him as hard as we can with it," she whispered.

My eyes widened. Shit, she was planning to do it just like that? "What? No. We have to actually plan this. We can't just hit him!"

She frowned deeply in anger. "This *is* a plan."

It wasn't. We couldn't just hit him without a plan. So many things could go wrong, and it had been tried in the past. "Violet, that's been done before without planning it through." I shook my head. "We can't, not now."

"Well, we can't do nothing. We have to. How can you say not now?"

"Have you ever seen someone being murdered right in front of you?"

She frowned. "What? No."

"Well, I have. That's how I can say not now." I stood up and walked into the bedroom. Cleaning seemed like a good idea for once.

The cellar door opened right on time, and my blood turned cold. Bile rose to my throat as he walked down the stairs, smiling, holding a bunch of bright purple violets. "Good evening, Flowers," he said. Those three words had the power to stop my heart. I stepped back behind the table and clung to the chair. Selfishly, I was grateful for Violet being here now; it meant he would take his place at the top of the table—the farthest from me.

Violet stared at him, her lip curled in hate and disgust. *Please don't*, I begged her silently. If she did anything, it would get her killed, and I didn't want that again. This Violet had to live.

Her eyes flicked to the empty vase sitting on the worktop. Too thin—it was far too thin and flimsy to do any damage. I doubted it would even hurt him at all. She caught my eye and nodded. I shook my head, eyes wide.

"Summer," Violet said, using my old name. *Shit. No!* My breathing slowed and I shook my head. He hadn't heard yet. He was too busy being greeted by Rose and Poppy. *No*, I mouthed. She didn't listen. Clover was standing sideways on to her. *Oh God, oh God.*

My breath caught in my throat as Violet swept the vase up and slammed it down on his head in one quick, swift movement. Rose and Poppy gasped as the flimsy plastic broke into only a few pieces and fell to the floor. Clover stumbled forward, but just a few steps.

This was it. My eyes widened in horror as he very slowly straightened up and turned around. Violet's mouth dropped open. His eyes were hard, cold, and fixed on her. I gulped and my hands shook.

20
SUMMER

Friday, January 21st (Present)

Clover slapped her cheek hard, and the sound echoed through the room. Violet cried out in pain and held the side of her face as she fell to the floor with a thud. I couldn't watch this anymore. I couldn't stand by and do nothing like I had with the other girl, and if he killed me too, then that was fine. Maybe he would be doing me a favor anyway.

I reached out to grab another vase. It wouldn't kill him, but that didn't even matter. This was about standing up for what was right. My fingertips had barely grazed the vase when Poppy grabbed my arm roughly and pulled me backward.

"No," she hissed in my ear. I struggled in her arms, but she had a tight grip on me. *I can't do this.* My legs gave way and I collapsed to the floor. It was too much. I was tired to putting on a smile and playing happy families.

Violet stood up straight, trying to seem confident and unafraid, but her hands shook with fear and her eyes were too wide. I admired her bravery, though. I'd never seen anyone look as terrified as her but she faced him anyway.

He took one small but purposeful step forward and something flashed through his eyes—something pure evil. Before I could blink, he launched himself at Violet and started punching and kicking her continuously. With each blow, she screamed a deep, throaty scream. Her arms darted in front of her face and she curled up in the fetal position to protect herself.

I watched, again. Whenever this happened, I couldn't tear my eyes off the scene even though it was the last thing in the world I wanted to see. And it never got any easier. Rose and Poppy still flinched and backed up, but they were used to it now. They didn't look like they were going to pass out or break down.

The sound of Violet's screams pierced right through me, rooting me to the spot. I gulped. My legs turned to jelly and I fell to the floor. Poppy dropped beside me and wrapped her arms around me. He was killing her. I wanted to help, but I couldn't move, and Poppy's arms held me tight.

Blood trickled from Violet's nose down her chin. The blows to her body were harsh and brutal and every single one tore through me. I burst into tears at the sound her painful cries. Grabbing her hair, he pulled her up. She screamed in pain and gripped her chest. He sneered and punched her in the face. She stumbled back, slammed into the wall, and sunk to the floor.

She gagged and spat red-stained saliva on the floor. Clover jumped back and wiped his forehead, eyes wide and nose turned up in disgust. The blood on his hand turned his face a pale white and he turned and ran up the stairs. Poppy released me as soon as he closed the door. I ran to Violet. She was limp on the floor and covered in blood. Her matted hair was tainted red and clung to her face in clumps.

"Violet," Rose whispered, gently placing her hand on her shoulder. "It's going to be all right. We'll get you cleaned up." Would it matter? Surely he was going to come back for her soon enough. "Towels, Lily," Rose ordered.

I jumped up and ran to the cupboard, eager to help in any way I could. I didn't know a thing about first aid, but I knew we needed to stop Violet's bleeding as soon as possible. Rose snatched one of the towels off me and pressed it against the cut on Violet's head.

"Take the other side," Rose ordered. Other side? I stepped over Violet and noticed what Rose was talking about. There was another deep cut on her head, almost exactly opposite to the other one. It was barely a centimeter long but blood flowed freely from it.

I sobbed, no longer being able to hold back my tears. "I'm sorry, Violet, I'm so sorry," I whispered and pressed down hard on the towel. She whimpered and hissed in pain. As much as I wanted to pull away and stop hurting her, I knew I couldn't. "Sorry." We all knew doing this was pretty much a waste of time. When he came back down, he would kill her if she hadn't already died, but we couldn't leave her. We had to try.

Poppy knelt down beside me with a plastic bowl of water, cotton balls, and thick padded bandages. "We should get her to bed as soon as we've cleaned her up. Hang in there, Violet." Poppy dipped a cotton ball into the water and very gently dabbed it around the cut Rose was tending.

"Ahh!" Violet cried out. "No, it stings," she said, gasping to catch her breath.

"I know, and I'm sorry. We need to clean these, though. I promise it won't take long, and I'll be as gentle as I can." Poppy brushed the cotton ball along the bottom of the cut. I grabbed Violet's hand, and she squeezed it tight—it reminded me of a woman gripping hold of her birth partner's hand. Blood seeped through the towel I had pressed on her cut with my other hand, staining my fingers red.

My chest felt like it was being squeezed. I was utterly terrified she would die. She was my only chance. Was this too bad? She could have internal injuries we couldn't see and her head looked really bad. I could still hear the loud thud as her head smashed against the hard wall. What if something happened to her? If she died then I didn't know what I would do. I should have tried to help her. Looking at her swollen and bloody face, I'd never felt so helpless before.

Poppy bandaged one cut and moved around to do the same with the one I was tending. I moved the towel and Poppy cleaned the cut. Rose stood awkwardly over Violet, holding the bandage up, ready to put it on as soon as Poppy was finished.

"Okay," Rose said once we'd cleaned and bandaged Violet's wounds. "Let's get her in bed." Rose and Poppy picked up either end of Violet's body, and I supported her back.

Violet cried out in pain, and the sound echoing through the

cellar made me flinch. She held her chest and breathed deeply. Broken ribs? "We're nearly there," I told her. We needed painkillers. If she had broken ribs as well as the cuts to her head, she was going to be in a lot of pain. He didn't let us just have pain pills, though. That was controlled by him—he only allowed us two at a time.

I ran ahead and pulled the cover back on her bed, ready for her to get in. Rose and Poppy carefully laid her down. I covered her to her hips, not wanting to go higher and lay it on her ribs. "Am I going to die?" she whispered. Her breathing was labored, and it sounded like she was struggling to take every one.

Shaking my head, I perched on the side of her bed. "No, you're not. You're going to be fine. We'll look after you." That bastard wasn't going to get his way. I would do everything I could to make sure she was okay. I wanted to make up for letting this happen. "Try and get some sleep." If she were asleep, she wouldn't feel pain.

Violet closed her eyes and continued breathing hard. I doubt she would sleep much, but at least she was getting some rest. Wiping my tears away, I took a deep breath to calm myself. What was going to happen now? He would be back eventually. Did he expect a body wrapped up in a black bag?

I gasped as I remembered. "We have painkillers!" When Poppy and Rose pretended I was ill, he had brought two down for me. Rushing to my bedside table, I grabbed them from the drawer and ran back. "Violet, take these!" Her eyes flicked open. She looked at the pills and opened her mouth, accepting them immediately. "Want water with them?" She shook her head. I couldn't take them without water—it was gross and they stuck to my throat. Violet had to have been in a lot of pain.

"Just one, Lily. We'll need to ration them," Rose said. As much as I wanted to give her both, I knew Rose was right. We only had two and getting more wouldn't be easy.

"Thanks," Violet whispered once she'd swallowed the pill I popped in her mouth.

Rose stood up from the bed. "We'll leave you to get some rest." I shook my head, not wanting to leave her on her own. Rose shooed me with her hand and widened her eyes—she wanted to talk about something without Violet. I got up and followed them out.

"What?" I asked as Rose shut the bedroom door.

"We need to think of something for when he comes back. He won't be happy with this outcome." Violet surviving. *The sick bastard!* "I'll speak with him and try saying Violet thought we were going to come to harm or something. I'm not sure yet."

I sniffed and wiped my eyes again. I was just holding it together. All I wanted to do was curl up in a little ball and cry, but I couldn't give up. I still had hope. "Will she die?"

Rose sighed. "I'm not sure. I truly hope not."

Violet couldn't die. I had only known her a few hours but down here that seemed like years. Everything down here seemed longer. She was the only one who was as desperate to get out as I was. I needed her.

My heart jumped into my throat as I heard the cellar door creaking open. I gripped Violet's hand and closed my eyes, saying a silent plea to Clover to leave Violet alone.

Someone opening the bedroom door made me jump. I leaped up but then sagged in relief as Poppy stepped in and closed the door. She was by herself. So he was listening to what Rose had to say?

"What's going on?" I asked.

"Rose is speaking with him now."

"Should we try and listen?"

Poppy shook her head. "No. If he came in and caught us, he wouldn't like it."

I clenched my jaw shut as the overwhelming urge to shout and scream at him flooded me. There were so many things I wanted to say to the bastard, but not one I could say without getting myself killed.

"How long do you think it'll take her to convince him?"

Poppy shrugged. "If she can, it could take a while. He doesn't change his mind often." His sick, screwed-up mind. Something really shitty must have happened to him, but that wasn't a good enough excuse to do what he was doing. I sat on my bed next to Poppy and we waited silently for Rose.

While we waited, I thought of so many things I would be willing to do if he just left her alone. I would never complain about being down here again. I would never again shout at Poppy or Rose for calling me Lily. I would never try to think of ways to hurt him.

I looked over at Poppy as we heard the cellar door open and close again. I didn't want to get my hopes up but he hadn't come for her—that must be good. Rose opened the door and smiled. "It's all right."

"What?" I asked, my eyes wide in shock. He wasn't coming back for her? I hoped but never expected it to happen.

Rose nodded and sat down on Violet's bed. "I explained that she was scared. Said she thought he was going to kill all of us and was just trying to protect us. He mumbled incoherently for about ten minutes. I couldn't understand a word of what he was saying." She stopped and frowned. "It was odd…and frightening." I gulped. Rose being frightened was frightening. "Eventually, though, I managed to convince him that she didn't know what she was doing. She hadn't understood that we're a family." I clenched my jaw. *We are not a family.*

"So he's going to help her?" Poppy asked. Her eyes were wide with surprise.

Rose bit her lip as she searched for the answer. "He's agreed to letting us help her. He won't be bringing any medication down for her as punishment." I sat frozen. He was going to leave her in pain. I felt the air leave my lungs as if I had been punched in the stomach. He wasn't being merciful—he was being vengeful. She had done something he didn't like, and he was making her suffer for it. My hate for him consumed me. I gritted my teeth. My blood boiled. I wanted to kill him. I wanted him to die in the way he had killed so many girls.

"Okay." Poppy nodded. "Well, it will be fine. We'll look after her. She will heal with our help." She would heal, but how long would she be in intense pain until then? I looked away to Violet's fragile, broken body. She would have been better off if she died. Living here, in her situation, was much worse than death. *I'm so sorry.*

We sat in the bedroom for hours. A loud bang followed by several thudding noises came from the main room. I gasped in surprise and my heart started racing. "What's that?" I asked, moving in between the door and Violet's bed. A shrill woman's scream answered my question. "No." He was doing this now?

Rose looked at the closed door with her mouth hanging open wide. There was something about only hearing what he was doing that made it so much scarier. In my head I imagined more blood, more gore, more violence.

"No, no, please!" the woman shouted.

Tears filled my eyes. "Rose, what do we do?"

She gulped. "You do nothing. I'll stand just inside the door and wait until it's over. He'll want to see at least one of us." Poppy walked with her, and they creaked the door open and stood at the threshold. My heart was in my mouth as I listened to the awful sounds of her crying and begging for her life. How could he not care that he was killing a person?!

"What's going on?" Violet rasped from behind me. Another guttural scream echoed through the room and I froze. "What's that?"

"Shh," I whispered, letting my tears drip to the floor. "That's the reason we do what we're told."

21
CLOVER

Friday, January 21st (Present)

I locked the girls' door with trembling hands and shoved the bookcase back to its place. Dirty—I was dirty and disgusting. I needed to be clean. I needed to regain control. My hands shook and my heart raced. The blood was smeared over my hands and splatters covered my clothes.

The bathroom was on the first floor, and I made it in a daze. Switching the shower on, I pulled my clothes off in a rush and shoved them in the sink. They were going to have to be burned. No amount of washing would get them clean, but it wouldn't matter; I had duplicates. I stepped into the shower, and the familiar sting of boiling hot water relaxed me. I could feel the germs being washed away. The anxiety and fear slowly subsided.

I got out of the shower and wrapped a towel around my body. It had hardened itself to the hot water. I used to feel tender after but not anymore. *Clean now. I'm clean now. I can do this. I will not fail. I can do this.* Mother was wrong. I didn't need her to survive. I was doing fine. *I'm not failing.*

Mother wouldn't like the girls, of course. She wouldn't like that they helped me, and she wouldn't like that they had my heart. She wasn't here, and she couldn't tell me what to do. I could do whatever I wanted now. I was in control of my life, not her. *Not you.*

The girls would be finished soon, so I dressed in clean clothes and bagged my dirty ones. The fire in the living room was already filled with coal and wood; I lit it and threw the bag straight in. I watched the flames grow and lick at the bag, turning it black in a matter of seconds. The clothes disintegrated into ash in front of my eyes, and my posture automatically relaxed. There was just one more thing to do before I could relax—get that filthy whore out of my house and away from my girls.

When I returned to their room, they were sitting on the sofa, reading. The whore was by the stairs, ready to go. Lily looked on over her book, staring at nothing. I understood this life was much different to the second-rate one she had with her former family. She had settled in just fine.

Rose smiled, tilting her head to the side and her long, dark hair fell half in front of her face. She was a very beautiful person, and very womanly and loving. To this day, I regretted how things had turned out. My life should have been different. Rose— Shannen—and I should be together. She should have been the one picking up the wool and clothes for the girls. She should have been the one I woke up to, rather than the cold, empty space in my bed.

Without saying a word, I picked up the body and carried it upstairs. Dead weight was heavy, but not as heavy as the price whores like her were costing society. There was one less of them in the world now. I knew there would be more; it was a never-ending cycle. Unlike the government and the police, though, I wouldn't just sit back and allow it to happen.

I carried the body out to the car and placed it in the trunk. It was dark—that was good.

The drive to the canal didn't take long. I had driven the journey so many times I didn't have to think about where to go anymore; it was natural. I could do it with my eyes closed. The murky water was the graveyard for the disgraceful.

Opening the trunk, I swept the body up in my arms and placed it on the ground. There was a pile of broken bricks, chalk, rubble, and concrete blocks nearby from the derelict buildings. This area was supposed to be developed in a years' time, but it had been rescheduled twice already. They should just leave it to fester.

I filled the body bag, weighing it down with as much as I could fit in, and dropped it into the water. The bag sank down and I sighed, content. *One more down...*

Monday, January 24th (Present)

"Good morning, Flowers," I said as I walked down the stairs. Lily sat at the table fiddling with her cutlery. She looked up and smiled halfheartedly. Her bright green eyes looked sad, worn down. Something was wrong with her. Perhaps she was ill.

"Good morning, Clover," Rose and Poppy replied.

"How did you sleep, Lily?" I asked, sitting down in the chair opposite her.

She looked down at the table. "Fine, thank you," she whispered.

"Are you feeling unwell?"

She shook her head. "No, I'm okay." I nodded and picked up my spoon as a bowl of granola was placed in front of me. We ate breakfast in silence.

"Right, I'm now going to work. Have a great day, and I'll see you all for dinner."

I arrived at the office forty minutes later. "Good morning, Christy," I said as I walked through reception. "How are you?"

She smiled. Her hair was pulled back in a tight bun and she wore the most inappropriate clothing. I didn't know why she was allowed to dress like a prostitute at work. "I'm great, Colin, and you?"

"I'm very well, thank you." I walked to my office and put my briefcase down. While my computer started up, I went to make a coffee. I passed Gregory Hart's office; he was a senior lawyer and started working for the company right out of college. He was talking with Christy—who seemed to have made a beeline for him first thing—and she was giggling. I took a step back so I could hear.

"So are you free tonight? We can try out that underwear set I was telling you about," Christy purred. My chest tightened. Greg was a married man with a heavily pregnant wife.

"Hmm, as a matter of fact, I am. Natalie's visiting her mum and sister for a few nights. I'll be all alone in that big house of mine."

Christy's face lit up like a child on Christmas morning. "I'll be over at seven. I'll just pop home first to change into something *less* comfortable."

I closed my eyes. Was that what my father said to his whore when Mother and I went shopping? Was he as excited to cheat on his wife as Greg Hart was? Turning on my heel, I stalked off into the kitchen. How dare that cheap little tart ruin a marriage?

Flicking on the kettle, I watched the water as it boiled, bubbling up like a volcano about to erupt—mirroring my temper. "There enough water in there for two?" Christy's voice made me cringe.

I turned around and smiled, swallowing my rage. "Of course. Why don't you go and sit down? I'll make these."

"Thank you, that'd be great. I've got a million things to do."

"I won't be long." Christy smiled and walked out just as Jane and Jessica entered. "Good morning, Jane, Jessica."

"Hi, Colin. We were just talking about that missing girl, Summer. They still haven't found her," Jane said, shaking her head in sympathy. "Her poor parents."

"Who could do something like that?" Jessica sighed. "It's just awful. Her whole family must be going through hell. And what about her? What's she going through? People always worry about the family, but what about her? She must be so scared."

"If she's still alive," Jane added.

Lily was better off with me than out there, where she would be corrupted by a society that found nothing wrong in sleeping around and behaving like selfish little whores. Lily was better off with someone who cared enough about her future and character to protect her. Even her so-called loving boyfriend allowed her to roam the streets alone at night.

"Now, we don't know the whole story. She could have run away." They nodded in agreement. "You two just make sure you keep yourselves safe," I said and picked up the two freshly made cups of coffee.

"There you go, Christy. Two sugars, just how you like it." I put her drink on the hot-pink coaster and noticed she was having a Skype chat with Greg. She minimized the screen before I could read it, though. *Something to hide.*

She looked up and grinned. "Thank you, Colin. Finally Friday, huh? Do you have plans for the weekend?"

"Not many. I have some DIY to catch up on. You?"

"Um, I'm seeing a friend tonight and possibly tomorrow too."

A married friend with a child on the way. "Well, have a nice time," I said through gritted teeth.

I walked away. My heart went out to Greg's wife and unborn child. What would she go through when she found out? Would she take it as well as Mother? She didn't cry, not once. She didn't cry when he left or when she found out he had rented a flat with the whore. She didn't even cry when their divorce was finalized. I cried once, until she hit me, and I realized that I needed to be strong and take control. Crying got you nowhere.

Something had to be done. Greg's wife deserved better than to arrive home and find her husband in bed with a dirty little whore. "Oh, Colin, I need to run out. Can you let anyone know if they ask? I'll be back in ten," Jessica called over her shoulder as she ran to the exit.

I smiled. Jessica would be out for ten minutes and her colleague, Miranda, in HR was on holiday. I put my coffee down in my office and walked up the stairs to the HR department. Their office wasn't big, and there was no window in the door, so I knew I wouldn't be seen.

Pushing the door open, I peered into the office. As I thought, it was empty. I stepped inside and closed the door. I had seen the employee filing cabinet from my appraisals, so I knew exactly where to look. I pulled the bottom drawer open and flicked through to Christy's file. Her address told me she wasn't far from my house—just a twenty-minute drive. I memorized the street name and number and put the file back.

My heart raced as I closed the drawer and stood up. The top floor was small and home to only HR and the managing director, Bruce. I hadn't seen Bruce this morning, but he often flitted in and out when it suited him. I reached for the door handle when the door swung open.

I froze momentarily. "Bruce, good morning."

"Hello, Colin. Do you know where Jessica is?"

"She just popped out, she'll be back soon."

"What are you looking for?"

"I wanted a holiday request form. I forgot Miranda was off until I got up here." I smiled and shook my head—*Silly me.*

He nodded and rubbed his bulging stomach once. "Ah, yes. The South of France she went to, wasn't it?"

"I think so. Lovely place. Have you been?"

"Can't say I have. I prefer to sit by a pool and drink a cool beer myself. Well, I'll see Jessica later." He nodded his head and walked out. I sighed in relief and left the office, closing the door behind me.

I knew dinner would be ready very soon, and I hated to be late, but I had to prepare for tonight. My duffel bag was open on the bed and already contained a body bag, thick rubber gloves, and cleaning products. My stomach turned at the thought of entering Christy's house and punishing her, but someone had to. This was her fault, not mine. *You're only taking control of a situation before it worsens.* Yes, that was all I was doing, taking care of something that needed to be controlled.

I combed my hair and repeated Christy's address in my head over and over. *I'm not weak. I can do this. Mother is wrong. Mother is wrong.* Placing the comb back on my dressing table, I straightened my shirt and walked down to the girls' room.

"Good evening, Flowers."

"Good evening. How was your day?" Poppy asked. Rose looked up at me and beamed. Her blue eyes glistened in the light. I tore my gaze from Rose and smiled at Poppy.

"Very good, thank you. Although I have something to do after dinner." I sat at the table opposite Lily. "And how are you?"

She bit her lip. "Fine, thank you."

"Here," Poppy said, placing my dinner in front of me. "Roast beef. One of your favorites."

"Yes it is." I smiled. Poppy was an incredible woman. She was caring and thoughtful, taking the time to get to know someone. I was proud to have her as part of the family. She had never disappointed me. I looked around the table and swelled with pride. All of my girls were beautiful, especially where it mattered, unlike that whore Christy.

I left my car in the parking area outside a nail salon; it was a thirty-second walk to Christy's house. She lived at the back of the butcher's, set off from the road. Aside from an old house that was currently being turned into flats, hers was the only residential property along the road. That meant, thankfully, I shouldn't have any interruptions tonight.

I folded my arms over my chest. The January wind was bitterly cold, and I longed to be back at home with the girls. Lowering my head, I threw my bag over my shoulder and quickly walked toward her house.

The only light in her house came from upstairs. It was a small house, and the upstairs looked like it was in the loft space. Although it wasn't a cottage, it had that feel to it. The house didn't suit Christy. It was warm, homey, and inviting—three things she was not.

Either side of the pinewood front door were faux olive trees, and not very good ones. They looked cheap and out of place. I lifted the right one up and sighed. Lying beneath the terra-cotta pot was a door key. *Oh dear, Christy, you really don't help yourself.* I stepped closer to the front door and heard Robbie Williams playing through the house. Mother used to put on her favorite music while getting ready to go on a date with Dad. I used to sit on the bed and watch her sing into the mirror as she applied her makeup.

Taking a quick glance over my shoulder, I slipped the key in the lock and opened the door. Christy's voice bellowed over the music as she sang her heart out. How could she be so excited to ruin a marriage? That was something I never understood. Why were women so callous when it came to other women's happiness?

My heart accelerated as I took the first step to find her. Adrenaline coursed through my bloodstream, giving me a lighter-than-air feeling—invincible. I stopped at the top of the stairs. Her bedroom was straight ahead, door wide open. Her long mirror was angled in the corner of the room, so she hadn't seen me in the reflection yet.

I gently placed my bag on the top step and watched her brush her hair. She was only wearing a skimpy, tasteless red bra and matching thong. Her body was toned and slender; it was her weapon. The thing she used to get her own way, especially with men.

I boldly walked forward. In the mirror, I saw her eyes widen.

She shouted out in surprise and spun around. Clutching her hand over her breasts she gaped at me. "C-Colin? What are you…?" She shook her head. "What are you doing here?"

I smiled and stepped into the room, closing the door behind me. "I'm very glad you asked, Christy. As you know, you've been a very naughty girl."

She gulped and took a step back. "What do you mean? What are you doing? H-How did you even get in?"

"Shh. Now is not the time for you to be asking questions. I'd like to ask you one, if I may?" I didn't wait for her reply. "Why are you sleeping with a married man?"

"What?" she whispered. "Greg? How do you know?"

"Have you met his wife?" She shook her head. "No, I didn't think so. Do you think she deserves the humiliation of her husband sleeping around?" Her mouth fell open and she backed up farther, her back hitting the wall. "That was a question, Christy."

"No," she answered.

"I didn't think so. How do you think she would feel if she knew what you were planning tonight?"

She trembled and a tear rolled down her cheek. "I-I don't… How do you know where I live?"

"I think that is enough talking." I didn't want to waste my time on her any longer. Without another word, I pulled the knife out of my pocket, and she screamed.

"No! What the fuck are you doing? Jesus, I'm sorry, okay? Please, Colin, what are you doing?" She held her hands up in front of her, body arched back protectively. "Think about this."

"Enough," I snapped. She flinched and whimpered back into the wall. I hated crying and begging. Mother hated crying and begging.

"Please don't do this, please. Please. I'll do *anything* you want, Colin, I swear." Anything I wanted. She was even offering sex when that was the very thing that had gotten her into trouble. *Dirty.* I growled as the anger inside reached the boiling point. With one quick whip of my arm, the knife slashed across her skin-deep beautiful face.

She shrieked and stared at me in horror. Her hands shook violently as she tried to touch her face. The screams had left a ringing in my ears. "Good-bye, Christy," I said and plunged the knife into her gut. As I pulled back, releasing her body trapped between the wall and me, she fell to the floor with a soft thud.

"No," she muttered, pressing her shaking hand over the knife wound. "Help me. Please?" she begged, gasping for breath.

"Christy, death is your punishment. There has to be a punishment or lessons will never be learned and society will never improve."

She gagged, coughing up blood, and threw herself forward in an attempt to crawl away. I turned as she shuffled past me, her fingernails clawing into the carpet. "Help me," she said, her voice squeaked, giving way.

Sighing, I stepped forward and nudged her onto her back with my foot. Her breathing was heavy and ragged. "Let me go. Please?" Her eyes filled with tears.

"Christy," I whispered and held the knife up. "It's time to say good night." She screamed as I brought the knife down with such force it cracked through her ribs. Her body turned limp and her eyes rolled backward. Letting out a deep breath, I closed my eyes. *I have control.*

I moved quickly, putting her body into a bag and cleaning up the mess. It had been a long time since I had scrubbed blood off the floor and walls. The body lay by the top of the stairs while I poured bleach over the carpet. I wasn't even sure why I was cleaning up. I only knew I couldn't leave it a bloody mess.

Once her room was looking better, I went to the bathroom sink and scrubbed my hands. *Dirty.* I was dirty. I felt dirty. Pumping the hand wash again, I scrubbed my hands for the third time. They were visibly clean, but I knew they weren't good enough. *You'll never be good enough.* I rubbed my hands together harder, washing furiously and gritting my teeth.

It was too much. I wasn't good enough—nothing was ever good enough. Throwing the soap dispenser against the wall, I gripped the sides of the sink and took deep breaths through my nose. *I can be good enough. I'm as strong as Mother. No, I'm stronger. I am a stronger person, and I will not fail. I. Will. Not. Fail.*

The music cut and the CD player loudly flicked to the next CD. I waited. A woman's voice filled the silence. I hadn't heard the song, but it was very mellow and calming. Whoever it was had a beautifully raw voice.

Turning around, I walked out of the bathroom and hauled the body over my shoulder. I dumped her outside her house and went to retrieve my car. The trunk was spacious and the body fit easily. The canal was only a short drive from here. It wouldn't be too long until I was back with my girls.

I threw my bag in beside the body and slammed the trunk closed. "Good-bye, whore."

22
LEWIS

Friday, January 28th (Present)

I woke up, startled by a loud thud. Looking at the clock, I saw that it was just before half past five in the morning. My heart leaped into my throat. *Summer!* Was it her? I jumped out of bed and sprinted down the stairs, almost bumping into Dawn and Henry. Daniel was ahead of us, already reaching for the front door. I missed so much—six months of her life, her seventeenth birthday. I didn't want to spend another second without her.

Daniel pulled the door open, and I held my breath, praying it would be her. My heart sunk when Detective Michael Walsh walked in. The grim expression on his face made my blood run cold. Something had happened.

"W-what? What's h-happened?" Dawn stuttered. Tears already rolled down her cheeks. "Where's my baby?"

Michael, as he'd asked us to call him, stepped into the house with another officer. He was the only one who let us call him by his first name. I wasn't sure if it was to make us feel more relaxed around him and trust him more or if he had a daughter Summer's age and felt more compassion. "Can we sit down, please?" I backed away and sat down on the sofa. Time stood still. The world stopped spinning. I almost didn't want to hear what he was going to say. "We've found Summer's cell phone," he started, "in a Dumpster by the canal."

The blood froze in my veins. *No it can't be Summer's.* "Are you sure it's hers?"

He nodded. "Yes. Someone found it and after seeing the background picture, instantly handed it in to the police." Her background picture was of us lying on her bed. She had taken the picture after our one-year anniversary dinner. That was the first time I was allowed to stay in her room overnight. Although the door had to be open *at all times.*

Dawn gasped. "Is it still on? She always had it on."

Michael's mouth set into a grim line, and I looked away. I gritted my teeth as searing pain tore through my whole body. She wasn't using it and that meant someone had her. Or someone had killed her. "We think someone else dumped the phone—not Summer. It seems unlikely a teenage girl with no known reason to leave home would throw away her cell. We're assembling a team as we speak, and as soon as it's light, we'll search the water. I'm so sorry I don't have any better news."

"You think my daughter's in the canal?" Dawn whispered.

Michael nodded his head and dropped his eyes to the floor. "That's a possibility. I'm so sorry."

I jumped up, finding some fight left. *This is all wrong.* "She's not dead. I would know if she was dead." Why the fuck wouldn't they listen to me when I told them that? My girlfriend was not dead. My throat went dry and I stopped breathing. *She isn't, is she?*

"Calm down." Henry stood up and stood in front of me. He

had the same color eyes as Summer. I wished it were hers staring back at me. "Her phone was found by a canal, Lewis," he said, tears welling in his eyes. Her *phone* not *her*. I would never give up hope.

I backed away from him and shook my head. "She's not dead," I repeated and walked back up to Summer's room. Summer was alive, and no one was going to make me believe anything else.

Since I was already up, I decided not to waste any time getting out there. There was never enough time. Every night when the sun set, I wished for just a few more hours of daylight, always wondering if we went home just five minute too early.

I walked out of the house and got in my car, eager to leave. I couldn't be there. How could they just give up on her?

The damn phone didn't mean anything. *She isn't dead.* I could tell what was wrong with her before she even knew it. She was such an open book—to me anyway. I could read her so easily. I could finish her sentences and understand what she was thinking just by looking at her face. We were too close for me not to know if she was dead.

Taking a deep breath, I put the car into first and was just about to pull off when I saw Henry in the mirror, running toward me and holding his arm up. *What now?* I wound the passenger window down but swung the door open. "If you're coming, Henry, just get—"

"No," he snapped, cutting me off. He got in the car and faced me. "You can't go. They found something."

For the second time in twenty minutes, my world stopped spinning. "What did they find?" I whispered, gulping down my fear.

"Two bodies. It's not Summer, but they're still looking."

"How do they know it's not Summer? They're sure?"

He nodded. "They've been down there too long for it to be her." My stomach turned. What would a body that had been in water for longer than five months look like? I scrunched my eyes closed in pain. "We need to go there, Lewis."

"Are they going to find her too?" I felt as if my chest were being cut open and my heart ripped out. I had never felt anything so painful—it took my breath away. Was I about to go and watch my girlfriend's body being dragged from a canal? "I…I don't…" Worlds failed to make sense. Nothing made sense. She was too young, too smart, and too beautiful to have her life ripped away from her like that. We had so much we wanted to do together to have it ripped away from us.

"We just need to go. Now." Henry slammed the door closed. "Follow my dad." Michael and the other officer rushed to their car and sped off. *Shit, this is bad.* "Go, Lewis," Henry growled. I jumped and looked up. His parents were already driving down the road. *Go, just go.* I pulled off and raced after them.

It was freezing outside. The freezing wind bit at my skin through my stupidly thin sweater. I walked slowly along the edge of the canal with Henry and Summer's parents. None of us were in any hurry to find out if our worst nightmare was about to come true.

Up ahead, police tape cordoned off an area of the canal just before a sharp corner. If we were made to stand there, we would barely see a thing. My heart was in my mouth as we approached the tape. I clenched my fists and held my breath.

"Daniel, go and find out," Dawn said, begging her husband. This was the first time she had come out. There was nothing anyone could have said to get her to stay behind this time. She had called her mum to sit in the house just in case, by some miracle, Summer called. I needed a miracle.

All of a sudden, the cops burst into action, running off in the opposite direction so I couldn't see anything. "What's happening?" I shouted.

"Stay there. I'll come and let you know anything as soon as I do," Michael said over his shoulder as he ran toward all the fuss.

"Summer!" Dawn screamed. *No! It can't be her.* "Not my little girl. Someone please tell me what's going on, Daniel!" she pleaded. Her voice shook as she sobbed hysterically.

The air left my lung in a big rush; I leaned down on my thighs and tried to breathe. If Sum was down there, how did she die? Was she in pain before? Was it quick? I took a deep breath and blinked rapidly. *Don't think about that.*

"Michael, what's going on?" Daniel called. I craned my neck around so quickly the muscles stretched.

Michael strode toward us. "It's not Summer." Closing my eyes, I let out a deep sigh of relief. Thank God.

Daniel shook his head. "So there's three now?"

Michael nodded and scratched the side of his head. "Yes. I can't say any more. I really do think you should wait at home, and I'll call you if there's any news."

Was he expecting to make that call? "Do you think Summer's in there?" I asked again, hoping someone would eventually say no.

"Lewis, I can't say. I sincerely hope not, but we will continue searching until we know this water is clear."

23
CLOVER

Saturday, December 19th (1987)

Mummy held my hand tight as we crossed the busy road. We were going to buy Daddy's Christmas present and buy the ingredients to bake cookies and cupcakes. "Mummy, can we make sausage rolls tonight too? I love sausage rolls!"

"That's a wonderful idea, Colin. Sausage rolls are Daddy's favorite too." I smiled wide and jumped up and down. Sausage rolls were all our favorites, and I couldn't wait to eat at least five in one go. "In here, sweetheart," she said and pulled me into a boring clothes shop. I hated going into clothing stores, but not more than I hated going into grocery stores. They were the most boring.

"What are we doing in here, Mummy?"

She looked down at me and smiled. "We're getting Daddy a pair of gloves and a sweater for Christmas."

I frowned. "But I want to get him a new car. He said his old one is *nearly dead*."

She bent down and squeezed my cheek. "That's very nice of you, sweetheart, but we don't have enough money for that. Mummy and Daddy will sort the car out in the new year, okay?"

"Okay. Can we get him blue gloves?"

"Of course." She ruffled my hair and stood up. She always

messed my hair up and then told me to flatten it so it was nice. I grinned. *Silly Mummy.* "What about these?"

I pointed to the better blue ones she was holding; the gloves in her other hand were a boring blue. "I like them."

"Then we'll get them. Come, let's look for a sweater and then maybe we can get a hot chocolate with marshmallows to warm ourselves up." I jumped up and down. I loved hot chocolate and marshmallows, and it was really cold outside.

Mummy chose Daddy's sweater and a pair of trousers and two pairs of socks. I wanted to leave and get the hot chocolate. "Right," she said when she had paid the lady. "Chocolate and then the supermarket for our ingredients."

"Yeah," I cheered.

I followed her, sipping my boiling-hot hot chocolate. I had already eaten the marshmallows—they were the best part and I always ate them first. Mommy stopped in every aisle, even after we had got everything we needed. She leaned over and smelled the flowers. "Do you want to smell, Colin?"

I turned my nose up. "No, they smell yuk."

She frowned. "Sweetheart, flowers are not 'yuk.' They're nature's most beautiful creation. Come on now." She picked up a really bright tulip and held it by my nose. I sniffed and it was okay. "See. It smells pretty, doesn't it?"

I shrugged. "It's okay, I guess."

Mummy stood up straight and looked at the old lady. "Can I have a bunch of the tulips, please?"

"A good choice, that one," the old lady replied to Mummy.

"I love to liven up the dark winter nights with colorful flowers." I looked around at the toy display because I was *really* bored. I wanted to go home and make cookies and sausage rolls.

"Ready, Colin?" Mummy said, tugging on my hand. "I think we're all finished."

"Ready." I grinned.

"What the hell is this?" Mummy's shouting made me jump, and I ran out of my room. She was looking in her bedroom. "Get out! Get out, you whore," she screamed.

My heart was beating really, really fast, and I was scared. What was a whore? "Mummy?" I called and started crying. She didn't hear me— she was too busy shouting. I stepped closer and saw Daddy in bed with the cover wrapped around him and another lady pulling her dress over her head. What were they doing?

"Beatrice," Daddy said. "I can explain."

"Shut up! Get the hell out. I don't want to see you ever again and take you dirty whore with you!" Mummy never shouted. I jumped into the corner of the hallway and sat on the floor. I looked up over my knees and saw the other lady run out of the room and down the stairs. Daddy followed but he stopped. "Get out and don't ever contact us again."

"Beatrice, please let me explain. I'm sorry, I'm so sorry. It didn't mean anything; it was a mistake."

"You're sorry you were caught, you sick bastard. You leave us alone."

"But Colin…"

Mummy laughed but it wasn't her happy laugh. "You don't love him. You don't love either of us. You picked that over us. Get. Out." My lip trembled. My daddy didn't love me and my mummy was mad. I closed my eyes, held my head, and cried.

Sunday, January 30th (Present)

I smiled tightly as Lewis and what looked like his brother approached. "Thanks for coming," Lewis said. "The groups have been organized already, but you can go with us."

"Okay," I replied. "I'll go wherever I'm needed. I'm Colin Brown."

"Lewis," he said, holding his hand out. I shook his hand and turned my attention to the person standing to his side. "This is my brother, Theo." I shook his hand too. "Let's get started then. I don't want to waste any more time."

I had no idea where we were focusing our search, but it didn't particularly matter. I just wanted to know what was going on and for people to see me helping find Lily. Lewis and his brother walked out of the town hall and across the road. The park was almost directly opposite.

We walked along the side of the park toward the fields at the back. There were four other people with us, all with maps and pointing at nothing in particular—it all looked very messy and random. As I walked past the park, I recalled when I first laid eyes on Lily. She was so beautiful, natural, and innocent, and her voice sang to me. As with all my girls, I knew instantly that she was part of my family. I knew she would fit in, and I was right.

"So is this your first time volunteering?" Lewis asked as he pulled back a branch to get a closer look at the bottom of the bramble bush at the entrance of the field.

"Yes, it is. When I heard the police search was slowing I thought I'd give my time." He pursed his lips. "You're angry about that. I can't blame you."

"It's all because of money," he spat. "My girlfriend is out there somewhere and they're worried about how much it costs to fund the search. It's disgusting." There are many things the police force didn't do. The people volunteering to search were the same as me, taking something into their own hands to make a positive change.

"Yes, this world is very money driven now. It's a shame."

"I appreciate you coming along. Are you alone? I didn't see you with anyone. Most people come in pairs at least."

"I'm alone," I confirmed. "How long will we spend in this field? All day or do we move on to somewhere else?" It was bitterly cold and we were out in the open. The field was the one behind where I found Lily. Long Thorpe was a short drive from my house, but even so, I didn't know it well.

"We'll move on soon. We've got the next two fields behind us to go." Ah, moving farther from the park. I admired his persistence. However, he should learn to take care of someone he claimed to love. "Do you need to leave?"

"No, I'm here for the day. I was just curious to know today's schedule." He nodded and went back to searching for goodness knows what on the ground. I mimicked his actions, moving over fallen leaves and twigs. Searching fields seemed pointless now. Surely the logical thing to do in a situation like this was to speak to people, search the streets, like the official search. This now seemed less planned out and more desperate.

"Do you have any thoughts on where Summer is?" I asked him. I didn't like using that name; Summer was dead.

He looked up at me and stared. I stood straight, my heart pounding. Why was he looking at me like that? I kept my posture firm and rigid. Finally, he frowned. "I wish I did. Wherever she is, I won't stop until I've found her."

I looked away. "Of course. Sorry, I shouldn't have asked." He was still looking at me; I could feel his gaze burning into the side of my head.

"Yeah, no worries," he replied and walked off. I heard him trudge along the crisp, frosty leaves. Why had he looked at me like that?

24
SUMMER

Friday, February 4th (Present)

I woke up to Violet whimpering and crying in pain. It had been *two weeks* since he hurt her. She had started to heal, but last night he had shoved her and she fell into one of the wooden chairs and hurt her ribs all over again—and it was all over dead flowers!

Rose held a cloth on Violet's forehead. It was only quarter past five in the morning. Poppy was still sleeping peacefully—I envied her for that. I pushed the cover off me and crept over to them. "How long have you been up?" I whispered to Rose.

She looked over at me, startled. "About half an hour. I'll change her bandages soon. Hopefully she'll wake up properly, and we can give her one of the pills. If not, I'll crush it and put it in her water." Violet's breathing was fast and heavy. Her face scrunched up in pain and her hand clutched at her chest. She really needed painkillers, but we only had four that we accumulated. We needed to make them last.

I nodded and turned my attention to Violet. "Are you okay?" Her eyes flicked open and landed on me; after a few seconds they closed again. She shook her head and whimpered. "I'm sorry. You'll be all right, though. We'll look after you," I promised her. No matter what happened, I would not leave her by herself again. If she tried anything like that again, I would help her.

"Hurts. It hurts," Violet whispered. Her pain was clear through her strained voice.

"I know it does. We can give you something now, if you want? Do you think you could swallow a pill?" Rose asked. Shouldn't she be healing better than this? Something wasn't right.

Violet nodded and winced at the same time. "Here," Rose said, holding the tiny white pill out. Violet opened her mouth; Rose popped it in and held the glass of water up for her. I hated that there was nothing more I could do to help her. Three pills were all we had left now and there was no way she would be healed by tomorrow!

She slumped back in her bed and hissed through her teeth in pain. Her eyes filled with tears, but the intense expression on her face told me she wasn't going to let herself cry. Violet was so strong—much stronger than me. "What's he going to do to me?"

Rose squeezed her hand. "Nothing at all. You're going to be fine. It's sorted, remember? He's not going to do anything to you." Was that really better? Living only meant living this "life." If I didn't have the tiniest bit of hope that I would see Lewis and my family again I would have let him kill me weeks ago.

Violet's eyes flickered to me for a second. She was expression-less, emotionless, like there was nothing there. I had no idea what she was thinking, and I wouldn't be able to find out until we were alone. I had a feeling she wouldn't want to talk in front of Rose and Poppy. I sat with her for as long as I could.

Poppy woke up and one by one we had a shower and changed into matching outfits. I helped Rose clean Violet's wounds and change the bandages. Her head wound looked bad, but at least the bleeding had stopped now.

"You're going to be just fine," Rose said and stroked a stray strand of hair from Violet's face. "We need to start breakfast now, but we'll come back after."

I looked up at the clock. He would be down here in half an hour. My chest tightened at the thought of being around a table with him. I hated him so much it consumed me. Whenever anyone mentioned his name, I felt my blood boil. "Lily, just make sure you're out here in twenty minutes, okay? We don't want him to come in here looking for you," Rose said and left us alone in the room.

"You gonna be okay?" Violet whispered.

"I'll be fine," I lied. "How are you feeling now?" I asked to shift the spotlight off me.

She shook her head and gasped in pain. "It hurts *so* much."

"The painkiller will kick in soon." I got her water and held the straw to her lips. I wanted to give her another pill but I knew I couldn't yet—only when she really needed it.

"Is he really leaving me alone now?"

"I told you, yesterday was about the bloody stupid flowers! You know Rose convinced him that you were scared and just trying to protect us." I looked down at the bed. "And that you didn't mean to hurt him." That part I hadn't told her before.

"Didn't mean to hurt him," she repeated, her eyes widening in disbelief. "I wanted to *kill* him. I still do." It was the loudest I had heard her speak in a long time. At least she had some fight left in her.

"Shh, they'll hear you," I hissed. "I know you do. I do too, but you can't say that to anyone else. Promise me." God, we had only just managed to get him to agree to let her live, there was no way he would agree again, especially if he knew the truth.

She looked away from me and stared up at the ceiling again. I didn't know what else to say. She hadn't promised, but she knew she couldn't risk doing something so stupid again. Violet still wanted to do something to fight back. Perhaps when she had healed we could plan something together. Poppy wouldn't stop us; I knew that now. Rose might, but she would be outnumbered.

"Lily," Poppy called from the doorway.

My breathing sped up and my heart felt like it was going to explode. *He's coming.* I wanted to stay and pretend I wasn't well, but I didn't want him to come looking for me and see Violet. Sure, he had said he would leave her alone, but I wasn't going to take any chances before she was better.

I very slowly pushed myself off the bed and walked out. "I'll be back soon," I said and closed the bedroom door.

"Why don't you just sit down now, Lily?" Poppy said and smiled too sweetly. She was trying too hard. She never tried too hard. I did what she said and prayed he wouldn't speak to me. He would, though, of course.

The cellar door opened, and I froze. He walked down with a huge smile on his messed-up face. "Good morning, Flowers," he said.

"Good morning," we replied in unison. It was like reciting a line in a play now. We said it automatically, without even thinking about it, as if he'd shouted *action*.

He kissed Rose and Poppy on the cheek and turned to me. I gripped the sides of the chair and clenched my jaw as he leaned down to kiss me. His lips pressed against the side of my forehead and my stomach turned. Every time he touched me, I wanted to scream and run, but of course that was impossible. It was something I would only do if I ever reached the point where I lost all hope of escaping and just wanted to end it.

Rose had prepared a big breakfast with pancakes and fruit salad—and I couldn't face eating any of it. When he kissed me, I could feel his skin on mine, his smell surrounding me, and his dark, beady eyes that burned into me. I managed as best as I could to feel that separate from Summer, to keep Lily and Summer as two different people. But it was hard.

I felt guilty, as if I were cheating on Lewis. I knew I wasn't, but it still haunted me. What would his reaction be? Angry, hurt, and sick were the obvious ones. Betrayed too? No, he couldn't feel that because I never wanted Clover and I never would. He took it. Lewis wouldn't feel betrayed. Would he?

"So, what have you got planned today?" he asked loudly, breaking me out of my thoughts. *We're going to look after the girl whose ribs you rebroke yesterday, you sick bastard!*

"We think some reading; we haven't done much recently," Rose replied and flashed me a warning look. I wanted to slap her, but I readjusted my hard expression, forcing myself to smile.

"I'll have to remind myself to purchase you some new material soon."

Rose nodded. "That would be great, Clover, thank you."

"You're welcome."

I wanted to puke at their sweet little exchange. I stabbed the plastic fork in a raspberry and took a deep breath. What would it take for me to be able to act properly around him? I always felt as if I wasn't hiding how much I hated him very well at all. I looked around the room, anywhere but at him. My eyes landed on the calendar—it was Lewis's birthday in one week. Would we spend that apart?

He wanted to go to the horse races for his birthday. We went with our families before we even got together and both loved it. He always said he wanted to go again so we had planned to go for his nineteenth. I hoped he would still go, even if I wasn't there. He wouldn't, of course, but I wanted him to have fun on his birthday.

"I was thinking of having a movie night soon," he said between mouthfuls of food. I almost fell off my chair. Movie nights were what normal people do, not him. "I've not spent much time with you recently, and I feel guilty." *Don't worry about it*, I wanted to say but bit my tongue.

"Sounds nice," Poppy replied cautiously, biting her lip.

He smiled for a second and then his face dropped to his new nervous, edgy expression. "Good. That's good."

Was it? I popped another raspberry in my mouth and chewed, staring at my plate. Rose and Poppy ate quietly as well, watching him too often. Usually there would be some conversation, but that was becoming rare. It was like they didn't know what to say to him now, or they didn't know how he would react to the things they would usually say.

Clover chewed his food for too long, his eyes darting around the room occasionally. He put his fork down, scratched his jaw, and then picked it up again. Rose watched him out of the corner of her eye, her head slightly down.

I bit my lip. My heart fluttered with unease. I kept myself small, eating what I could silently. I felt like we were all waiting for a volcano to erupt.

"Nice," he muttered under his breath and shoved a forkful of beans and sausage into his mouth. No one responded, because he hadn't said it to us. I wasn't even sure it was about the food. I was anxious to get back to Violet and away from him.

"Well, thank you for breakfast," he said and abruptly stood up. "I'll see you for dinner. Have a good day."

Rose and Poppy busied themselves saying good-bye and getting up to clean. They were jumpy and moved too fast, as if they wanted everything to be clean doubly quick in case…what?

Deciding to skip the cleanup and not wanting to drive myself crazy worrying and overthinking why they were so on edge, I went straight into the bedroom and sat on Violet's bed.

"Hi," she whispered, her eyes flicking open.

"Hi. You okay?" She nodded, although she clearly wasn't okay. She looked pale and her hair was messy and greasy. "Want a shower?"

She frowned for a second. I could tell she was desperate for one. "You mind helping me?"

I rolled my eyes. "You know I don't." Standing up, I held my hands out for her and helped her out of bed. She tried to hide her pain, but her eyes scrunched up. "We're reading today apparently."

"Fabulous," she replied, making me laugh. If it weren't for Violet, I didn't know what I would be like. She kept me sane— well, as sane as you could be down here. She understood how suffocating it was because she was just as eager to get out as I was.

"There you go," I said as I pushed the bathroom door open. "I'll just get you some oh-so-glamorous clothes and a towel."

Violet grinned and switched the shower on. "Thanks."

I gave her a fresh towel and the clothes that matched ours and went back into the bedroom. One week until Lewis turned nineteen. His last birthday being a teenager. It was something I desperately wanted to celebrate with him. How many other birthdays would I miss? Taking a deep breath, I flattened my already perfect hair and prepared for another boring day. *Everything will be okay.*

Wednesday, February 11th (2009)

Theo answered the door. "Where is he?" I asked.

He smirked. "It's ten in the morning, so Lewis will still be in bed."

I scowled. "But it's his birthday," I said, tugging on the Happy Birthday balloon. I loved birthdays, anyone's birthday.

Theo shrugged. "What can I say, my brother's a lazy arse."

"Well, I'm making him get up." I strode in past Theo and stomped up the stairs. Who the heck slept in on special occasions? I pushed open his bedroom door and grinned at him sleeping with one arm thrown over his face. "Happy birthday!" I shouted and launched myself on his bed.

He gasped and jumped awake, looking around disorientedly. I giggled. He looked so funny when he was woken up. "What the…?" He groaned. "Sum, what're you doing?"

I thrust the balloon string at him. "Happy birthday." Flopping back on the bed, he groaned again. "Oh, no, you don't. Get up! Come on, it's your seventeenth! You can legally drive now. Well, after you pass your test, but you can learn." I shook my head. "Anyway, what do you want to do to celebrate?"

"Sleep," he mumbled, his voice muffled by the pillows.

"Wow, you are *not* a morning person." I sighed and climbed on his lap. His eyes shot open. Well, that got his attention

"Hmm, I like this idea too." *Of course you do.* He ran his hands up my thighs, biting his lip.

"I'm sure you do, pervert, but unfortunately for you, I'm not easy. Get up. Your mum's making pancakes and they smell so good." I leaned over and kissed him. My heart was doing somersaults. "Come on." I hopped off him and stood at the side of his bed. "You want me to go down and get you some while you get dressed?"

"I love you, Summer," he said, looking deep into my eyes and completely ignoring my question. My heart felt like it was trying to burst out of my chest. Sometimes I didn't believe him when he said it. Actually most of the time. He was…well, *him*, all gorgeous, tall, dark, and unbelievably handsome, and I was just me.

"Love you too, birthday boy."

He chuckled and got off the bed, pulling me into his arms. *Whoa half-naked!* He only had on cotton pajama pants and nothing else. I gulped. My hormones seemed to be in overdrive and my body burst into flames. *Wow, wow, wow!* I was secretly grateful for all the football and training he did because it did wonders for his chest.

"Now who's the pervert?" he teased, smirking at me. I rolled my eyes and got up again, opening his wardrobe. "I kinda feel like a piece of meat."

"Well, either get used to it or cover up," I replied and threw a T-shirt at him.

He caught it just before it smacked him in the face and pulled it over his head. "Let's get this over with then. And thanks for that," he said, nodding at the balloon that was now stuck to the ceiling.

"You're welcome. That's not your present by the way."

His eyes lit up. "Is my present you?"

I sighed, discouraged. "Downstairs. Now." He saluted and marched out of the room. Following him downstairs, I grinned like an idiot to myself. I had wanted to be with him for years and now we were *finally* together. This was the first birthday we would spend together, where I could get him something decent because now he knew how crazy I was about him.

He stopped suddenly at the bottom of the stairs. "Did you know about this?" He questioned, gesturing his hand to all the birthday decorations.

"Of course I did. I chose most of them," I said, smiling proudly. He frowned. "Don't be a pain in the arse, Lewis. It's your birthday and everyone's excited!" *Me mostly.* Spending his birthday with him—properly with him—was like a dream come true so he could suck it up. Nothing was going to take away the excitement I felt, not even a grumpy arse.

"Fine," he said and sighed dramatically. I wrapped my arms around his neck and he kissed me. "I know I said this like two seconds ago, but I really do love you." He pressed his forehead against mine and smiled.

"I know I said this like two seconds ago, but I really do love you too."

25
CLOVER

Monday, February 7th (Present)

I woke up early. The sun was still working its way over the horizon. My mind immediately flitted to the search for my Lily. Yawning and rubbing my eyes, I forced myself to get out of bed. I had to go to work. I had to keep it up. No one could suspect a thing. My whole family was on the line, and I had to continue my normal routine to protect us.

Looking in the mirror, I tried to recognize the man I was when Mother was alive. I wasn't as strong, but I wanted to be. I tried to be. I didn't want to let her down. I *could* make the world that little bit better while making *my* world a happy one. A nagging voice at the back of my head still chanted *"Failure,"* and I knew I would never stop until I had succeeded. *I will prove her wrong and make her proud.*

I showered, washing myself thoroughly twice—and dressed in black trousers, a blue shirt, and blue tie. I didn't look in the mirror again. All I saw now was a shadow of a man, barely holding on. *You don't need her; you can do this alone.* I did need her, though, but I didn't want to.

Growling in frustration, I slammed my bathroom door shut and went down to the girls. I needed to see them, to see how much they needed me, how they appreciated our family and me.

"Good morning, Flowers," I said and walked down the stairs. The room was filled with the heavenly scent of toasted hot cross buns.

"Morning, Clover," they replied in unison. Lily looked to the floor. Her shyness was both attractive and endearing. I did have hope for her coming out of her shell a little more, though. There really was no need for her to be so shy when she was among family.

I sat down and a plate of warm buns smothered in melting butter was placed before me. "Thank you, Lily."

She smiled and muttered, "You're welcome." There was something sad about her. The smiles she offered never quite reached her eyes. "Are you not feeling well, Lily?"

"I'm fine," she replied and sat down. Somehow I didn't believe her. She was the type of young woman that didn't complain at every ailment. I respected that. She was strong.

"So, what do you have planned today?" I asked them and took a large bite of the hot cross bun, closing my eyes at the comforting taste of the warm bun.

Rose smiled and it lit up her beautiful blue eyes. "We're going to do some knitting. We haven't done any in a while. Which reminds me, do you think you'll be able to pick us up some more wool? We're getting a little low."

"Of course, I'll get some after work."

"Thank you," she replied.

I took her hand over the table and gave it a squeeze. "You're welcome. It's my pleasure." Rose's blue eyes danced with happiness. My heart constricted. Every touch from her meant so much to me—much more than anyone else's. I wished I could go back in time and handle our meeting better.

"How is work?" she asked.

"Boring but fine."

Work wasn't the problem. The fact that everyone now knows about the bodies is what concerned me. It was only a matter of time before the police would want to talk to Christy's colleagues—which I was one of. If she hadn't been such a disgusting whore, none of it would have happened. She deserved it.

Finishing my last bite, I stood up, not wanting to put off the inevitable any longer. The girls hadn't finished, and I knew I was being rude by leaving, but this was too important. "Forgive me for not staying, but I have something I need to tend to. Thank you for breakfast."

"Okay," Rose said. "We'll see you tonight. Have a good day."

I gave her a nod and smiled. "You too. Thank you."

I arrived at work and walked straight to my office. "Morning, Colin. Would you like a coffee?" Jemma asked as she pushed my door open.

"Good morning, Jemma. That would be lovely, thank you."

She left the room, and I turned on my computer. There were so many folders in my tray. *What now?* I thought and flipped the first one open.

When are they coming? I looked out of my window to the parking lot. Nothing. I tried to concentrate on work, but I couldn't. My foot tapped the floor of its own accord and everything outside caught my attention—birds, a cat, cars, people, anything.

Jemma came back with a cup of coffee and placed it on my coaster. "Terrible about Christy, isn't it? I can't believe anyone would hurt her."

"Thank you. Yes, it is. She was such a bright young woman." Who made disgusting choices. "Are you okay?"

She shook her head. "In shock. I just can't believe it. So many women in the canal too. It's scary."

"You just make sure you're safe."

She nodded. "Oh, I will be. My boyfriend is picking me up now. I don't feel safe walking anywhere while a killer is on the loose." I blinked in shock and Jemma walked out of my office. *Killer.* That wasn't what I was. There is a huge problem out there, and I act accordingly. Did people just think of me as a killer?

A knock on my door pulled me back. Sarah, the receptionist, pushed the door open. "Mr. Brown, the police are in reception. They'd like to speak to everyone, starting at management level. Can I show them in?"

My heart raced. I hadn't seen a police car. Glancing out the window, I saw none. Front of the building perhaps. "Of course, Sarah. Please show them through." She nodded her head and retreated back out of my office. I took a deep breath to mentally prepare myself and then straightened the papers on my desk.

A minute or two later, two police officers entered my office and

Sarah closed the door behind them. "Good morning. Please sit," I said, gesturing toward the two chairs against the wall.

"Thank you. We won't keep you long; we just have a few standard questions to ask."

I nodded. "Anything I can do to help." One of them, the female officer, flipped open a notepad and clicked the top of her pen.

"Thank you. I'm Detective Inspector Brook and this is DI McKinney," the man, Brook, said.

"Christy was a lovely woman, always willing to help—never turned you down if you needed a chat. It's such shame she got herself tied up in that awful mess."

"Mess?" the male officer asked. "What mess was that?"

"Oh, I assumed you would know by now. Christy and Greg Hart, also an employee here, were having an affair." They both looked up and the woman quickly scribbled something down on her pad. *Good girl.*

"Do you know how long this was going on for?"

I shook my head. "No, I only found out recently, when I heard them argue in his office."

"What were they arguing about?"

"I didn't catch it all, but Christy was saying she wanted their relationship to be exclusive. I guess she wanted him to leave his wife. Mr. Hart's wife is pregnant. I assumed Greg had come to his senses and decided to make things work with his family."

"And what did Mr. Hart want from Christy?" he asked.

"I'm sorry, I can't speak for him, but it didn't sound like he wanted the same. He told her he didn't want a relationship with her. Like I said, I got the impression he'd realized he'd made a mistake having an affair. You don't think Greg had something to do with this? He wouldn't hurt a fly." *Come on. Come on.*

"When was the last time you saw Christy?" he asked, ignoring my question.

"At work, she left slightly early. It was about four forty-five, I think. When she didn't turn up the next morning, I assumed she was just ill."

"And no one heard from her? She didn't call in sick?"

"I can't say. I don't take those calls. You'll have to speak to someone from HR for that—Jessica Peterson."

He nodded and McKinney wrote something else down. "Have you ever heard Mr. Hart mention any other women?"

I smiled. Their line of questioning was focused on Greg. "Not to me. He did mention going out to dinner regularly. I assumed his wife wasn't a good cook." Brook smiled.

They continued their questions; most were about Greg, trying to find out what kind of a person he was and his relationship with others—particularly with women. When asked where I was, they were satisfied with my "at home watching *Ocean's Eleven*" answer. They would look into it, of course, but I knew the movie was on at the time Christy died. "Well, I think that's all for now, Mr. Brown. Here's my card if you think of anything else." He handed me his card as the stood up. "Thank you for your time."

I took the card and smiled at them both. "Absolutely." That was almost too easy.

26
SUMMER

Wednesday, February 9th (Present)

I looked up at the clock, only half past eight, still too early for bedtime. If I went to sleep too early, then I would wake up early—and spend the extra few hours stressing over how long until he came for breakfast.

Six months I had been living in the same hell, doing the same thing in the same four depressing walls. I didn't even know how I was still sane. Maybe I wasn't. Maybe I was too insane to realize that I was insane!

The cellar door creaked open. I knew him coming down here after seven wasn't a good thing—only for breakfast, lunch, and dinner. Was he going to kill again? He had killed too many women. I didn't understand how he was getting away with it.

A high-pitched scream rang through my ears, and I gulped. Which poor girl was it this time? I had almost closed off from it. Watching someone being killed made me sick, but I pretended it wasn't real, fake blood, just like the movies—my *coping mechanism* Poppy called it. Whatever it was called, I didn't care. It helped. I stood up and moved to the wall close to our bedroom and the others followed. We should do something. We should always do something, but we didn't. Fear was powerful. It was why he hadn't been murdered down here by four women.

He pushed the girl downstairs roughly, making her cry out in pain. She had a short, pixie haircut, not something Clover thought was *womanly*. He liked long hair. Her clothes were short, revealing, and tight. She never stood a chance. Clover didn't know why she was selling her body, and he didn't care. He was judge, jury, and executioner.

As she sobbed, mascara-stained tears poured down her face. She stumbled down the stairs and clung to the wall. Lifting her head, she saw us and her eyes widened in surprise. "Help me," she begged, her voice trembling. My eyes prickled with tears. She looked so scared and helpless. We were just as scared. I wished that there was something I could do, but I knew it was useless. I would never be able to overpower him alone.

He kicked her hard in the stomach, making her scream in pain. Something cracked, and I pressed my fist to my mouth as a wave of nausea hit me. I slumped down on the sofa and crawled back, curling up into a ball.

"Don't talk to them. They're not like you," he spat. His face was red and his eyes so cold he looked dead. He had to be dead inside to do what he did. He kicked her again, and she screamed through another crack. I gulped and hugged my legs.

Why was he doing that? He used to just stab them. Why was he hurting her like that first? Did he enjoy it? "P-please don't," she muttered. "Let me go, please." Her breathing was heavy and labored. He smiled in return, cocking his head to the side. His enjoyment in tormenting her sent a shiver down my spine. I hated him so much.

"You're the one making me hurt you! If you didn't ruin innocent peoples' lives, I wouldn't have to do this," he growled and punched her in the face. She fell to her knees from the force and spat out blood onto the floor.

Horror flashed through his eyes at the sight of the blood splatters on the floor. *Oh no!*

The veins in his neck popped out and strained against his skin and his face went red with rage. He pulled out his knife. *This is it.* She screamed and thrashed her arms and legs around trying to keep him away from her. "No, no, no! Please don't. No, please." Her eyes were wide, like a kid trying to prove her innocence. That wouldn't help her. He never let any of them go

Tears rolled down my face so quickly it felt like one long, neverending tear. I knew what was coming next. He kicked her hard in the side, in the same place as before. She gagged and held her ribs. As she looked down, he plunged the knife into her stomach, retracted it, and stabbed her again. Blood pumped from the wounds. I heaved, fighting the overwhelming urge to throw up.

She choked and blood splattered on the floor from her mouth. Her body slumped to the floor, and she made a throaty scream that made my entire body tremble. With one last gasp for air, her body stilled. My lip trembled. *Don't think of it as a person,* I told myself. I pictured a slab of meat on the floor, the remains of a slaughtered animal. I had to turn it off.

"Clean this. Now," he barked and sprinted back up the stairs.

Would he still kill if he were the one that had to close their eyes and mop up the blood? A pool of blood seeped out from under her body and trickled toward me. I watched it with morbid fascination. So much blood was inside the human body, bright red liquid swimming around in our veins. It didn't even take losing much to fuck you up either.

"Lily," Rose's voice snapped me back to reality. "Come help, please?"

I nodded. "Okay." Walking toward the body slowly, I crouched down. The smell of blood filled my lungs, and I gagged. My eyes watered, and I jumped to my feet. "I can't, sorry," I muttered and ran for the bathroom.

I threw up in the toilet. Tears flowed down my face as I leaned over the toilet. I gasped, trying to get my breath back. I couldn't do this. I couldn't clean up after his murders. "Lily?" Poppy called through the door. I squeezed my eyes closed. *Just leave me alone!*

Slumping against the wall, I gripped my head in my hands. I felt as if I were suffocating. I hated him, and I hated being down here. Poppy walked into the room and knelt down in front of me. "I can't do this," I said. The lump in my throat grew, and I started sobbing, chest heaving.

"Shh, it's okay. You can, Lily. You have to."

I shook my head. I didn't have to at all. "N-No I don't," I replied, gasping for air.

"Don't. You don't think like that, okay? We'll be fine. We will all be fine." I curled up in a ball, hugging myself tight. I'd heard "It will be fine" so many times. When was it actually going to start being fine? When Lewis said it, it was true. When he held me, everything seemed to be all right, even if it was only for a while. He wasn't here now, and I needed him more than ever.

My head pounded. It felt like someone was repeatedly bashing me in the skull with a hammer. I wiped my tears away with the back of my hand and took a deep, ragged breath. "I can't help you do that."

She stroked my hair. "I know, and you don't have to. Stay in here, and I'll come get you when it's done. You clean yourself up for when he comes back." She got up and left the room. I wanted to clean myself up, but not for him. I felt gross and could taste bile in my mouth still.

Pushing myself up, I turned the cold tap on and stuck my mouth under it. The cool water made me feel a little better. I pulled away and splashed my face. My eyes were red and puffy from crying. I looked awful. How was I going to make it another day? Especially when I didn't have a clue when it would end—or even *if* it would end. I could be down here for years. If I knew how long, then I could make a decision. The one thing I didn't ever want to happen was for me to grow to accept this. I would sooner die than be okay down here.

"Lily, we're all finished. Can I come in?" Poppy said, tapping on the door. That was quick. Only ten minutes. If there were a world record for the quickest murder cleanup, they would get it. I opened the door and she smiled. "You look better." Yes, *looked*. I didn't feel better. She sighed. "Have your shower now. I'll tell him you're feeling unwell and having an early night."

"Do you think that would be okay?"

"We can sleep when we want, Lily." Well, when it didn't conflict with his meal times!

The main room was spotless when I walked out of the bathroom. It was hard to believe just half an hour ago a girl was murdered in this room. It almost made it seem unreal, as if I had dreamed it. Sometimes I second-guessed things because it all seemed too surreal. Had I imagined him killing her? My sense of reality blurred every day, and I was terrified that it meant I was starting to lose it like Rose. Not once had she or Poppy asked me to call them by their real names.

On the side table was another newspaper, but I refused to look at it. It was torment to see my family's faces.

I went into the bedroom, ignoring Rose watching me, and climbed into bed. I started to think that I was the one worse off. Sure, Rose and Poppy didn't have anyone looking for them—that we knew of—but that also meant they didn't miss anyone so much it made them feel sick. I missed all the special little moments I had with my family and the things I'd done with Lewis, even the silly things, like going bowling or shopping on the weekends.

Rolling onto my stomach, I buried my head under my pillow. Had I really reached a new low where I wished I had no one? My heart broke, and I sobbed into the sheet.

Saturday, June 5th (2010)

"Lewis, come on. You need to get up," I said, shaking his arm gently. Every time we had to go somewhere or do something early, I had the same battle to get him out of bed. He was worse than a child!

He groaned. "Baby, you gotta let me sleep."

"Nope. Up," I said, pulling the quilt off him. He groaned again and rolled over, burying his head in the pillow. We were going to his aunt's wedding and needed to leave in an hour. I had already been up over two hours, had breakfast, showered, got dressed, brought my dress to his house, done my makeup, and straightened my hair. "Lewis, seriously, we have an hour."

"An hour?" he mumbled into the pillow.

"Yes!"

"Then wake me up in thirty minutes."

I sighed in frustration. He was so impossible in the mornings. I suddenly thought of something that would get him up. "Okay. You sleep. I just need to take this bra off—it's so uncomfortable," I said casually and removed my top. I saw him twitch, but he didn't look over—he didn't think I would actually do it. I smiled and dropped my top to the floor. The noise got his attention. He rolled over at ninja speed and pushed himself up on his elbows.

"Hey, I thought you were taking your bra off?" he said, narrowing his eyes playfully.

I shrugged. "It's not hurting now, but since you're awake, you should just get up." I jumped back as his arms shot out to grab me.

"That's not fair. Tease!" I giggled to myself and walked away. "Summer?" I turned around and gasped at how close he was to me. I hadn't heard him get up over my laughing. He wound his arms around my waist and pulled me against his chest. "I love you," he said, staring into my eyes, making me feel like I was floating.

"I love you too. Now get ready!" I pushed his chest and he must not have expected it because he stumbled backward. He groaned and pouted, making me roll my eyes at him. Man-child.

We arrived at the church ten minutes late and had to sit at the back. I was so annoyed with him as everyone stared at us. I scowled at Lewis and he mouthed, "I love you" to try and get back in my good graces. *Not happening, buddy!* I frowned and turned my attention to the bride and groom.

His aunt Lisa and her almost husband, Brian, read out their vows. They had written their own and they were beautiful. I loved weddings, especially when they were so personal.

"Are you crying?" Lewis whispered, bumping his shoulder against mine. He looked like he was trying not to smirk. Every time I cried at something happy he teased me.

"I'm sorry I'm not dead inside like you!" I hissed. He burst out laughing and quickly turned it into a cough. Everyone in the church fell silent and turned around to look at us. My eyes widened and my face burst into flames. Being with Lewis felt like bloody babysitting sometimes—most of the time.

"Sorry," Lewis said, faking another cough and slapping his chest. Could I move seats without anyone noticing?

Once the ceremony ended, everyone made their way outside for drinks, canapés, and photos. Lewis grabbed my hand, rubbing my palm with his thumb. It was hard to stay mad at him. "Late as always hey, Lewis?" Lisa teased, pulling him into a hug.

"Yeah, sorry. Summer was taking ages doing her hair." I stared at him with my mouth hanging open. Was he *seriously* blaming me for this?

"Don't worry, hon. I know the truth," she said and winked at me.

"Good," I replied and narrowed my eyes at Lewis. "Anyway, congratulations!" I hugged her, kissing her cheek.

"Yeah, what she said," Lewis said, nodding his head toward me.

"Thank you," Lisa replied sarcastically and pinched Lewis's cheek. He frowned, turning his nose up and batting her hand away. *Ha.* "Well, I'd better keep moving, gotta get around to everyone before I have too many drinks." She smiled at us and walked toward Lewis's parents.

"Come on, baby, let's get some champagne. I'm gonna need the alcohol to survive this." He kissed my temple and put his arm around my waist. Yeah, Lewis's family could get a little… extravagant when they were all together. I still had flashbacks from the Irish dancing incident at his mum's birthday party.

I rolled my eyes. "You're far too young to be this grumpy, you know." He also didn't like how his gran had a million stories about him when he was a baby. Personally, I loved it.

"Oh, now I'm young? You're always teasing the crap out of me for being old, so which one is it?" He raised his eyebrows and waited for an answer.

I shrugged. "That all depends on my mood." He chuckled quietly and pulled me into a kiss.

27
LEWIS

Thursday, February 24th (Present)

I lay awake in Summer's bed. It was two thirty in the morning, and I had only slept for about an hour. I had a shitty feeling in the pit of my stomach. All I could think was, *There's something really wrong*. Even more wrong than her being missing. Today marked the seventh month she had been gone. Was that too long to find her alive? I couldn't think there was no chance. Statistically the chances sucked, but I had to believe she was still alive.

She had to come back soon. I couldn't think straight. I hated every second she was out there wondering if we were still looking for her. Whenever thoughts of what she was going through slipped into my mind, I felt sick, angry, and just wanted to punch someone or something. Someone knew what happened, but no one was coming forward. I hated them. I hated everyone—most of all myself.

I shouldn't have let her go to that fucking gig. Not that I could have ever stopped her doing anything she wanted, but I should have. I should have been the arsehole boyfriend and made her stay with me. She would have hated me, but she would be here.

Sitting up in bed, I rubbed my temples, feeling another headache coming on from the lack of sleep. I hated waking up every morning knowing I faced another day desperately searching, knowing at the end of the day I would be going to bed alone in Summer's house while she was out there living God knows what hell.

"Lewis," Henry said and pushed the bedroom door open. "I was thinking about going to Hart's." *Finally!* I had wanted to go and see Greg Hart ever since the police released him after questioning. He should never have been let out, especially after finding eight bodies in the canal. They believed the murders spanned over four years. The search wasn't even over; the cops thought there could still be more bodies.

"Pretty sure I already know the answer, but are you coming?" he asked.

I cocked my head to the side. It had been my idea in the first place, but Henry had refused and spouted off a million reasons why it was a bad idea. I had no doubt that it was a bad idea, but that wasn't going to stop me. I couldn't relax or eat or sleep until she was found. Time was standing still, and I was stuck until we knew.

"You know I am." If I could just talk to him, maybe I could get him to tell me where Summer was.

"Henry, the guy that helped with the search, Colin Brown, do you think there's something weird about him?" Theo said I was being stupid and looking for answers wherever I thought I could find them, but the guy was creepy. I couldn't get his face out of my head.

"Not really. What do you mean 'something weird' anyway?"

"I don't know," I replied and sighed deeply. Maybe I was just looking for anything and looking in the wrong places. "He just seemed so…closed off. Everyone else that's helped with the search did it because they want Summer found. It seemed like he was doing it because he thought he should."

Henry frowned. "How did you get all that from talking to him once?"

"I dunno. He was…" I shook my head. I didn't even know what I meant. "Never mind."

"Maybe he just didn't know how to react. Forget it, Lewis; we need to concentrate on getting Hart talking. He's under police surveillance so it won't be easy. We'll think of a plan in the morning. Sleep," he ordered and left the room.

Sighing, I laid back down and stared at the ceiling. Maybe Henry's right about Colin. I needed to concentrate on Hart, the one real suspect—or person of interest, whatever he was now—the police had.

Sleep was impossible. I couldn't relax, even though I was exhausted from walking around searching all day. I glanced over to the bedside table where Summer kept a framed picture of us. We looked so happy—we *were* happy. She drove me crazy but I love her and would do anything for her. Looking at it was torture but I couldn't put it down; my eyes were fixed on her perfect face. "Tell me where you are, baby," I whispered, swallowing the lump in my throat.

"Lewis," someone shouted through the door. I jumped awake from my half-asleep state. "Breakfast is ready. Hurry up. I wanna leave soon," Henry added.

I groaned and rubbed my eyes. "All right, I'm up." It was six in the morning. The last time I had looked at the clock that morning, it was 4:23. My eyes stung from having hardly any sleep, and I felt drained. I needed food and a couple energy drinks. Stretching my aching limbs, I took one last look at Summer's picture and prepared for yet another day wondering where she was.

My stomach was tied in knots. I was nervous to speak to Hart. I almost didn't want to know. It would make it too real. Mum and Dawn were the only people in the kitchen when I came down for breakfast. I sat at the table and forced down a few bits of toast. It was no use, though; I felt too sick to eat.

"I'll take a couple cereal bars," I said, dropping my half-eaten toast back on the plate. Everything tasted like shit now anyway.

Dawn frowned. "Make sure you do." The circles under her eyes had darkened. I don't think she slept much either. I often heard her walking around in the early hours of the morning.

"Where are you going today?" Mum asked.

"Back to town and then maybe farther toward the city. I don't really know yet."

"Ready, Lewis?" Henry asked, leaning against the kitchen doorframe.

I got up, eager to go. "Yeah."

Dawn nodded and swiped a tear from her face. "Keep in touch and be careful."

"We will, Mum," Henry replied. "See you later." I walked ahead of Henry and got in my car.

"So...plan?" I asked. "I guess we should plan something, although I just want to go and beat the shit out of him."

He scratched his jaw and frowned. "Err, no. You got any ideas?"

"No," I replied, shaking my head. "We're just going to have to get there and see how well the police are watching him."

"Yeah. We are doing the right thing, aren't we?"

"For Sum, yeah. You think we could sneak into his house?"

"Maybe. We'd make shit robbers," he said, laughing humorlessly.

"I feel like I'm in a movie."

"Vin Diesel's gonna burst round the corner in some souped-up sports car and start shooting at us."

Six months ago, I would have driven like a dick and Henry would have pretended to shoot things out the windows. I would love to go back to being an idiot.

The closer we got to his house, the angrier I became. I felt rage coursing through my veins. We parked the car along the road so he wouldn't see from his house and watched. "I don't see the police," Henry said, looking up and down the road.

"That's the whole point, Henry," I muttered dryly. I shook my head and looked back at his house. He was there. I clenched my jaw and felt every muscle in my body tense. He stood outside, picking up a newspaper from his doorstep. I had planned to keep calm, but seeing him made my blood boil. I just wanted to rip his fucking head off. Adrenaline pumped through my body, and I jumped out of the car.

In that moment, I didn't think about trying to stay calm and get him to confess. The man that took Summer from me was just feet away, and I was going to kill him. Even the threat of prison wasn't enough to stop me. I didn't care.

He looked up and saw me as I ran toward him. His hands shot up, telling me to back off. *Not fucking likely.* I lunged forward, grabbed his shirt, and punched him as hard as I could in the jaw. The satisfaction of hearing his jaw crack lasted only a second. He still had Summer.

"Where is she?" I shouted and drew my arm back to punch him again. I couldn't think straight. I wanted answers, someone to tell me where she was and what happened, and someone to pay. I wanted someone to pay. "Tell me where she is." I punched his face again and his lip split open. I couldn't even put into words how much I hated him.

"I don't know. I haven't done anything, I swear!" he shouted back and shoved me back away from him.

"I swear to God if you don't tell me where she is…" I growled and gasped as I was suddenly grabbed from behind and slammed to the ground. I expected it to be Henry, but when I looked over my shoulder, I saw it was some police officer. I didn't care that I was about to be arrested. I only cared that they stopped me too soon.

The officer read me my rights and clamped handcuffs on my wrists tight. "I swear to you, Lewis, I haven't done anything to Summer," Hart protested.

"Don't you fucking say her name. Just tell me where she is. Tell me where she is."

Henry stood beside me looking lost and shocked. *Nice one, Henry, cheers for the help, mate!* "Wait, you can't arrest him," Henry said. Finally. "He's only doing what everyone else wants to do."

"Shut up, Henry!" What was the point of him speaking up now? I pulled against the handcuffs and winced as it bit into my wrist. "I'll walk myself," I spat as one of them pushed me forward, toward the unmarked car half-hidden behind a neighbor's hedge. I walked to the car in disbelief. That bastard could go back in his house and have a cup of tea while I was being hauled off to the police station.

"Don't tell anyone," I said to Henry as the car door was slammed behind me.

Lying back in the car, I closed my eyes. Summer would go crazy if she knew I was being arrested. I pictured her angry face and smiled. Her eyes would narrow and she would get these two little vertical lines between her eyebrows as she frowned. I had seen that face a million times, especially when I wouldn't get up in the morning.

Minutes later, we arrived at the station, and I realized I had my car keys. How the hell was Henry going to get back home? I hoped he would call Theo and not his parents. I didn't want them finding out. The door was opened for me, and I got out, feeling like a damn criminal. What the hell was I going to do if Hart pressed charges? I knew I shouldn't have punched him, but I couldn't control my temper when I saw his face.

Michael looked up as I was led into the station with my hands handcuffed behind my back. He did a double take and said something to his colleague, walking toward me. "What's going on?" he asked, looking between me and the officer holding on to my arm.

"We picked him up at Hart's. We actually pulled him *off* Hart."

Michael nodded once. "I'll take it from here. You can remove the cuffs now." The officer who had arrested me looked put out, and I tried not to look smug. The cuffs dug into my skin again as they were removed. I held back a wince. "This way," Michael muttered and walked down the corridor.

He pushed a door open and nodded for me to go into a small interview room. His face was hard and grim. I felt like I was back at high school being sent to the head master's office. I sat down on one side of the dark wooden table. "Wait here," he said and left the room.

I looked around and wondered if this was the room Hart was interviewed in. Was this where he managed to convince them he was innocent? Leaning back on the hard plastic chair, I rubbed my wrist. What the fuck was Michael doing?

Ten minutes later he came back in and sat down opposite me. "Well?" he said.

I sighed and leaned my elbows on the table. "I just wanted to get him to tell me where she is."

"And you thought punching him was the best way to do that?"

"I didn't plan it. When I saw him I lost control. Seeing his smug face." I seethed. "I wanted to kill him." *I want to kill him.*

Michael held his hand up. "You need to calm down. Now I've just spoken to Mr. Hart, and he's not going to press charges. But don't think you're getting away with it. If you try anything like that again, I'll arrest you myself. You're getting off very lightly here, Lewis, but it won't happen again."

"Getting off lightly?" I repeated in disbelief. "My girlfriend's been kidnapped, we have no idea where she is or what's happened to her, and you think I'm getting off lightly?"

"You know exactly what I mean, Lewis. I'll remind you that Mr. Hart has not been convicted of anything." He leaned forward. "Look, I know this is hard for you. I know you want answers, but you have to let us do our job."

"And when exactly are you going to start doing your job?" I hissed. "It's been *seven* months."

His face hardened. "You may leave now, Lewis."

I jumped up, knocking the chair over in the process and stormed out of the room. *Fuck this!* Henry stood by the front desk, having an argument with some officer. "Henry," I called, pulling his arm. "Let's go."

"Hey, what happened?" he questioned, running after me. I needed to get away. They were doing nothing. They didn't care enough.

"Nothing. No charges. Where's Theo?" I asked, spotting my brother's car.

"I dropped him back off at work after he picked me up. He loaned me his car. So they're doing nothing?"

"Apparently *Mr. Hart* doesn't want to press charges." I got in the car and slammed the door. "Let's go into town with her picture. We can pick up my car on the way home. I don't want to waste the whole day."

"Sure. Lewis, you won't give up, will you?"

I frowned. "No. Why do you ask?" He shook his head. That would never happen. I couldn't move forward without knowing where she was and what happened. My throat dried and eyes stung. *Do not fucking cry!* "Do you want to give up?"

"No, she drives me crazy, but I won't stop looking until my annoying little sister is found." He laughed at some memory. "She really did do my head in."

I grinned. "I know. I had to listen to the arguments."

"She started them," he said, and we both laughed. I would give anything to hear them shouting at each other and Summer slamming her bedroom door every day again.

Henry parked on Main Street. "Split up or stay together?" he asked.

"Together for the straight road and we can split up at the end." We started along the street, and I saw Colin walking out of a door. He was holding two bags, one full of books and the other one with what looked like yarn. What the hell was he doing with yarn?

"Henry," I said, nodding my head in his direction.

"Your weird dude?"

"Mmm. There's definitely something weird. Look what he's bought. What would he be doing with that?"

Henry shrugged. "Knitting books, I dunno."

"Lewis, Henry," Colin said, stopping in front of us.

"Hi," Henry muttered.

"How are you both?"

What are you hiding? I shrugged my shoulders, not wanting to get into how shitty I felt.

"I've been meaning to stop by and help with the search again."

"We'd appreciate that. The more people we have looking for her the better," I replied. I wanted him to come along. Maybe then I could figure him out.

"Do you still meet at the same place?"

"Yeah," I replied. "Long Thorpe town hall, seven o'clock every morning." Weekends were better, but during the week we still had a decent turnout. There were a lot of people that cared about Summer and just wanted to see her come home safely.

"I'll come and help this weekend. How are your parents holding up?" he asked Henry.

"My dad spends every waking second searching for Summer and Mum spends every second crying," he said honestly.

Colin nodded sympathetically, but his eyes showed no emotion. They were empty. He looked bored. Something was wrong, and I couldn't ignore it this time. Normal people were sympathetic—they had something to say. Even the ones that couldn't find the words at least looked sympathetic.

"Well, I hope you find her soon, and I'll join the search on Sunday."

"Yeah, thanks," Henry replied. Colin turned around and walked in the opposite direction. I watched him gripping hold of his bags as he went. His knuckles were bright white where he was holding on too tight. Why? I fought the urge to follow him.

"At least we'll be able to spend some time with him on Sunday. Maybe he'll let something slip."

Henry frowned. "Let what slip?"

"I don't know yet. You think we should follow him?" He wouldn't of course.

"What? You can't just go around stalking people. Jesus, Lewis."

I clenched my jaw. *The fuck I can't!* "I'm trying to find my girlfriend. I'll do whatever I need to and *stalk* whoever I need to stalk." I would have thought he would understand. He loved Summer. How could he not be willing to do anything to find her too?

"Excuse me," I said, stopping two old ladies that tried to walk past. I flicked to a picture of Summer on my phone. "Have you seen this girl?"

28
CLOVER

Sunday, February 27 (Present)

I arrived at the town hall where the search for Lily was based. There were a million things I would prefer to do today, but I wanted to know what was going on with the search. I wanted to be seen helping. There was something about the way that Lewis looked at me that left me with an uneasy feeling. I constantly felt paranoid that he knew. My heart wouldn't let up, and I checked out the window multiple times a day. It was taking over my life, and I had to put an end to his suspicion. He couldn't know.

The plain, cream room was crammed with people. I frowned. There were still a lot of people looking for her, even after the official police searches had died down. Why couldn't they just leave her be? She was better off with me. They all were. I shuffled into a space away from a disease-ridden homeless man coughing up his lungs near the door. He was probably here for the warmth rather than to help.

Moments after I arrived, people started filtering out, studying maps as they went. I had arrived a little late on purpose. Lily was splashed over posters pinned to a corkboard. She was pretty in her picture, very fresh-faced and natural. It was nice to see a teenager without a thick layer of makeup on. However, it was only a matter of time before she felt the need to paint her face like the trampy women in magazines.

"Colin, thanks for coming." I jumped and looked over. Lewis cocked his head to the side. His eyes darkened and his posture straightened. "We appreciate you helping us find Summer." His lips pulled into a tight, forced smile. *He knows something. He can see through you.*

I returned his smile and chastised myself. He couldn't know. Matching his posture, I held out my hand and he briefly shook it. "It's no trouble. Really. Anything I can do to help, I am more than willing to do. I'm going to get started right now," I said, turning to get away from him.

"Great," he replied, effectively gaining my attention again. "Your group is ready."

My group? I frowned and looked on. They still had enough volunteers to make enough groups. I had hoped I could go alone this time.

Lewis frowned. "You're with Dan, Kate, Rick," he said, reading their names from a piece of paper. He looked up and smiled. "And me." I gritted my teeth and nodded. "Let's get started. We're meeting the others outside."

My heart spiked in panic. I knew it was not accidental that I was in his search group. I had to look at it as a positive. Today I would convince him that I was only trying to help. Today I would fool him too. "Let's go then," I replied. He smiled tightly and turned. I followed him out the door. "Where are we starting?"

He looked forward, avoiding my gaze, tense. Too tense. "A field a few miles away, on the edge of town." I smiled. *Miles and miles away from my home.*

"Any reason why there? It's quite far from town."

He sighed. "The logical places have been searched and searched. I'll cover every inch of the country until I find her. I don't care how far away it is." The tragic thing was, he did love her. If he were a better boyfriend, then perhaps she would have been safe with him. Lewis was the sort of person who only realized his mistakes afterward. He didn't think or plan forward—he was all hindsight—and that was exactly why I was the best person to take care of Lily.

Dan drove his car out of Long Thorpe through the miles of farmland and fields, toward town. I sat in the back with my side pressed firmly against the door. Dan's wife, Kate, was a plump woman who had let herself go. It was hard to keep any distance in the back of their small hatchback.

"So do you want us to split up in the field or stick together?" Kate asked Lewis. Her hair was scrunched back in a messy tie and her makeup looked days old. She had yellowing teeth and her breath smelled of cigarettes and coffee. I gulped. I wanted to be anywhere but here. My foot tapped against the floor and I only realized I was doing it when Lewis looked over. I stopped and stared forward.

"Stick together. We'll start on the edge and walk at the same pace a few feet apart," he replied. "Look for…anything. There's nothing in the field, so searching should be easy and quick." He sounded like a professional.

I lined up between Lewis and Dan and very slowly walked forward. I kept my eyes on the ground, pretending to thoroughly search the area in front of me. Pausing occasionally, I bent down and picked up any old piece of rubbish, proving that I was searching hard and double-checking anything that caught my eye. The day was going to pass painfully slowly. When I could have been spending time with the girls, I was out in the freezing cold, searching a field for someone who was safe in my home.

Lewis looked over. "Thanks for helping again," he said and looked back at the ground.

I swallowed. Why was he thanking me again? "Like I said, I just want to help. It's really no problem. I wish there were more I could do."

He frowned and a pained expression dominated his face. "Life goes on, apparently," he replied quietly. Life was moving on for Lily. She was doing well. She was a part of my family and that was where she was staying. They had nothing to offer her now.

"I suppose it does. You've not stopped to work?"

"Nothing's more important than finding her." He looked up again. "I won't stop until I find her and bring to justice whichever sick fucker took her."

My throat ran dry. Why did it sound like he was saying that *about* me? I looked to my right, away from him. *He knows. He's found you out. Mother's right, you can't do anything properly. You're useless. Pathetic. A failure.* I pursed my lips, ignoring the agonizing tear in my heart. "She's very lucky to have you. Some people would have given up by now."

"I'm the lucky one. Do you live alone? No one missing you today?" I was taken aback by the sudden change of conversation.

"I live alone. I'm free to come and go as I please."

"Hmm." Where was he going with this? Why did he want to know that? He was trying to find out if I had a wife. Why? He was planning something. *He's coming to get you.*

"Why do you ask?" I kept my voice calm and controlled, though underneath I was anything but.

"Sorry, I shouldn't have. I've just never seen you with anyone and didn't want an angry wife at home waiting for you to get back." That's not why he asked. *He knows you have her. He knows what you've been doing. Put him off. Take control.*

"I'll have more time to give now I'm back," I said, sweeping my foot over a small mound of mud in an effort to look thorough.

"Oh?" Lewis asked, his eyebrows rose momentarily. I had spiked his interest.

I nodded. "Yes. I've been away for the past two weeks. Our Edinburgh office needed assistance. Their accountant left suddenly." Yes, in Scotland. He couldn't possibly think I would have Lily if I'd left the country for a fortnight. A frown set into his face. It seemed his only expression, other than the one of surprise.

"The police still have nothing solid on Hart," he said. "He must have had something to do with it." *Why is he moving on to Greg?* Did he now believe that I had nothing to do with it, or did he just want me to think that? Was he trying to make me feel secure—pretend he no longer suspects so I would slip up?

I smiled through my internal debate. "I'm sure he will be brought to justice if he's proven to have had any involvement in Summer's disappearance." I prayed that they would have enough circumstantial evidence to charge him. There was no guarantee, though. The police couldn't catch me, so I had little faith. It was only because of me that they had their one and only suspect. I had given them enough; it was now up to them to prosecute him with the evidence. It wasn't as if Gregory Hart was an honest and innocent man. He deserved to be punished.

"I hope so. She needs to be back with her family," he said, taking a deep breath as if he was struggling to keep his emotions in check.

She is with her family.

As soon as I got home, I had a quick shower and went down to the girls' room. Lewis was relentless in his search for his "girlfriend," and I was exhausted. How someone could care so much but be so careless was beyond me. If you loved something, you protected it. There was no use in wanting to do so once they were gone.

"Clover, hello," Rose said, blinking in surprise. "Are you okay?"

"I'm absolutely fine, thank you. I'm sorry I missed dinner. Time got away from me."

Rose shook her head. "It's fine. Would you like something to eat now? We have your plate in the oven."

I took her hand in mine and smiled at how thoughtful she was. My Rose. My Shannen. My…wife? Perhaps. "That would be lovely." She grinned and went to prepare my dinner. Poppy followed and got some cutlery to set the table. "Where is Lily?"

Poppy spun around. "In the bedroom. I'll just go get her." She skipped to their bedroom and disappeared behind the door. Lily must have been with Violet, looking after her. Violet still had to earn my forgiveness. I wasn't sure if she was a good fit for our family. Time would tell, though. If it weren't for my beautiful, loyal, caring Rose, she wouldn't be here. Giving Violet a second chance was a favor to Rose, a gift from me to her. I couldn't give her the life I wanted for us, but I could give her this.

Lily entered the room behind Poppy, and I smiled. I could see why Lewis loved her. She had natural beauty, one that she embraced rather than plastering on thick makeup. When would women understand that layers of makeup made them look like cheap whores?

I stepped forward and took her hand. Her body stiffened. "Are you unwell?" I asked her. "You're very tense."

She bit her lip. "I have a headache. I'll be fine, though."

"Lily, I'll bring you some aspirin. I don't want you suffering."

She stared on with a bemused expression. "Thank you," she muttered. I brought her hand to my lips and kissed her knuckles. Her eyes flicked to the floor. *Still so shy.* I sighed. How long would it take for her to feel confident and at home? Perhaps it wasn't us, though. If her parents hadn't socialized her properly, then she would be shy around most people. Lily had only been with me for seven months, but I wished she had been with me longer—for her sake.

I sat down on the sofa and patted the cushion beside me. "Come and sit, Lily." I needed to help her more than the others. She needed more guidance. She slowly made her way to the sofa and sat down, looking at the floor and holding her hands on her lap. Looking into her eyes at that minute, I had never hated anyone more than her family. She was a bright and beautiful young woman, but her personality didn't always show it.

"How are you feeling really?" I asked her, placing my hand softly on top of hers. "Is it just a headache, or is there more?"

She sat hunched over. "Just that."

I sighed in frustration. She never looked me directly in the eye. *It's rude.* "Look at me when I speak to you, Lily," I said forcefully.

Her eyes widened and she looked up immediately. "Sorry," she whispered, her body turning rigid beside me. That was more like it.

"That's better. I like to look into those beautiful eyes."

"They're my mum's," she muttered.

"Clover, do you think you could get us another, please?" Rose asked, cutting into my conversation with Lily. She held up a wooden spoon, split down the middle.

Were they all tired? Their manners had slipped in a matter of minutes. "I'll go right now," I said and stood up, taking the spoon from her outstretched hand. I kept a stock of things in the

276

built-in a ceiling-high cupboard, so I had replacements for most things. I liked to be prepared.

Locking the door behind me, I walked to the bottom drawer and picked up a new wooden spoon. From somewhere behind me, I heard a soft thud. My heart leaped, and I spun around. Who was here? I scanned the room. There was a small bag of yarn on the floor. It was sitting on the side table waiting to be put away. I sighed and relief flooded my system. It must have been on the edge and fallen.

Was that it, though? Could it have been something, or someone, else? Lewis. Was he here? Did he know where I lived? Was he following me, spying on me? I placed the spoon on the table and slowly walked toward the door. My ears pricked as I concentrated hard on listening for any noise. Poking my head around the door, I saw my empty hallway. *This is ridiculous.* Lewis had made me paranoid. *He is watching you.*

I stormed back into the room and picked the spoon up. *He is not going to ruin this for me. I am still in control. He is not taking my family.*

The girls were chatting when I got back. Lily seemed to have brightened up and joined in their conversation. "Your spoon," I said, placing it on the worktop.

Rose stood up. "Thank you. Your dinner is ready."

I ate quickly; my foot tapped on the floor automatically as I forced down mouthful after mouthful. *This is Lewis's fault. It's all him.* "His fault. It's his," I shouted, jumping up out of my seat.

The girls gasped. "What is?" Rose asked cautiously. Her voice was barely a whisper.

"Lewis," I spat, glaring at Lily, caught up in the moment.

Lily's face fell. Horror swept across her eyes. "What?" Anger built up and up and up, and I felt like I was going to explode. I was wound up, a coil. I breathed in and out heavily. My heart raced and the tips of my fingers tingled. I couldn't control it. I wanted to smash something, smash everything. I had never been so on edge and ready to burst before. It was terrifying.

"What's he done? What are you going to do?" she asked, her eyes filling with tears. The desperation in her voice made me sick.

"Shut up," I bellowed. "Just. Shut. Up." *You're losing it. Everything is going to be ripped away from under your feet and you'll be left with nothing. You'll be a failure.* I growled from deep in my throat in frustration, picked up my plate, and launched it across the room. It hit the stairs and smashed. My heavy breathing was the only noise in the room. My hands shook and teeth ground together. The girls stood frozen.

You need to take it back. You've lost control. They would find the girls and me. They would take them and stop me. I knew they would.

"No," I snapped and ran up the stairs, slamming the door behind me.

I pulled over to the side of the road and waited. They would come to me; they always did. Looking in the mirror, I slicked down my wild hair with the palm of my hand. My hands twitched, foot tapped, and I was unable to relax. I barely recognized myself anymore. Physically, I looked the same, but beneath that, I was a shadow of a man, desperate to break free.

A tap on the window made me jump back to reality. I looked to who it was and smiled. "Hi," the dirty whore purred, causing my stomach to turn. She smiled, fluttering her false eyelashes. "I'm Cantrell. What can I do for you then?" *You. You're going to repair me.*

Without a word, I gestured toward the passenger side and she got in. I gripped the steering wheel and drove toward the woods. She hadn't even asked me where we were going. "So what's your name, darlin'?"

"My name is of no concern to you."

"Mmm, I love the feisty ones." Did she? Did she enjoy this lifestyle, or was it all for my benefit?

"Aren't you going to ask if I'm married?"

She laughed loudly, from the pit of her stomach. "No, darlin'. All I need to know is if you've got the dough for the ho!" My mouth dropped at her brashness. Pride. She had pride in what she was and what she was doing. I took a deep breath. My mind clouded with a red mist, and I could barely concentrate on driving. I wanted her gone.

My fingers twitched around the steering wheel and my heavy breathing threatened to give me away. It had to be now. The feeling of losing control, being a failure, weighed me down, threatening to consume me. I used to pride myself on patience. I'd waited long enough to get the girls, but I couldn't wait now. *Home is too far.*

The turnoff couldn't have come sooner; I took the muddy track and drove into the woods I knew so well. She didn't seem concerned at all; if anything, she seemed bored of driving, looking out the window and pursing her lips. Bored of waiting. I stopped the car and turned the engine off.

"So how do you want me?" she asked and licked her bottom lip.

"Hood," I replied through gritted teeth.

She giggled and opened the door. "Oh, I like your style."

I shuddered in disgust and nodded my head, gesturing for her to follow me. My knife was in my pocket; I touched it through the thick material of my coat. She walked toward me slowly, swaying her hips. I fought the urge to jump forward right then and plunge the knife into her black heart.

She stopped in front of me. I pushed her down onto the hood and she looked up at me, breathing heavily. Was she enjoying this? No, she couldn't be. "Lift up your top," I instructed and she obliged immediately. I tasted bile in my mouth. Her flimsy, hot-pink top covered a tiny pink bra. What had happened to her to turn her into this?

I turned my nose up, pulled the knife out of my pocket, and rested the tip over her windpipe. She gasped, her eyes widening in terror. "W-What are y-you doing?"

"I'm taking control," I replied and pushed the knife down, lightly piercing her skin. Her body began to shake and tears welled in her eyes. I scored her skin, creating a shallow red line from the middle of her neck to the middle of her breasts. She whimpered and hissed through her teeth, panting heavily to absorb the pain. Her eyes were as wide as I'd ever seen.

"P-Please, stop. I'll do whatever you want," she stuttered, body trembling in fear.

I sighed. Didn't she understand what I wanted? "I want you dead, and I want to be the one that kills you."

"No." She whimpered and broke into a loud sob. The noise was like music to my ears. This was what I was good at doing. With this, I couldn't fail.

"No, no, please!" she begged.

I rested the knife over her heart. "Shh." Her eyes bulged even wider. I gripped the knife with both hands and, with as much force as I could muster, shoved it down through her chest. She made no noise as her body sagged in front of me.

I took a step back and watched her body slide down the hood of my car, falling to the ground in a heap. I closed my eyes, exhaling deeply.

I have control.

29
LEWIS

Monday, February 28th (Present)

Dawn sat at the kitchen table staring at pictures of Summer scattered across the counter. "She's beautiful, isn't she?" she said, not looking up from where her eyes were fixed.

"Yeah," I replied.

She ran her finger over one of the photos. "I need to see this smile again."

"You will, Dawn. Can I get you another cup of coffee?"

"Yes, thank you." I took her empty mug and flicked the coffee machine on. "How long have you been up?"

"Not sure. A while. Summer was never happy with her hair, was she? I don't know why. It always looked perfect to me."

I laughed humorlessly. "She's a teenage girl. I think it goes with the territory."

"Do you still cry?" she asked, taking me by surprise. "I feel like I'm the only one. Although I know I'm not."

"You're not," I whispered.

She smiled sadly. "You won't give up, will you? We can't give up, no matter how long it takes."

I was a little hurt she had to ask. She knew how I felt about Summer, and I had spent the last seven months of my life devoted to finding her. Why would I suddenly give up now? I was stuck. I couldn't move on until we had her back or knew what happened. "Never."

She swiped away a tear with the back of her hand. "I hate the idea of her being scared out there somewhere. She does know we'll find her, doesn't she? She knows we wouldn't just leave her. I couldn't bear it if she thought we had given up."

"Dawn, she knows we wouldn't. Sum knows how much we all love her." *I* wasn't sure. I hoped. There were no guarantees in this. Everything was down to hope. Knowing Summer, she would probably hope we had given up so we would be happy. That couldn't happen. This wasn't like when someone died and you got to say good-bye. We don't know where she was or what had happened to her. We had no answers, so there was no ending.

"You know you'd be getting a lecture about caffeine overdosing if she was here right now," I said as she took a big gulp of her coffee.

She smiled halfheartedly and nodded. "Yeah, she had a thing about that, probably because caffeine made her hyper. You remember when she had those Red Bulls and was practically bouncing off the walls?"

I laughed. "Yeah, I remember. You all went to bed and left me to deal with her. At one point, she wanted to go out for a run, then swimming, then to Disneyland. In the end I managed to get her to watch movies instead—chick flicks! I think it was about four in the morning before she finally stopped talking at me and went to sleep."

"We'll take her when she gets home, to Disneyland," she said, nodding her head. Would Summer still want to go when she got back? We had no idea what she was going through. It could be bad. I clenched my jaw and forced out images that I really didn't want to see. The thought of her being hurt was too much. *She'll be fine.* No matter what she was going through, whatever it was, I would fix it.

I drove past Colin's house slowly and stared in at his front yard. There was no car in the driveway, but there was a garage. Could he be in? It was quarter past four in the afternoon, so odds were he was at work.

Summer could be in there. But surely she could leave if he was at work? It didn't really make sense. Maybe he had her somewhere else. But maybe there was a clue inside. I got out of my car and looked back over my shoulder, double-checking that you definitely couldn't see it from the road.

Adrenaline coursed through my veins as I stepped around the shoulder-height hedge that surrounded the house. Why did he need a hedge so tall? His house was the only one around and certainly couldn't be seen by the nearest house down the road. Who was he trying to keep out? Or in?

It struck me how normal his house looked. He had no family, but this was a big family home. Why would he need something this size if it were just him? He didn't seem that wealthy and didn't splash his cash around. Why buy a huge house for one, non-rich, single person? Unless he didn't buy it and it was inherited. I mentally kicked myself. Maybe the freak just liked it! Most people would buy the best they could afford. I was reading too much into it, as Theo always said.

I ran around the side of the building. My heart thumped against my chest, and I felt slightly sick. I didn't really know what I was looking for—just anything. There was a huge possibility he was innocent and his weirdness was just weirdness. Other than a gut feeling, I had nothing on him at all.

The first window was a large one; I peered through it, holding my breath. I could hear my pulse pounding in my ears. The room was a large living room decorated in a traditional way but seemed in keeping with the time. Two large leather sofas faced each other with a dark wooden coffee table between them. A wide fireplace dominated one wall with a large mirror hanging above it. Nothing out of the ordinary at all.

"Come on, you bastard," I whispered. There had to be something. I passed the second window on the sidewall, a bathroom wall, and arrived at the back of the house. The back had three long windows across it, two separated by the back door. It was all the kitchen and dining area. I studied the room, taking in every detail. Nothing. Was it all normal because there was nothing or because he was hiding something? I had too many questions, and it was driving me fucking crazy.

I moved to the other side of the house and found nothing. One room was a utility room and the only thing that seemed out of place was a pile of folded clothes. From the neatness of the rest of the house, I would have expected them to be put away, but that hardly meant he was a kidnapper. In the other room was a table, a dark red, high-backed chair, and a half-height bookshelf.

There was one strip of glass beside the door. I peered inside and saw the hallway and stairs. I frowned and moved closer. By the stairs were four boxes of shoes from New Look. What the hell would he be doing with women's shoes? Summer had dragged me into that shop a million times before. What would a thirty-odd-year-old man be doing shopping there, and for who?

I spun around as I heard a car. "Shit," I muttered and sprinted toward the hedge to the left of the house—closer to my car. My heart felt as if it was going to rip through my chest and my stomach did somersaults. The hedge scratched at my face as I shoved into it just in time to see his car pull into the drive. Could I get all the way through? The bottom of the hedge was bare, but it had started getting dark out. I hoped I could get out without him seeing me.

His engine cut out, and I heard him get out. I froze, half-buried in the damn hedge. I watched him walk to his front door with his briefcase. As soon as he was inside, I covered my face and pushed all of my weight against the branches, forcing my way through.

I ran to my car and started the engine before I'd even closed the door properly. Could he hear the engine? I sped off toward Summer's house, hoping Colin didn't hear me. Damn, that was too close. It was worth it, though. I now knew he was hiding something.

"Hello," I called out and shut the front door to Summer's house.

"Kitchen," Dawn replied. She sat at the table, poking spaghetti with her fork. "Nothing then?"

Yes. Possibly. I shook my head, not wanting to give her false hope.

She nodded. "Your dinner's in the microwave. Your parents will be back soon."

"Where are they?" I asked and turned the microwave on to heat my dinner.

"Shopping."

"Daniel and Henry?"

"Daniel's still out, and Henry's taking a shower." I sat opposite Dawn, and we both picked at our food; neither of us were hungry. I couldn't remember when I was. "I want to be out there too."

I nodded. Being in her position must be the hardest. There was nothing she could do but sit around. Someone had to be here in case Sum called or came home. "I know you do. But we might hear something. If Summer came home, she would want to see you."

Dawn looked up, titling her head and smirking. "Lewis, if Summer walked through that door right now, you would be the first person she ran to. I used to think teenage love was fickle until I saw how much my daughter loved you. Just the way she looked at you. It's how I look at Daniel. I knew then I was wrong about young love."

I swallowed. That was hard to hear. I never thought she *really* loved me, not in the same way I loved her, and not because she didn't say or show it, but because it didn't seem possible.

"I hope we're still together hundreds of years on, like you two." Her mouth pulled up into a grin. "I love her, Dawn, and I won't ever give up. Besides, I told her I'd marry her at Disneyland."

"Marry her at Disneyland?"

I smiled. We weren't going to say anything to anyone —besides it was just a dream—but I wanted it now more than ever. "I know. I don't think I've ever seen her as excited as she was when she found out you can get married there."

"Do it as soon as she gets back," she said.

In any other situation, Dawn would be telling me I was crazy for talking about marrying her seventeen-year-old daughter. I envied people that had problems that small. You never know what's around the corner. I would never again not do something just because I was worried about what other people would say or think.

After I forced down half of dinner, I went to Summer's room. I wasn't sure what to do next. All I wanted to do was go back to Colin's and search every inch of his house. "Where have you been?" Henry questioned the second I walk into the room. He sat on her bed, obviously waiting for me.

"You know where."

He sighed, shaking his head. "And?"

"Couldn't see much through the windows, but I did see four pairs of women's shoes stacked in boxes by the stairs."

"How do you know they were women's shoes?"

"New Look boxes. Colin is definitely hiding something." Henry opened his mouth to start the lecture, so I held my hand up. "His place was creepy, man. I'm not exaggerating or looking too far into it. He's a single man living alone and buying women's shoes. His house is a spotless family home surrounded by high hedges and trees."

"Okay, the shoe thing's weird. I'll give you that."

"But?" I prompted, raising my eyebrow.

"But it doesn't prove anything."

I walked over to Summer's dressing table, where she had a few photos of us stuck around the edge of the mirror. "I know it doesn't. That's why I'm going back in the morning. I need to get inside."

Tuesday, December 30th (2008)

"I'm starving, walk quicker," Henry snapped.

"I don't think you'll die between here and Pizza Hut, which is about three feet away," Summer replied sarcastically, rolling her eyes.

"Okay, why are you with us again, Sum?"

"Well, actually there are *two* of my friends and *one* of yours, so what are you doing with us?"

"Okay," Kerri yelled. "Both of you shut up." Sum and Henry fought all the time. They loved each to death, but most of the time, they wanted to strangle each other. If I were their dad, I would have gone crazy by now.

Henry opened the restaurant door and walked ahead. I hung

back with Summer, holding the door open for her. "Thanks," she said, smiling up at me. I gulped and smiled back. As we walked in, I made sure I was close enough so my arm "accidentally" brushed against hers. For a while now, I had suspected she wanted more than friendship, and as soon as I found out, it hit me like a fucking bus—I wanted more too.

Henry, Kerri, and Beth were already following a waitress to a table. Man, Summer walked slow. "So, you hungry?" I asked. *Oh God! How stupid is that? "So, you hungry?" Jesus, Lewis!* I winced, mentally kicking myself.

Summer laughed. "Yep."

"Getting your weird pizza?"

She stopped, turned to me, and scowled. Her lips pouted the tiniest bit, and I wanted to grab her and kiss her, bite that lip. "It's not weird. Try some and you'll soon see the way." My heart raced as I pictured her feeding me the slice of pizza…naked.

"Um…" I trailed off, all coherent thought had fucked off, and I was left with the very nice image of a naked Summer. She rolled her eyes and sat down in the booth. I sat next to her and pressed my leg against hers. She tried to hide her smile by biting the inside of her mouth, but she didn't do a very good job. She grabbed a menu even though she'd just admitted she already knew what she was having. Summer's pizza was chicken, sweet corn, pineapple, and bacon. I'd drop all the yellow crap. I didn't know how she could eat it.

"So this pizza?"

She turned and smirked at me. "Yeah?"

"How the hell did you get there?"

"I dunno, I just like all that stuff. Trust me, it's good."

"You gonna feed me some?"

"Why? Haven't you learned to do that for yourself yet?"

I laughed and shook my head. Yeah, I should have expected that one. I pouted. "Nope. I'll need your help."

She smirked. "You need someone's help."

"Coming from the girl that's mixing chicken, pig, corn, and fruit together."

"He's got a point, Sum. It's pretty gross," Henry said, siding with me. Summer rolled her eyes and muttered *whatever*.

The waitress arrived and took our order, and I spent the whole time trying not to stare at Summer like a stalker. It annoyed me how much I liked her. If I'd never realized she liked me, I wouldn't be obsessing about her constantly. I hated that I felt like a damn teenage girl when it came to her.

I watched her face as our food was brought to our table. Her bright green eyes lit up and she grinned, eager for food. I dragged my eyes away from her and dug into my normal person's BBQ pizza. "Try it," Summer instructed, holding a slice of hers out to me.

Turning my nose up, I bit into the pizza. It wasn't bad— nowhere near as bad as I thought it would be—but I definitely wouldn't be ordering it. I chewed slowly, turning my nose up.

She rolled her eyes. "It's not that bad. You're lying. It's the best."

I swallowed. "No, Sum. You're just weird."

"Liar. You like it." She nudged my side with her elbow. I grabbed her arm and she squealed and wriggled in her seat. Her side was pressed against my chest. I held her close and faked trying to tickle her.

"Picture," Kerri shouted. Summer stilled and looked at Kerri, smiling. We were in the same position, her lying against me and my arms around her but we were both looking at the camera. If it wouldn't make me such a pussy, I'd ask for a copy of it.

30
LEWIS

Tuesday, February 29th (Present)

"We shouldn't be doing this," Henry muttered, tapping his knee and shaking his head. He'd said that about four fucking thousand times already.

"We need to do something. You know there's something off about Colin."

My car was parked in the field near his house, hidden by the tall bush. We could just about see the opening of his driveway. I didn't know what time he left for work, so we had been parked here since seven in the morning—one hour and twenty minutes ago. "How long do you think he'll be?" Henry whispered.

"You know we're in the car, right? He can't hear us, and I don't know how long," I replied, staring down at his house. He lived alone in the middle of nowhere. He could have easily done something to her.

"It's him, isn't it?"

My heart dropped. "Yeah. Why're you so sure now?"

He gulped. "I've run out of alternatives. I just want to find my sister, even if she's not…"

"She's alive," I snapped. Henry blinked, shocked.

"Sorry," I muttered, running my hand over my face. "I just can't take people assuming she could be dead."

"It's all right."

"She not dead, Henry," I said more forcefully.

He nodded. "I know. Wait, did you hear that?"

"Hear what?" We fell silent and heard the quiet roar of a car engine. "Come on, you bastard," I whispered, watching his house. A minute later, a silver BMW backed onto the road. Colin was alone in the car. He stopped to change gears and drove off. "Let's go," I said as soon as his car was out of sight.

We got out and walked toward the house. "How are we going to get in?" he asked.

"There'll be a way."

"How do you know?"

I stopped in the middle of the road, facing his drive. "For fuck's sake, Henry, we'll get in somehow." What the hell was wrong with him? "Go back to the car if you don't wanna do this."

"She's my sister. I'm doing it."

"Stop whining then." His house was large and well kept. The grass was cut and the garden was tidy. "Let's try the back first." We walked along the side of the house. The backyard was just as neat, with large bushes and trees lining the boundary, like a giant, natural barbed-wire fence. This was his way of keeping his life private without it being suspicious. The guy was a creep, but an intelligent one.

"This is eerie. Too normal," Henry whispered. It was. Without knowing Colin, you would think a family lived here. He had made it *too* normal. So why had no one else ever realized? "There. Look!" He pointed to the kitchen window; above it was a smaller rectangle window—which was open.

"You're smaller than me," I said and grinned, nodding to the window.

He sighed. "Bloody knew you were going to say that."

"Shouldn't have wasted that gym membership. Go on, I'll help you up." He placed his hands on the glass and one foot in my hands. I gritted my teeth as he pushed up. Henry was skinny so I thought he would be quite light. I was wrong. "Christ. How much do you weigh?"

He ignored my question and shoved the window fully open. "Push me up," he said. The muscles in my arms flexed and strained as I shoved Henry's foot into the air. He gripped the window frame and shuffled through the tight gap. I couldn't help grinning as he hung upside down on the other side of the window. He fell onto the floor with a thud

"All right?"

"Yeah, was only a hard tile floor," he replied sarcastically, rubbing his elbow where it had smacked the ground. He smiled and turned the key in the back door. "Very helpful, Colin." I pushed the door open and walked inside. The kitchen was immaculately tidy, nothing sat on the countertops. It looked like a show home. "Where first?"

"You take down here and I'll go upstairs," I said and headed out of the room. "Check everything, okay?"

"Got it."

I took the stairs two at a time, desperately eager for answers. I pushed the first door open and stepped inside the room. The smell of lemon washed over me. It smelled worse than a hospital and started giving me a headache almost immediately.

The bathroom gleamed. I could practically see my own face in the sink. He certainly didn't live like a single man. I don't think I've ever picked up a bottle of bleach. Two bottles of hand sanitizer sat at the side of the sink. Germ freak. I stepped back out and closed the door. The smell was too overpowering; it burned my nose. How the hell could he live in it all the time?

I opened the door to the next room and heard Henry rummaging through cupboards. Was he searching for Summer or robbing him? "Henry," I called.

"Yeah?"

"If you move anything, make sure it goes back in exactly the same place. He'll know."

"Right," he replied. "Will do."

I walked into the overly tidy room and my eyes widened. The room was painted in a peach color. It was just as clean but very old-fashioned. The bedding had a disgusting floral pattern with matching bedside lamps. Whose room was this? Definitely not his. This was a female's room, and an old one. Did he really live with someone? His mum or gran? I froze. Shit, was someone in the house? Surely we would have heard them already if there were. I didn't want to tell Henry in case he freaked. We couldn't turn back now.

I was about to leave when something on the chest of drawers caught my eye. A line of white, wooden picture frames covered the surface. I took a step closer and my stomach turned. They were all pictures of Colin and a woman that looked like him—his mum? *Kissing!* The final picture was one of them kissing. *What the fuck?*

I turned around and left the room, swallowing my discomfort. If he did that with his mum, what was he doing to Summer?

"Have you found anything?" I called. I couldn't have cared less if anyone else was in the house; I needed to find Summer right now.

"Not yet," Henry replied. He sounded as frustrated as I was.

I ripped another door open and continued searching the house. I was in a rush, desperate to get her out of here. What if she's not here? *No, she is. She has to be.*

Every room was immaculate and empty. In the final room, there was nothing but a wall of built-in mahogany wardrobes. I gulped. My heart raced as I eyed them, imagining all kinds of fucked-up shit behind the doors. Stepping forward, I held my breath and reached out to open the doors.

Women's clothes? Why would he have a full wardrobe of women's clothes? The first wardrobe was filled with dresses and cardigans. They were too modern to be his mum's, going by her old-fashioned room. Nothing looked like anything Summer would wear. She was a jeans and T-shirt girl and rarely wore dresses or skirts. Why did he have these? A thought flew through my mind. What if *he* wore them? It seemed unlikely, but still possible.

Could that be his reason for being so private? I slammed the doors and opened the ones next to them. If that was it, then he didn't have Summer, and I had hit a brick wall again. I pulled a box off the shelf. No, he definitely wasn't a cross-dresser. The box was filled with packs of tampons and maxipads. This stuff wasn't his. I quickly pulled each box out and rummaged through it. Makeup, loads hair stuff, moisturizing cream, and tubes of toothpaste.

"Lewis." My heart leaped, and I jumped around. I'd been caught.

"Jesus, Henry, you scared the shit outta me!" His face was ghostly white. "What?" I whispered.

He held up a bunch of newspapers. Well, a few pages from newspapers. All with Summer's face on them. I took them and flicked through the papers, every single one was an article about Sum, dating back to the first headline in July.

I looked up and saw Henry looking at the sanitary box still on the floor. "It's him," he said, and I nodded. My body went numb and the blood drained from my face. He'd done something to her. This stuff suggested that she was still alive, though. She would need these things. But where was she? Did he have her somewhere else? That would make more sense. "Where is she then?"

A chill ran down my spine. We were so close to finding her— or finding out what happened. Throwing them back at Henry, I ran from the room. "Summer," I shouted at the top of my lungs. "Summer, it's me, baby. Shout if you can hear me!"

"Damn it, Lewis! What the hell are ya doing?" Henry shouted and pulled me to a stop on the landing.

I shoved his chest to get him off me. She was close. "What does it look like I'm doing?" I hissed. "Summer!" I flew down the stairs and into the first room I saw. "Summer!" Henry followed me, looking around, lost and completely unsure of what to do.

"Christ, Lewis, she's not here. Will you stop?" he snapped. "You've lost it! Just calm down. We *have* to do this properly."

I stopped and pulled my phone out of my pocket. "You're right."

"What are you doing?" he hissed.

"Calling Michael," I replied. The police dogs would be able tell if she was here or had been. They'll find her. They will.

His eyes widened. I grabbed his arm as he tried to snatch the phone out of my hand. "This is crazy. Lewis, hang up!"

"Go, Henry."

"What?"

"Get out," I hissed. "Go." Henry shook his head at me as if I'd lost it. "Just go." Sighing, he turned and ran as Michael answered my call.

I stood by the back door and waited. They couldn't get here soon enough. *Come on.* My heart was in my throat, and I couldn't breathe properly. "It won't be long now, Summer," I whispered, praying that she would hear me, although I knew she couldn't.

Michael appeared at the back door, making me jump. Why didn't I hear the police car? He shook his head, his mouth pressed into a pissed off line. "What are you doing, Lewis?" he asked calmly.

I held my hands up. The last thing I needed was another lecture. I needed him to listen. "Look, just listen to me, okay? He has all these women's clothes and…products. He keeps old newspapers.

They're all of Summer. He's kept them all. Why? Why would he do that?"

Michael sighed. "Lewis, you can't go around breaking into people's houses."

House. "Will you listen to me? Summer is here, or was here." I groaned and squeezed my eyes closed. "I don't know. I don't know anything anymore. But it's weird. *He* is weird. Please just search the house for yourself and you'll see."

"The clothes could be his wife or girlfriend's, and plenty of people keep old newspapers or forget to throw them out."

"Ah, yes but he's too much of a neat freak for that. Take a look around for yourself."

Michael rubbed his hand over his face. "I can't just do that. You need you to come with me right now."

"Why?"

"Because you can't just break into someone's house!" he hissed, exasperated.

I held my hands up again. "You said you wouldn't give up."

"I'm not giving up, but you can't do this. We can't arrest and search everyone that keeps old papers, that's not how it works."

"Maybe the way you do things needs to change!"

"I'm not here to argue that." He sighed. "I get it, Lewis. If I were in your position, I would be the same. Look, I'll speak to him again, that's the best I can do."

"So this isn't weird to you?"

He shook his head. "Not really. You need more than this to obtain a search warrant. Now, did you find anything of Summer's?"

My heart plummeted and shoulders slumped. They weren't going to do anything. "No, I didn't."

"I will question him. You need to come with me," he repeated.

Michael led me outside and closed the back door. I walked to his car with a sick feeling in the pit of my stomach. What did this mean now? Would Colin know we were there? He opened the back door, and I got inside. Staring back at the house, I wondered if Summer would ever be found. She wasn't in there.

Michael got in the front and turned the engine on. "You're arresting me?" I asked.

"No, but don't let this happen again. I mean it. Next time I won't just pick you up. Understand?" I nodded and looked back as we drove off. *I'm so sorry, Sum.*

31
SUMMER

Thursday, March 3rd (Present)

I stood in front of the bathroom mirror applying concealer to my black eye. The bruise on my arm was fading quickly, and you could barely notice it anymore; there was just a light yellow mark left. Clover was getting worse. His mind was always somewhere elsewhere, and his hollow eyes were even more emotionless than ever. Something was weighing heavily on his mind, and I wasn't sure what. With him, it could have been anything. I hoped it was because the police were getting closer to finding me—finding us. I clung to that with everything I had.

My hopes of being found increased as his nervousness increased. I wanted nothing more than to feel safe in one of my dad's hugs, to smell my mum's sweet perfume, to hear Lewis tell me he loved me, and even to hear Henry yell at me because I was annoying him.

I turned my head so I couldn't see myself anymore and walked back into the room. Rose, Poppy, and Violet sat on the sofa reading books. "You okay?" Rose asked, putting her book down and standing up to look at my eye.

Not really. "Yeah, it's a lot better today."

She gave me a sympathetic smile and pulled me down on the

sofa. It was a tight squeeze with all four of us, but it made me feel safe. He hadn't been down for dinner, and it was now half past eight at night. His dinner sat in the cold oven, waiting to be reheated if he made an appearance.

Rose looked up at the clock. "Where is he?" she muttered to herself.

"Maybe he's not coming," I said and prayed I was right.

She frowned. "I'm going to clean the kitchen." Keeping busy was what took her mind off things. I could always tell when something was weighing on her mind because she would clean and then reclean. Poppy got up to help like she always did now. Violet turned to me and mouthed "bedroom." She wanted to talk in private.

I followed her and we sat down on her bed. "Something's going on. What if something's happened to him?" Her eyes widened in horror. "Shit, Lily, what if he's dead?"

If he was dead, we were screwed. I hated him more than anything, but we relied on him. "I don't think anything's happened," I replied. "He probably just forgot to tell us he had something else to do, that's all." I sounded calm and convincing when inside I was terrified of the thought of something happening and us dying down here. "Maybe he's polishing his crazy of the year trophy," I joked, trying to lighten the mood.

"But…" She shook her head.

"Violet, don't panic. He's only missed dinner."

"He was distracted at breakfast." That's because he's a sick psycho. "Lily, something *is* wrong."

I nodded. "I know, but we need to stay calm, okay?" She took a deep breath. A few months ago, it was me panicking and Poppy and Rose trying to calm me down. "Whatever's going on, we'll be all right."

"If he's gone crazy…"

I snorted. "If?" Violet half smiled, not allowing herself to laugh. "The crazier he gets, the better for us."

"How's that?"

"He might start making mistakes." She nodded, and I smiled. "See? We'll be fine. Now don't say too much to Rose or Poppy. If he's losing it even more than usual, then we have a chance."

"To bash his head in?" Violet asked.

Whoa, okay. "Um, if we have to, I guess." She was deadly serious; her expression showed no emotion. Could I kill someone? The thought made me sick, but if it was a matter of life or death, I think I could. Him I could.

"Wanna watch *The Notebook*?" I asked her, trying to change the subject. It was Violet's favorite movie, and I hoped it would take her mind off everything. I think I knew it word for word now.

She nodded her head, smiling a sad smile. "Yeah, sure." I stood up to go back in the other room when she grabbed my wrist. "Do you think Lewis is still looking for you?"

Her question surprised me. "I hope not," I replied.

"But you love him."

"I do, and that's why I hope not." She looked at me as if I was crazy. I wasn't crazy. I loved him. He couldn't be happy if he was still searching for me. Deep down, I had a feeling he was, though. I knew

I would if it were the other way around. I walked out of the bedroom so she couldn't ask anything else. I didn't want to talk about it.

Rose and Poppy were wiping down the counter—a sparkling clean counter. I was about to ask if they wanted to watch the movie too when the cellar door unlocked. I stood still and my heart took off in a sprint. He was late. What did it mean that he was here now?

"Clover, is everything okay? We have your dinner in the oven if you're hungry," Rose said and pulled off her yellow rubber gloves as he walked down the stairs. My eyes flicked to the cellar door and widened. It wasn't shut. My heart leaped. There was about an inch gap. He hadn't closed it. Did he even realize?

He kissed Rose's cheek and turned to face us all. Violet walked out of the bedroom and stopped beside me. "Something has happened, but I don't want any of you to worry about it. I've thought of a way to keep us together," he said, looking at each of us. *What? What's happened?*

Violet's hand found mine and she squeezed me tight. I could sense her fear. She was terrified of what he had planned. What did it mean, *a way to keep us together*? He was going to try to run with us? My heart leaped. They knew about him.

He looked around and waved his hand. "There are some people that want to split us up, but I will never let that happen," he said far too calmly. He was too calm, as if he was discussing the weather. "We won't be separated. We can't be separated," he muttered. It was a promise, and it sent chills down my spine. His eyes were dark and distant. In that moment, I knew that he wasn't going to try to run with us. He was going to kill us. *All* of us.

My blood ran cold and heart plummeted to my stomach. Were they coming for him now? Was that why he needed to do this now and break his precious routine? *Keep him talking.* My throat was tight, but I knew I had to speak. "Clover, no one can separate us if we don't want them to." Violet's hand tightened into a vise-like grip.

His eyes snapped up to me and he cocked his head to the side. "No, Lily, they're going to."

"But we can tell them we want to be here." He frowned, as if that was news to him. Did he really believe we wanted to be here? Surely, he wasn't that delusional. I started to question if he even understood right and wrong anymore, or if he lived in his own world where he was always right.

"Lily, you're not listening to me. I've told you, they want to split us up. Now, I need you all to be good girls. I promise this will be quick and it won't hurt too much." He pulled out a knife from his pocket. The air left my lungs. He didn't react. He was dead inside already. Defeated.

Violet whimpered and pulled me back with her a step. Poppy also moved back, more toward us, but Rose stood still. *Move, Rose. Damn it, move!* I needed her to get out of his way. As much as she frustrated me sometimes, I couldn't stand the thought of something happening to her. Over time, she had become like family too. Like an older sister.

"C-Clover," Rose whispered and shook her head. Her hands trembled with fear, and I heard her gulp.

He smiled at her. "You understand we can't be apart, don't you? I can't live without you and you can't live without me. It won't hurt, I promise," he repeated and took a step closer to her. She didn't even flinch. Shit, she wasn't going to try and stop him. I could see what was going to happen play out in my head just like a movie: Clover stabbing her. Rose falling to the floor. I couldn't let that happen. I jumped forward, grabbed the top of her arm, and pulled her back. She slammed against my chest, and I yanked her behind me.

Clover glared at me. His face turned hard as he realized I wasn't going to go down without a fight. If I was going to die down here, it was going to be trying to escape with Poppy, Rose, and Violet. "Clover, please, don't do this. We can find another way. No one is going to do anything if we tell them we're a family and we're here because we want to be," Poppy said, trying to reason with him.

"You do not beg, Poppy!" he shouted, and I jumped back in surprise. The door wasn't locked; we could all make it out of here. I kept that thought in my mind. His breathing was heavy and ragged. The way it was when he killed. I looked around the cellar for anything at all we could use to hurt him or distract him long enough to get out. Nothing!

He suddenly lunged forward and grabbed Violet from beside me. A silent scream pierced through my head. I tried to pull her back but he was too fast, he slammed her into the wall and raised the knife. Poppy and Violet screamed so loud it rang in my ears. Through their cries, I could just about hear Clover chanting something, but I couldn't make out what it was. Everything happened so fast, I was powerless to stop it. Violet tried to grab his wrist but he was too quick—he plunged the knife into her stomach and she slumped to the floor.

"No!" Poppy screamed. I dropped to the floor and tried to look at the wound. Would she be okay or had it gone too far in? My vision blurred. I fought to swallow the lump in my throat but it was no use. I cried, my chest heaving with sobs.

Looking up, I gasped. Clover very quickly stabbed the knife into Poppy's side. Poppy stumbled, one hand clutching the wall for support and the other holding the knife wound. Blood seeped through her fingers and she started hyperventilating. She looked so scared—scared to die.

Jumping up, I grabbed Rose and pulled her with me. We ran behind the table. He was between the stairs and us. Out of the corner of my eye, I saw Poppy hobbling toward us, her face twisted in pain and tears streaming down her terrified face. I swiped the tears from my cheeks quickly and stared at him. His menacing face looked like pure evil, like there was no humanity left in him at all.

I didn't want to leave them behind, but I had to do something or we would all die down here. If I could just get into the house, then I could find something there to stop him. His face softened and he smiled. "It's going to be okay. Don't be afraid. We're doing this together, as a family."

"We are not a fucking family!" I snapped and gasped. *What have I done?* Keeping him on my side was harder than I thought. He turned his whole body to face me, and I knew while his attention was on me, Rose had a chance. "Run," I whispered under my breath. *Go, Rose!*

He walked around the table slowly, and I stood my ground. I planned to kick him between the legs when he got close enough. That was what Henry used to tell me I should do when guys came up to talk to me. "Kick them hard and don't slow down. Follow the kick through." Those were my brother's words, and I planned to follow them—for once.

Clover moved in front of me. I'd never been in a fight before, and I was pretty sure I wouldn't be any good at it, but I felt strong now. My hate for him was busting from every pore in my body. I clenched my jaw, determined. He retracted his arm, and I knew he was about to hit me. I stopped breathing as I flung my own arm out, successfully blocking his blow.

I couldn't believe I'd blocked him, but I didn't have time to gloat. I pictured every horrible thing he'd done to me and all the other girls, and with as much strength as I could muster, I shoved my fist in his face.

Gasping as pain shot through my hand, I jumped back. Clover stumbled to the side, shooting his arms out to steady himself. I knew I was going to die, and I wanted it to be while I was fighting back, showing him I didn't want what he had done to me. I wanted him to know how sick and evil he was.

"You little bitch," he spat in a voice that was so angry and aggressive it didn't sound like his own. I took a deep breath, positioning myself better, ready to follow Henry's instructions and kick with everything I had left.

Adrenaline pumped through my body, and I went to raise my leg. Rose grabbed me and pulled me back. *Shit, no!* Why was she stopping me? Why hadn't she left when she had the chance? My eyes widened as his fist raised and slammed down on my face.

My vision blurred, and I blinked hard. I was shoved backward hard and slammed into the wall. My head smashed against the bricks, and I fell to the floor. A black mist fell over me, and I couldn't see. I rubbed my eyes and ignored the throbbing pain in my head. *Where is he? Where are they?*

Pushing myself up, I narrowed my eyes to try to see what was going on. I felt like I was falling. This time it was peaceful. There were so many voices around and loud screams, but I couldn't focus on anything. The only thing I could smell was the usual lemon, but it wasn't that strong anymore.

I was drifting, floating. The pain was subsiding. Suddenly through all the noise, I heard a loud bang, followed by thuds. Flopping down on the floor so I was lying, I tried to see who had come in. The darkness clouded my view even more. I felt exhausted. I just wanted to sleep. Closing my eyes, I felt someone move me. "Stay with me, Summer. Everything's going to be okay. You just need to stay with me." *Summer?*

All I could feel was movement, no pain. I was being carried. Carried by someone that called me Summer. Was I dreaming? I fell further and then there was only darkness.

32
LEWIS

Thursday, March 3rd (Present)

I pulled up at the hotel and rubbed my eyes. For the past few days, I'd been driving all over the country checking out possible leads and sightings of her. The police covered it too of course, but the longer she was gone, the more I lost faith in them. For seven months, since she disappeared, I had been in limbo and I couldn't move on until I knew what happened. Someone knew where she was.

I yawned and got out of the car. London was an impossibly large place to find one girl, and I doubted Summer was here, but I wasn't going to risk not looking.

The police search for her had slowed down even more; there weren't many officers still on the case, and the search was now funded by donations and volunteers. It meant we would have to go back to work to get the money, only part-time, though.

Thankfully, I only spent one night in a jail cell for breaking into Colin's house—to teach me a lesson, I think—and there was nothing on my record. I didn't want to think what would happen if I couldn't get a job and then couldn't help fund the search. I would have failed her.

One good thing came of Michael arresting me; the police had promised to question Colin. The sleaze was on their radar now. Something was definitely weird about him, and now it was only a matter of time before whatever he was hiding came out.

My phone vibrated in my pocket and started ringing. I swiped it out and answered it immediately. "Hello."

"Lewis, they've got a warrant. They're going in soon," Daniel said.

"What?" *Finally!* "How did they get it?"

"They found him with a box of different phone chargers and women's clothing. Apparently, he was on his way out somewhere with them. Lucky they turned up to re-question him when they did or that probably would have been gone."

"Did he have a charger for Summer's phone?" I whispered into the phone.

"I don't know. They wouldn't say."

I sighed and pinched the bridge of my nose. I was getting a headache. "Okay, call me the second you hear something. Anything at all."

"Of course I will."

"Thanks," I said and ended the call. If they didn't find anything, then I had no idea what to do next. Keep following every lead that fizzled into nothing? "Hello," the receptionist said. "Are you checking in?"

I debated. Did I stay here and search or go home? "Actually, no. Sorry." I waved over my shoulder as I jogged back to the parking lot. I had a long drive back—to possibly nothing. But I had to be there in case.

My heart leaped at the thought of seeing her again. I didn't want to get my hopes up too much; it would crush me all over again if she weren't found. *Please be okay, baby. I'm on my way.* Theo had said I was putting too much on Colin, and I was—but I had nothing else.

I tried turning the key in the ignition, but my hands shook so badly it took three tries. *Fuck's sake! Come on!* Finally I managed to start the car, and I sped off. The damn car couldn't go fast enough. I should have never left town. I was so damn stupid.

My phone rang and my heart jumped. "Lewis," Daniel said. His voice was thick with emotion, as if he had been crying. *No!*

"Yes," I whispered and took a deep breath. My world stopped.

"They…they've found her. They found her. They have her," he said, repeating himself in disbelief.

"What? What happened? Where is she? Is she okay?" I questioned. My heart soared. They have her!

"In his house—his cellar. She's alive, Lewis." He broke down, sobbing. "She's alive."

Was I dreaming? Everything around me was in slow motion. Daniel's voice seemed too far away, too dreamlike. I had imagined this moment millions of times over and had it felt this unreal. Tears pooled in my eyes, blurring my vision. "Where is she?"

"Hospital. We're on our way now. She hit her head, but she's here. She's here. There was a struggle and she was hurt. I have to go, we're here now, and I need to be with her. Just get here as soon as you can."

"Bye," I muttered and ended the call. His words echoed through my head. *She's here.* That was all I had wanted for the past seven months. Now I was in London, fucking hours away. Frustration built up. I hated myself for not being there. I slammed my hand on the steering wheel. "Fuck!" There was a struggle and she was in the hospital. How badly was she injured? She hit her head. A serious hit? She *had* to be okay. We couldn't go through over a half a year of hell only for her to die. I needed her.

I felt sick with guilt and wished I were with her already. If she was awake, would she ask for me? What if she hated me for not finding her sooner? I promised I would take care of her. I blew out a deep breath that I didn't even know I was holding in. She's okay. I blinked heavily and felt tears roll down my face. Everything was going to be all right now. She's alive and I would do anything to make it up to her. I was overwhelmed and couldn't figure out how I felt. Relieved. Scared. Happy. Angry. Ecstatic. Guilty.

I gripped the steering wheel with one hand and wiped my tears away with the other. Whatever happened to her in those seven months would be okay, because she was home. I pushed my foot down on the accelerator.

"Where is she?" I demanded of Theo the second I walked through the hospital doors.

"This way," he replied, jogging beside me.

"Have you seen her?"

"No."

"Has anyone? She's okay, right?"

"She's awake now. Daniel and Dawn are with her. Lewis, before you go in there, Henry wanted to speak to you."

"What?" I shook my head. What the fuck? I didn't want a chat with Henry; I wanted to see my girlfriend! "I'm not waiting to speak to him."

"He's waiting for you outside her room and you *need* to speak to him first." Why? What did that mean? Was Summer angry? We turned a corner and went through onto one of the wards. It smelled too clean and clinical. Henry stood outside a door on the ward and my heart stopped. Summer was the other side of that wall. My heart swelled.

"Lewis," Henry said and walked toward me. He held his hands up. "Not yet, man, we need to talk."

I sighed. "Why? I just want to go and see her. Is she okay? Does she not want to see me?"

"Just come to the café with me, and I'll explain."

"Henry, I don't want to sit and have a fucking coffee!"

"Okay, let's take this into the corridor then." *Take this into the corridor?* He sounded like he wanted a damn fight or something. "Lewis, please. For her sake, please. You need to understand what happened before you go in there. She's not…herself."

My face fell. "What do you mean she's not herself?"

"Back up, and I'll tell you."

I looked at the door. She was just feet away, but I still couldn't get to her. I sighed. "Fine. Okay, fine." I followed him back. Theo stayed behind, going into a room opposite hers. Waiting room maybe? "What then?" I asked, as the ward door closed behind us.

"She's different." He frowned. "It's like she doesn't properly recognize us. She doesn't respond that well. All we've heard is her asking for Rose, Poppy, and Violet."

"What?" I frowned, shocked "She wants flowers?"

Henry looked at the floor. "No. They're the three other girls she was locked up with." My eyes widened and mouth dropped open. "She said her name was Lily."

What? That didn't make sense. I couldn't get my head around it. Why was she calling herself Lily? "Look, we've not got the whole picture. None of them are saying much, but it seems that Brown, or *Clover*, changed their names."

"I..." Shaking my head, I tried to make sense of it all. "Clover? What the hell, man? I don't..."

"Neither do I. Listen, she's not herself, so don't expect much. We just need to help her snap out of it, help her remember who she is." She forgot who she was? What the fuck did he do to her to make her like that?

"I want to see her. *Now.*" Helping her remember I could do. I just needed to see her, to hold her and smell her. I wanted to wrap my arms around her and magically make everything better.

We stopped at her door and my heart took off.

33
SUMMER

Friday, March 4th (Present)

My whole body felt heavy, like I was made of concrete. A dull pain throbbed through my head. I tried to open my eyes, but they wouldn't move; it was as if my eyelids had been glued together. What was going on? A dark fog spread across me, and I peacefully drifted back to sleep.

I woke in the dark again; my body still refused to move even an inch. *Just open your eyes. Focus on opening your eyes!* Voices of strangers surrounded me, and I slowly began to hear what they were saying.

"She's strong. She'll be fine." Me? I didn't feel strong.

"I thought we'd lost her." Whose voice was that? My dad's? Was that him? What happened? As things around me started making sense: the clean, clinical smell—no strong lemon—and the strange but familiar voices of my family. I was out of Clover's prison and in a hospital. But how?

I blocked everything else out. I could work all that out later; now I needed to focus on waking up. My body didn't want to respond to the demands I was making, but, finally, I managed to flutter my eyes open for barely a second. A brief ray of bright white light flashed in front of me before it went black again.

A sea of voices filled the room as everyone spoke at the same time. Did they see?

"Summer? Summer?"

Open your eyes, I screamed at myself and tried again, forcing my eyes to open. This time they didn't close again, but I felt exhausted from the effort. I winced at the bright light. Everything looked blurry, but the room slowly came into focus.

"Summer? Sweetheart?" Mum's voice sounded so strange. I had remembered her voice only well enough for me to vaguely recognize it. She sobbed, and I tried to smile to soothe her. Being free felt as dreamlike as when I had first entered the cellar. "Sweetheart, are you okay?"

I couldn't talk—I didn't have enough energy—so I nodded my head as best I could. "I'll get a doctor," Henry said. I couldn't see him, but I had remembered my annoying brother's voice perfectly. I smiled weakly.

"Oh, you're okay." Mum stroked my hair. I turned my head slightly so I was facing her a little better. She looked older, like she had aged eight years in almost eight months. Her hair was almost fully gray and she had deep, dark circles under her eyes. Was that my fault?

A stranger wearing a light blue nurse uniform looked over me and smiled as if I were her daughter. "Hello, Summer. My name's Tara. How are you feeling?" I opened my mouth but only a groggy mutter came out. My throat was dry, like I'd swallowed sand. I shrugged. Tara smiled. "Are you in any pain?" I nodded. Everywhere but mostly my head. "Okay, I'll get you something for that. There's water on the side table."

"I'll do it," Dad said. I smiled. Of course he would want to do something practical.

The nurse nodded. "I'll go and get something for the pain and bring a doctor in to check her over."

"Thank you," Mum said, gripping my hand. "Summer? Honey…" She stopped talking and wiped the tears that flowed freely down her face. I blinked a couple times as my vision blurred. My head pounded and I just wanted to sleep.

Dad poured water in a cup and put a straw in it. *What am I, three?* I opened my mouth, grateful for the cool water. I'd almost drained the whole cup before my throat felt normal again.

"How are we doing?" another nurse asked as she walked into the room. She held a syringe in her hand—the pain medication. I sighed in relief. *Give it!* "Summer, I'm Brieanna. Don't worry. I'm not going to ask you to do anything; you'll receive the medication through the IV." She stuck a needle into a tube and nothing happened. How long did this stuff take to work exactly? "Okay, the doctor will be with you shortly. Call if you need anything." She left the room and we were alone again.

Clips of the events flittered through my mind, but I couldn't piece them together properly. Where were Rose, Poppy, and Violet? "Wh-what…happened?" I asked.

Mum, Dad, and Henry moved closer, sitting on the edge of the bed. They loomed over me, and I squirmed uncomfortably. I shouldn't feel uncomfortable with my family. "Do you remember anything, sweetheart?" Dad asked.

"Clover. He attacked Violet, attacked us. Where are they?"

"The other girls?" Mum asked. Her voice was soft, like she thought I was made from glass and would break at any loud noise. Dad and Henry stepped forward again.

My heart stopped. Where were they? "I need to see them. Can you find them?"

"Summer, calm down."

"Where's the nurse?" I pushed myself up and pain shot through my head. I groaned and flopped back down, wincing. "Find them, please," I whispered, my eyes filling with tears.

"Honey, calm down," Mum whispered. She exchanged a look with Dad, and I couldn't tell what it meant. "Your dad will go and find out what happened to them."

Someone knocked on the door and walked in. She wasn't a nurse; she was wearing black trousers and a fitted black shirt, but she had a hospital ID hanging around her neck. "Hello, Summer. I'm Cecilia. How are you feeling?"

"Where are they?" I asked.

She smiled. She knew about them. Was she looking after them? "I've just been with Poppy, and she's up and walking around. She's with Violet. Violet's in a critical but stable condition."

I gulped. Critical. That was bad. Really, really bad. "Rose?" I whispered.

"Physically, she's fine."

My eyes welled up. Of course, she needed him. "I have to see them."

"As soon as you're feeling better, I'll arrange that."

"I feel fine. Please."

She shook her head. "I'm sorry. Rest for a while, and then I'll see if we can get you to Violet."

She had only used my real name, not theirs. Had Poppy not told them who they really were? I almost wanted to be called Lily—to be the same as them again. For almost eight months they were all I knew, and being away from them made me feel vulnerable. Summer seemed like someone I was a lifetime ago. I didn't want to keep his name, though. I didn't want anything to do with him—just them.

"Is he in prison?"

Cecilia looked at my parents. "I'm afraid I don't have that information, Summer. Perhaps you can talk to your parents." She flipped over my chart and wrote something down. After checking me over she straightened up. "Right, I'll be back to check on you again soon, and we'll have an in-depth chat a little later, when you're feeling better." Definitely not a nurse.

"Are you hungry?" Mum asked as soon as Cecilia left the room.

"No. Where is he?"

"The police have him," Dad replied. "You're safe now, Summer. He won't hurt you again."

Every time someone called me Summer, I expected someone else to answer, expected them to be calling someone else. I didn't feel like Summer. It was as weird as being called Lily in the beginning.

The door opened, and I jumped. Being outside, back in the real world, was strange. Scary almost. My family hadn't left me alone, but I wanted them to. I didn't want to be alone but I didn't want to be with people that constantly stared at me and made me feel like I was a freak show.

"Summer," Henry shouted, waving his hand in front of my face. "You okay? I've been calling you for the last couple minutes."

I frowned. *He was?* "Um. Yeah?"

He smiled and sat on the edge of the bed. "Lewis is on his way." Lewis. My heart leaped and stomach fluttered. He was coming here, now. "Err," he said, frowning. "Do you want to see him?"

Do I? For the past seven and a half months, seeing him was the only thing I wanted to do; now it was possible I didn't even know how I felt or what I wanted. Not if he was going to look at me like they all were. I didn't want pity, especially not his. I wanted Rose, Poppy, and Violet. I wanted to feel safe. "Where are they?"

"Where are who?"

"Rose, Poppy, and Violet?"

"I don't know, Sum. Lewis is on his way, though," he repeated and looked at me as if I were crazy.

Mum sat down opposite Henry and grabbed my hand. I pulled away and played with my fingers. Her touch felt strange. "Honey?"

I chewed on my lip and tried to figure out what I wanted. Everything was so confusing and absolutely nothing made sense. My emotions were blank. "Can you all leave? Please."

"What? What's wrong, sweetheart?" Dad asked.

"Just go," I whispered and covered my eyes with my hands. I wanted to curl up in a ball and sleep.

I was left alone for a grand total of twelve minutes. Henry still hadn't come back in, but my parents sat on the chairs against the wall—about as much space as they were going to give me. They hadn't said anything since they told me they weren't going to leave me. It was almost as if they weren't here. It wasn't quite enough, though. I didn't want them here. I felt guilty for being so confused whenever they looked at me with sadness and confusion in their eyes. At least Henry would make stupid small talk.

The door opened, and before I even looked up, I knew it was Lewis. Everything changed. The atmosphere spiked; my heart rate spiked. My parents both sat forward, and Henry marched in front of my bed and looked back to the door. What were they expecting? Did they think Lewis had the magic cure that would fix everything? I wished he did, but I wasn't that naïve anymore.

He's here. My breath caught in my throat and everything stopped. I felt nervous, confused, and scared—not excited. I felt like the air had been sucked from the room. I could hardly breathe.

Neither of us said a word, and I still hadn't looked up. It became painful to be in the same room. His footsteps grew louder as he approached. I felt the bed dip and, out of the corner of my eye, saw his leg. I gulped and looked up. The first thing I saw was my family standing just inside the door. We weren't getting privacy for this, then.

I turned my head, and he came into view. I stopped breathing altogether. I had remembered his face perfectly, down to the faint little scar just under his eyebrow.

"Summer," he whispered. I closed my eyes. The way he said my name was how I had imagined it so many times when I was in the cellar, how I pictured him saying it, how his eyes shone when he said it. My name suddenly didn't feel as strange anymore.

His beautiful green eyes pierced into mine, and I felt weightless. He still looked at me the same way. How? Did he really wait for me? I wanted to believe it so badly, but seven and a half months was a long time. How long ago did he think I was dead? Had he started to move on? He was still searching for me, but did that mean he wanted me?

I had so many questions, and I didn't feel that I could ask him any of them. He opened and closed his mouth a few times. I guess he couldn't find the words either. He was just as lost. I always thought our reunion would be romantic—rescued girl jumps into guy's arms and they kiss.

"Lily?" I leaped forward at the sound of Poppy's voice. She looked around nervously, avoiding eye contact with everyone. I threw the thin blanket off my legs and got out of bed. My head swam as I stood up, and I stumbled trying to walk.

Lewis gasped. "Summer!" My mum started fussing, and I was ordered to get back to bed. I ignored my family's demands and rushed into Poppy's open arms. She started crying. I wanted to go home. Not to the cellar, but somewhere with Rose, Poppy, and Violet. I didn't feel safe without them.

"Are you okay?" I asked, looking her up and down frantically. He'd stabbed her!

She nodded. "Fine. It wasn't deep. Violet…" She let out a big sob. *What?*

"What about her? You've been with her. They told me you were with her. Is she okay?" Poppy sobbed harder on my shoulder and shook her head. *No.* "But…she can't be…" *Violet's dead.* Clover had killed her.

I collapsed against Poppy. My body started to shake. It hurt so much. After all of that, Violet died anyway. I burst into tears. Why couldn't it just all be over? "Rose, where's Rose?" I sobbed, my chest heaving. She would need us too.

"She's in the hospital, but they won't let me see her."

Pulling back, I wiped my tears, but it was useless; fresh ones replaced them straight away. "I want to see her. We need to find someone."

"Summer, stop!" Henry grabbed my arm. I pulled my wrist from his grip and stepped back. "You need to get into bed."

I turned away from him. My own brother felt like a stranger to me. "Do you know where she is?" I asked Poppy.

She shook her head. "No, I've asked a million times, but no one will tell me anything."

The door opened yet again and Cecilia walked in. "Poppy, you can't be in here." She shook her head. "And you need to be in bed, Summer."

"Lily," I corrected and froze. Lily? I recoiled, shocked at myself. What? *No.* Turning in a daze, I climbed back in bed. Why did

I say that? "Can you just please find out how Rose is?" My eyes welled up with tears again. "Please?"

Cecilia nodded. "I'll do my best. Back to your room now, Poppy. You can visit later, I promise."

Why weren't they calling Poppy, Becca? Had no one come to see her to tell the doctors the truth? My heart sunk. I was so sure her family would come forward. Poppy left without a fight, and I was alone again. Well, not really alone.

Out of the corner of my eye, I could see Lewis staring at me as if I had gone crazy. I probably actually had, but I couldn't tell anymore. Did I want to talk to him? I did, but I didn't know how. What could I possibly say to him? Things must have changed for him now—it had been seven and a half months! We'd never technically broken up, so I wasn't sure what we were. What did I want? Together. I definitely wanted to be together, but I didn't know how to be anymore. I wasn't the same Summer he fell in love with. I had nothing to offer him.

My eyes stung. *He's here with me.* I wanted to rush to him but I was scared. "Can you give us a minute, please?" I asked, staring down at the bed. They would know I meant leave me with Lewis. My family left the room, and he sat on the edge of the bed, facing me. We had reached a point where I had to look at him. There were no distractions I could use anymore. *This is Lewis. Why am I so scared?*

"Sum," he whispered. My name didn't seem so wrong when he said it. It had meaning, and I remembered all the times he had called me before. "Look at me, baby."

The air left my lungs. *Baby.* I couldn't find my breath. Gulping, I looked up. He stared at me with love and relief in his eyes. I saw my future there again. That hadn't changed. My heart fluttered, and I felt alive again.

The atmosphere changed again—charged with such a high sense of relief and longing. I had missed him so much. There wasn't one day that I hadn't thought about him. I had heard that true love is realized after a couple has experienced and overcome something huge. Was this it? I still loved Lewis so much, and it looked like he felt the same way. I wasn't naïve enough to think I would leave this hospital with him and live happily ever after—after all, perfect endings were for fairy tales—but I had more hope for things working out.

Lewis's lips slowly turned up into the most beautiful smile I had seen in a long time. "Hi, you," he whispered.

I grinned, mirroring him. "Hi." This was a little weird. We had never been weird before. Because I knew him before we got together, we had always been comfortable around each other.

We lapsed into silence again. I played with the soft material of the hospital gown I was wearing. *Please say something better than hi!* Would it be like this for a while? Maybe we had to get to know each other again. I knew I wasn't the same person, and I didn't know if I ever would be again.

"How are you?" He frowned at himself and shook his head as if he was telling himself off. *Yes, Lewis, stupid question.*

"I'm fine." He raised an eyebrow. "What do you really want to ask me?"

He bit his lip and sighed. "Sum, I have a million questions, and there's so much I want to say, but I can't find the words." He shuffled forward and my heart leaped. *What's he doing?* "Right now, I just want to hold you. I've missed you *so* much."

I moved so I was sitting forward, giving him permission. His arms shot around me and pulled me against his chest. His hand gripped my hair so desperately it filled my eyes with fresh tears. I buried my head in his chest and let go, bursting into tears. All of the horror, heartache, and fear over the last eight months poured out, and I sobbed until my throat was raw.

Lewis held me, kissing the side of my neck occasionally. "It's okay, baby. You're safe now. I love you so much." He must have been uncomfortable in his odd bent-over position, but he didn't move an inch. I felt his body shake, and I knew he was crying too. Lewis didn't cry. I had never seen him cry. It broke my heart.

I wanted to comfort him and beg him to stop crying, but I couldn't stop myself. My sense of relief was so huge—I was completely overwhelmed. He was really here and this wasn't a dream. I wasn't sure how long we held each other, but it felt like hours. His scent surrounded me and I was home.

When he finally released me, I collapsed back on the bed, exhausted. I hadn't even done anything, but I was so tired. "Sorry, you need to rest," he said, pulling the blanket up over me. He looked at me, taking in every inch of my face. I bet I looked a terrible, with cuts and bruises all over me. I dropped my eyes to the blanket, seeing him look at me like that was too intense. I felt too vulnerable. Lewis could see through me better than anyone else—probably because I told him everything. There was no bullshitting him.

I bit my lip and played with my fingers. "Are you leaving?"

He shook his head. "I'm not going anywhere. Ever again, actually."

I smirked, closed my eyes. "Stalker." His quiet chuckle filled the room and he took my hand, pressing his lips to my knuckles. I smiled as I fell asleep.

34
SUMMER

Saturday, March 26th (Present)

I knelt down and laid the daisies on Layal's grave. Becca did the same for Rose, laying down a large bunch of red roses. She would have still wanted roses. Poppy—Becca—and I had been calling each other by our real names since we left the hospital, but calling her Becca and hearing her say Summer was still weird.

I missed Rose and Layal so much it made me feel sick. They had become my family, and I still woke up every morning expecting them to be there. I had a lot of guilt that I couldn't help Rose, but I wasn't sure if there was anything I would have been able to do anyway. She had been down there too long. She couldn't be anywhere else. But even so, whenever I thought about the day that I was finally back with my family being looked after while she was alone, swiping medication and overdosing, I hated myself.

"I'm sorry," I whispered to them both. Sorry for not finding something that could have helped Rose, and sorry that I hadn't been able to fight Clover off Violet long enough.

Becca grabbed my hand. "It wasn't your fault, Sum." I knew it wasn't, but I still felt awful. Survivor's guilt, apparently. They died and I managed to get out alive. "We should go. You've got to be home soon."

I nodded. My family had barely let me out since I got back. They watched my every move, and I couldn't even go outside without one of them following me.

"I'll come back soon," I promised Rose and Violet. We walked back toward the road. "So, you're definitely coming tonight?"

Becca nodded. "Yeah, I'll be over at six thirty."

"Good girl." She rolled her eyes and linked her arm though mine. Over the past ten days, we had spent most of our time together. We were both on very friendly terms with each other's families. Our situation united us all. Becca and Henry had also been growing closer. I had a feeling it wouldn't be long before they were together—if Becca could get past her fear of not being good enough. I wanted that for her—even though it was gross her being with my brother. She deserved to be happy. I reminded myself to tell him to buy her a cottage so she could finally live the life she dreamed of.

Becca's brother's car was parked next to Lewis's, where he was waiting for me. He jumped out of the car as we walked through the gate to the parking lot, worry etched on his face. I was surprised he hadn't gone prematurely gray. "Okay?" he asked.

"I'm fine. I just want to go home and relax," I replied and got in the passenger side. I saw him frown, hurt, as I got in the car before going to him. *Take your own advice.* Since Clover, I hadn't felt good enough for Lewis. Surely, he was only with me because he felt sorry for me? He knew everything, so how could he want me? He was in love with the old Summer, and it was only a matter of time before he realized I wasn't her.

Lewis got in the car and turned to me. Becca's brother drove off, and I watched them disappear around the corner. "I love you," he whispered, turning and looking directly into my eyes. I didn't doubt it, but it wasn't love for me now.

"I love you too, Lewis."

"But?"

"No buts."

He raised his eyebrows. "I know you, Summer. I know there's something you're not telling me."

I sighed in frustration. "Lewis, can we just forget it and go home, please?" We stared at each other. I wasn't going to back down. I didn't want to admit how I felt in case he confirmed it. "Becca's coming over tonight."

"Okay. You think we could have a night alone soon?" I froze. Alone to do what? "I don't expect anything!" he exclaimed and frowned. "Summer, you never have to do anything you don't want to with me, ever. I don't expect anything from you. Fuck, I wanna kill that fucking bastard!"

I smiled. "Language."

He smiled too, visibly calming down. "Sorry. You never have to do anything you don't want to with me. You know that."

"I do know. Look, Clover was…" I trailed off, not knowing how to put it. There was no way I could put it nicely. "With him I didn't have a choice and now I feel…um…" I didn't want to say the words aloud; it would make it more real. Dirty, sick, used, worthless. "I don't feel sick about you being…close with me, but I'm not ready for anything like that. I don't know when I'll be ready. Or if I will."

"Summer, listen to me. Please. I will never rush you. I can wait as long as you need. Not every guy is ruled by his dick. I don't need sex. I do have some self-control, you know."

I smiled. "Right. Sorry. I know you do. I just don't want you to get bored."

"I'm definitely not getting bored. I didn't ever think I'd see you again, Sum. Sex really isn't a priority for me. Please just forget it, don't worry about it. In fact, I won't ever say anything about it. Whenever you're ready—if you're ready—we can talk again then."

I gulped. He was willing to do that? "Really?"

"Really. Now, you wanna watch something scary or funny?" he asked, effectively changing the subject.

Was there anything scary in the movie world anymore? Everything that frightened me before just seemed so stupid now. Once you'd lived your own personal horror movie, nothing else measured up. "Whatever you want."

"Why don't we let Henry decide?"

I shrugged. "Yeah, whatever." He grinned a full, face-splitting smile.

"What?"

"You said whatever. Not heard that in a while." I rolled my eyes.

"What do you wanna watch?" Lewis asked Henry as he walked into my bedroom. He was right on cue.

"*Halloween?*" he replied and frowned. "Summer, err…"

I rolled my eyes again. "I'm not a baby. Put whatever you want on."

"But isn't it…"

"Henry, just put it on. I don't need any special treatment. Okay?" I had been through a shitload, but that didn't mean I wanted everyone to treat me as if I were made of glass. Before Clover, they would have just teased me for being scared of the "fake blood and screaming actors." If I was going to move on and find Summer again, then I needed people to treat me the same as they always had.

Henry didn't say anything else; he put the movie on and sat next to me. "Scared yet?" Henry teased. It hadn't even started.

I smiled, silently thanking him for being normal. "Not yet but I'll let you know, and where's the popcorn?"

He grinned. "Mum's bringing it up in a minute."

The movie started, and I waited, hoping that it would scare me so I knew there was at least a little part of me still in there. When the people in the movie were being murdered, I didn't even flinch. Watching it felt like watching Mum bake a cake. It was something I had seen too many times for it to affect me. Would I still feel nothing if someone were actually being killed in front of my eyes? I partly hoped so. I didn't ever want to go back to that pure terror I felt at seeing someone's life ripped away from them. I'd reached a point where I could almost completely switch it off, especially if they were a stranger.

"You okay, Sum?" Henry asked, smirking at me.

I frowned. "Fine. It doesn't scare me anymore." I knew they would be making faces and feeling sorry for me, so I focused on the TV. The second the credits rolled, Henry ran from the room. I think it was my fault after telling him I wasn't scared anymore. It was a stupid thing to say, and I should have just kept it to myself.

Lewis smiled at me sadly. Not him too! "I want to go to Ethan's party thing tonight," I said, hoping to take his mind off whatever was going through his head. Kerri had told me about a very, very small party her boyfriend, Ethan, was having, and I had debated whether to go or not. I used to love getting together at his house with my friends and messing around for the evening. "I need to work things out with Rachel."

Lewis looked down at me, his eyes weary. "Why?"

Did I not just say? "To work things out with Rachel…"

"I got that, Summer. Why, though?"

"Because she's my friend and she feels bad. What happened to me wasn't her fault." He flinched and looked down at the bed. He blamed himself. "Lewis, it wasn't anyone's fault but Clover's. Please stop beating yourself up," I whispered, shuffling toward him and laying my head on his shoulder. "I love you."

He sighed and wrapped his arm around me. "I love you too, Sum. I just—"

"Shh," I hissed. "Please don't. You couldn't have known. I hate that you feel so guilty for something you had no control over." He smiled tightly and nodded. I knew he wasn't really listening to me, and I wished there was something I could do to make him realize it wasn't his fault, but he was a stubborn arse and needed to get there himself. Hopefully soon, because I hated him feeling crappy.

"So you really want to go to a party?"

"Yes." There would only be about five or six of my friends there, chilling at Ethan's and playing Guitar Hero. It was hardly a rave.

"Okay," he replied slowly. "We'll go."

"I was going anyway."

He grinned in amusement, making his eyes light up. "Stubborn as ever."

"Back at ya. Becca's coming too."

He nodded. "Wait. Do you want to start getting ready?" He looked at his watch, and I knew what was coming. "There's only five hours until we need to leave," he teased.

I rolled my eyes. "I don't take that long and you know it."

"I'm so proud of you." What? Where did that come from? Complete change of subject. "You're dealing with all this so well. Better than any of us." *Do I have another choice?* I didn't want to let him ruin my life. Deep down, I knew I was dealing with it too well. I had the number of a *good* therapist on a leaflet sent home with me from hospital. I was just enjoying being *okay* right now.

"I think I'm gonna have a bath before tonight."

Lewis frowned. "Okay. Everything all right?"

"Yes, Lewis." If I had a pound for every time someone asked me if I was fine, I would be a billionaire right now.

He reluctantly nodded and unwound his arms from around me. I looked back at him as I walked out. He looked worried, as usual. I still couldn't believe he spent every day looking for me.

While I was down there, he had been in the house. I wished I had known that at the time, just to know I was so close to him again. That didn't matter anymore because we were together now and I was back to normal—whatever normal was going to be.

I locked the bathroom door and looked in the mirror. I felt like two people. Lily was the one that was hurt and abused; Summer was the person I went back to. Clover had done that at least, made me disconnect from what happened by giving me a false name. How long would it be before Summer and Lily collided?

Clover was now locked up in a secure psychiatric unit. I wondered how he felt being locked up, if he felt scared and suffocated the way I had. I hoped so. At least he would get whatever help he needed to sort out his screwed-up head. At first I was pissed off that he wasn't going to stand trial—because he's not mentally stable to stand trial, no shock there—but as long as he was locked away and couldn't hurt anyone else, I could accept it.

Lewis squeezed my hand as we drove past the park toward Ethan's. My stomach tightened as I glanced over to where Clover had kidnapped me from. My blood ran cold as I remembered him calling me Lily for the first time and dragging me to his van. I squeezed my eyes closed. *Don't think about it.*

"Are you sure about this?" Lewis asked and pulled the car into Ethan's driveway.

"Yep. Let's go." I was sure, but I was also nervous about seeing everyone again. Henry followed behind with Becca. He kept close to her and she seemed to be happy.

Kerri sprinted out of the house and ripped open my door. "Summer!" she gasped and yanked me toward her. I smiled and hugged her back as I was pulled into one of her tight, lung-crushing bear hugs. I had really missed those bone-crushing Kerri cuddles.

"Hi," I said, gasping for breath.

She pushed me away at arm's length and grinned. "I'm so glad you came. I wasn't sure if you were going to." Kerri and I had spoken twice since I got back, but we'd texted almost every day.

"I wasn't sure until a few hours ago. Is Rachel here?"

"Yeah, she's inside. You're not mad at her, are you?"

"No. You know I'm not." Why couldn't people believe that I really wasn't angry with anyone but Clover? No one had a crystal ball and saw what was coming. "Let's go in. It's freezing."

I walked in the house after Kerri. Lewis trailed behind me as usual. I held my breath as Ethan, Beth, Rachel, and Jack looked up at me. "Hi," I muttered nervously.

Ethan held a bottle of Malibu up. "Thirsty?" And just like that, I had my friends back.

"Think we can talk?" I asked Rachel. We had been sitting in the living room drinking and eating junk for half an hour, and I really wanted to sort things out with Rach. She had been quiet, rarely making eye contact with me.

"Okay," she replied. "Kitchen?"

We walked next to each other awkwardly. I bit my lip and sat down at the breakfast bar. "Summer, I am so sorry—"

I held my hand up. "Rachel, stop. I don't want you to apologize." I didn't want anyone to. "It wasn't your fault, so please, please don't say you're sorry. I just want us be okay." God, I felt like a parrot, repeating the same thing over and over.

Her mouth dropped open. "But how? After what happened to you, what he did to you… If it wasn't for me, you would have never been there…"

"There are too many what-ifs. It happened, and it was *all him*. Okay?" Tears welled up in her eyes and I felt my heart squeeze. Great, we were going to cry! "Don't cry 'cause I will too."

She wiped her eyes. "I can't help it. Are you okay, though?"

Yes and no. "I will be."

"Are you seeing anyone about what happened?"

"No, but I think I will soon."

She nodded. "I think that would be a good idea."

"Deep down, so do I, but I want a little bit longer living in denial."

"Denial is popular."

I smiled and leaned over the breakfast bar. "Totally get why. Shall we go back in there?" Becca had Henry, and they were in their own little world, chatting to each other, but I didn't want to leave her alone too long. For me as well as her.

"Sure. We're fine, right?"

I nodded and slipped off the stool. "Totally fine," I replied and gave her a sideways hug as we walked back to the living room.

Sunday, April 10th (Present)

I walked downstairs when I heard Lewis's voice. He had barely left my side since I got back, but last night I made him stay at his house. I was a big girl, and although I didn't like sleeping on my own, I *had* to. Things were a little more normal. Well, on the outside anyway. Everyone still stepped on eggshells around me, but it wasn't as bad now. I managed to get a minute to pee in peace before someone came looking for me.

Lewis beamed as he saw me and my heart skipped a beat. I still felt the same for him, but something had changed. Me. I had changed and I was no longer the girl he fell for. He told me that didn't matter to him; he loved me just as much now as he did before, more even, apparently. We were trying, and as long as he was in, so was I.

"Hi," he said and wrapped his arms around my back, burying his face in my hair. He kissed the side of my neck. It was more intimate than usual, and although he said he'd wait as long as I needed and even be celibate for the rest of our lives—which was ridiculous because what guy would do that—I felt guilty for not wanting to be with him.

"Hi. See? I made it," I teased. I didn't know what he thought was going to happen to me in the night if he wasn't there. I *slept*—that was it.

He cocked his head to the side and his light eyes danced with humor. "Glad to hear it. You didn't miss me, then?"

"Did I miss someone's elbow digging in my side, you mean? Hmm, no I bloody didn't."

"Thanks. I feel so special," he replied sarcastically.

I grinned. This was so normal—how we used to act around each other. "Anyway, outside."

He frowned, bemused. "You wanna fight?"

"No, idiot. Bar-be-cue," I said slowly.

"In April?"

I shrugged. "It's warm, and Dad has a lot of steak." Did you even need a reason to barbecue anyway? I liked being outside after being trapped underground for seven and a half months. At first it almost hurt; my eyes stung and I felt too exposed, but now I couldn't get enough of the freedom—although I didn't ever want to be alone and outside.

"Fair enough."

"I spoke to Michael today."

Lewis stilled, frowning. "What did he say? Was it about that fucker?"

That fucker was all Lewis would call Clover or Colin, whatever you wanted to call the freak. "Yes," I whispered and continued, ignoring his less than amused expression, "apparently he's responding well to treatment."

"Hmm." It was almost a growl. "You believe that?"

"I believe his doctors believe that." Clover was intelligent and a master at acting normal. I had no doubt that he could pull the wool over his doctors' eyes. It wouldn't help him much, though; he wasn't ever going to be released.

"You okay? You know no matter what happens, he'll never get near you again, right?"

"Of course," I replied, lying.

I smiled and turned to walk outside. Lewis followed, gripping my hand tight as if he wasn't sure if anyone would be able to help me if Clover got out. I had no doubt that if he managed to escape or was released, he would want us back. To him, we were family, and he proved every time he kidnapped or killed just how far he would go for his family.

For now I wasn't going to worry, though. For now I was going to eat steak with the people I loved and enjoy the warm April afternoon, and for a while, I wouldn't have to pretend to be okay.

Loved *The Cellar*?

Don't miss the latest gripping, high-stakes thriller from Natasha Preston

1

SCARLETT

Imogen nudged my arm, nodding toward the classroom door. "Finally, some talent," she whispered.

She wasn't wrong. The guy standing by Mrs. Wells's door was gorgeous—like, *shouldn't even be at our school* gorgeous.

"Welcome to Fordham High, Noah," Mrs. Wells said. "Take a seat over there." She pointed to the empty space next to me, and Imogen gripped my forearm. "Scarlett and Imogen, you have most of the same classes as Noah this year, so please show him around and make him feel welcome."

Im's face lit up. "Absolutely."

Good luck, Noah.

He walked to our desk at the back of the classroom, demanding everyone's attention and owning the room, but his focus was on me. I squirmed in my seat, heat flooding my face. He looked older, the way he carried himself with an air of *I don't give a crap.*

"Hi," he said, still staring just at me.

"Hey. I'm Scarlett, and that's Imogen," I said, pointing to my best friend beside me. "I guess we're your tour guides."

"Thank you," he replied. He even sounded older—he pronounced a lot more of each word than most of the kids here did. "Although this school is so small, I doubt anyone could get lost here."

"So true!" Imogen said, leaning over the desk so Noah could see her past me.

Bobby turned around in his seat. "You like wrestling, Noah?"

Noah's forehead creased.

I held up my hand. "Bobby's a WWE freak; he's not offering you a fight."

"Definitely not," Bobby confirmed. "You look like you can handle yourself."

Noah grinned. "Handling myself is what got me expelled from my last school."

He didn't seem like the fighting type, but then again, I'd known him for five seconds. Maybe he was repeating a grade.

"How old are you?" I asked. "You look older than fifteen or sixteen."

"Sixteen," he replied. "What about you?"

"Same."

"She's *just* sixteen," Imogen cut in, clearly annoyed at being ignored. "I am too."

I wanted to roll my eyes. As if he were going to take her over the desk right now just because she'd been the same age as him that little bit longer.

"Yeah, it was my birthday last month," I explained.

Still ignoring Imogen, Noah said, "It was my brother's birthday last month too. What date was yours?"

"Thirteenth. Thank God it wasn't a Friday this year."

He laughed. "Are you superstitious?"

I nodded once. "Big time. I won't walk under a ladder or cross paths with a black cat. I wave to magpies, depending on how many there are, of course, and throw salt over my shoulder." He cocked his eyebrow. I shrugged. "My parents are kinda superstitious too. And suspicious."

"Wow," he said. "Well, you never know what's out there in the big, bad world."

Out there in the big, bad world. Déjà vu. I'd heard that somewhere before, but I couldn't place it.

The bell rang, making me jump. "Ready for English lit?" I asked Noah, ignoring the odd feeling inside.

"Not really. You are sitting next to me, right? You're my tour guide after all."

Imogen stalked off ahead, in a foul mood because she didn't have Noah eating out of her hand.

I smiled. "Sure."

"So where did you move from?" I asked Noah as we walked to our next class.

Throughout our fifty-minute English class, Noah had quizzed me relentlessly. It was as if he was trying to learn every last thing there was to know. New kids weren't usually this chatty. But I liked it and wanted to know all about him too.

"Hayling Island."

"Cool. What's it like there?"

"Small," he replied.

I'd learned about it in geography when we briefly covered the British Isles. It really was small.

"What made you move to Bath?"

"My dad's job. Hayling wasn't much fun, so it's nice to be here."

We reached the science block, and I turned to him. "Well, I'm glad you're here." My eyes widened to the point of pain. *Why on earth did I say that out loud?* I cringed. You didn't tell a guy you kind of liked him right away—especially when you'd only known him an hour.

He shoved a hand through his fair hair, moving it out of the way of his forehead, and smiled. His light blue eyes sparkled. Actually freakin' sparkled. I used to think I was more of a tall, dark, and handsome type of girl, but it was *definitely* tall, blond, and handsome for me now. His jaw looked like it had been carved from stone, and his lips... Well, those things would have any girl gaping.

He stared down, a full head taller than me. "I'm glad that you're glad."

Sucking my lips between my teeth, I took a small step back. I liked him. There was no question of that, but he looked dangerously close to kissing me, and I was in no way ready for that.

We were called into the classroom, and Noah took a seat next to me. The Bunsen burners were out, which meant I was going to have to really listen because it looked like we were doing an experiment. I hated experiments.

"You good at chemistry?" I asked.

He chuckled. "There is a bad joke in there somewhere. I'm okay, yeah."

"Good, because I suck. I'm failing so badly, I don't know why they continue to make me attend. I think my presence alone dumbs down the rest of the class."

He chuckled. "You can't be that bad."

"Oh, wait and see."

"Settle down," Mr. Gregor said. "Welcome, Noah. Have you covered—"

And that was where I switched off. I couldn't be any less interested in chemistry if I tried. I'd learned more watching *The Big Bang Theory* than I had at school.

I switched back on when Noah poured something into a test tube.

"What's the point of this then?" I asked, nodding to the Bunsen burner.

"You really don't like science, do you?"

"No."

"Me neither, actually. There is too much unexplained that science doesn't have an answer to."

"What do you believe in?"

He shrugged. "I'm not sure yet. Anyway, I might not like all this, but I do understand it, so I'll explain while I work, and you can make notes. Let's see if I can help you pass this class."

Yeah, again, good luck, Noah.

I popped the lid off my pen, trying to concentrate on what he was saying rather than his deep voice and the way his crooked smile made me swoon. There was no way he was going to be able to help me with chemistry—the subject anyway.

As he worked, his eyes kept flicking back to watch me like I was the most interesting thing on the planet, like he was scared if he took his eyes off me, I'd be assassinated.

He turned to me once everything was set up. "Tell me something about yourself."

"We're supposed to be making those chemicals...do something." *And there's not a whole lot to tell.*

He shrugged. "We've got a minute. Come on."

There *was* one thing. I didn't like to bring it up much because it was weird and I always got the same *how can it not drive you crazy* question. Sighing, I replied, "I remember nothing before the age of four."

His eyebrows shot up. "What?"

"There was a house fire and we lost everything. My parents got me and my brother, Jeremy, out, but we were hospitalized for smoke inhalation. When I woke up, I couldn't remember anything."

"Nothing?"

"Nope. All I remember is waking up in a yellow room. I didn't even know my family."

"When did you start remembering?"

I frowned. "I didn't. They filled in the blanks with stories of stuff we'd done, but I don't actually remember any of it."

"That's crazy. Hey, they could've told you anything."

I laughed. "Yeah, they could've had fun with that one. 'We're a normal family and you and your brother fight like cats and dogs' is pretty boring."

"They could have made you a princess. Or you could really be a princess and they stole you away to—"

"Okay," I said, cutting him off, "you have an overactive imagination."

Smiling, he replied, "Sorry. It's just a bit weird."

"Totally weird. I repressed everything because of the traumatic experience, apparently."

"Think you'll ever get your memory back?"

I shrugged. "Probably not. Doesn't matter though."

"I suppose not. I would just hate to have *four years* and a lot of experiences I couldn't remember."

"It bugged me before but not now. Lots of people don't remember much of their childhood. I just don't remember the first four years."

"Did you try therapy or get hypnotized?"

I laughed. "Nope. It's really not that big of a deal. I tried remembering, but there's nothing there."

He smiled. "One day you will remember."

I gave up believing that about four years ago.

ACKNOWLEDGMENTS

I'd like to say a huge thank-you to my readers who have given me incredible and valuable feedback from the day I started writing *The Cellar*. To the Wattpad team, particularly Seema, Eva, and Allen, for everything they've done to get this book to print. To Sourcebooks for taking a chance and publishing this book, especially my fabulous editor, Aubrey. And to my friends and backers, who have been there for me, offering support and the occasional kick up the bum as I went through rewrites, edits, and "should I kill this one?"

ABOUT THE AUTHOR

UK native Natasha Preston grew up in small villages and towns. She discovered her love of writing when she stumbled across an amateur writing site and uploaded her first story and hasn't looked back since. She enjoys writing romance, thrillers, gritty YA, and the occasional serial killer. Visit www.natashapreston.com.

ABOUT WATTPAD

You might not realize it, but the book you're holding started as a story on Wattpad, a social reading platform. It was written by someone just like you, someone who might not have necessarily thought they were an author until they shared their story with the world's largest community of readers and writers. Download the Wattpad app today to discover other stories like this one that you can read for free on your phone or tablet, or on your computer at www.wattpad.com.